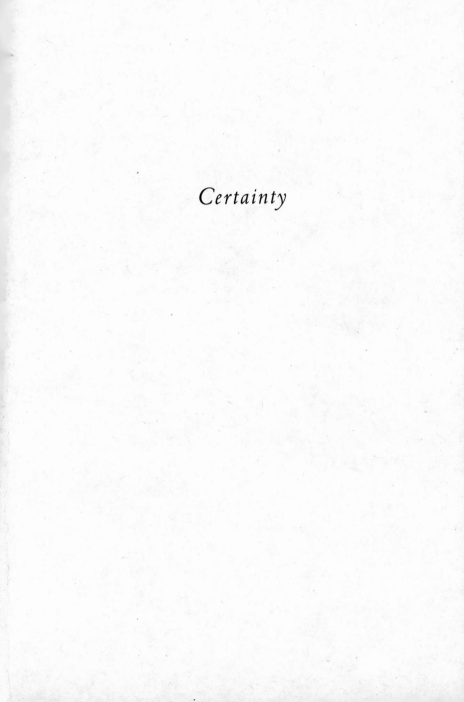

Certainty

Madeleine Thien

Certainty

McCLELLAND & STEWART

Library and Archives Canada Cataloguing in Publication

Thien, Madeleine, 1974–
Certainty / Madeleine Thien.

ISBN-13: 978-0-7710-8513-0
ISBN-10: 0-7710-8513-3

I. Title.

PS8589.H449C47 2006   C813'.6   C2005-907274-1

We acknowledge the financial support of the Government of Canada through the Book Publishing Industry Development Program and that of the Government of Ontario through the Ontario Media Development Corporation's Ontario Book Initiative. We further acknowledge the support of the Canada Council for the Arts and the Ontario Arts Council for our publishing program.

The author gratefully acknowledges the support of the British Columbia Arts Council and the Canada Council for the Arts.

Typeset in Bembo by M&S, Toronto
Printed and bound in Canada

This book is printed on acid-free paper that is 100% recycled, ancient-forest friendly (100% post-consumer recycled).

McClelland & Stewart Ltd.
75 Sherbourne Street
Toronto, Ontario
M5A 2P9
www.mcclelland.com

1 2 3 4 5   10 09 08 07 06

for Willem

For we convinced physicists the distinction between past, present, and future is only an illusion, however persistent.

Albert Einstein, from a letter of condolence to the family of Michelangelo Besso

He said we could face the worst if we simply renounced our yearning for certainty. But who among us is capable of that renunciation?

Michael Ignatieff, from The Needs of Strangers

1

Chaos

VANCOUVER, CANADA

In what was to have been the future, Ansel rolled towards her, half awake, half forgetful. He curved his body around hers and Gail's warmth drew him back into sleep. Morning passed into afternoon, the rest of the world waited outside, but he and Gail were just rising from bed, they were fumbling into their clothes, they knew that the day was long.

Some of her work, the tapes and reel-to-reel, are in the house. Some in the attic of her parents' house, and some in her former office. When Ansel listens to them, the finished and the unfinished work, the quality of the recording is fine, as if Gail is in the room herself, her voice preserved on a quarter-inch strip of tape.

There is a sunroom at the front of the house where Ansel drinks his coffee. Across the street, their neighbour is crouched on the ground, snipping the grass with a pair of scissors. Because of the noise, she says. A lawnmower makes far too much noise. She is in her mid-sixties and the wide brim of a sun hat shades her face. Gail, who had grown up in a house a block away, once told Ansel that she remembered this same woman snipping the grass when Gail herself was a child. "All the kids would come with their plastic scissors and help her out. It was a kind of neighbourhood haircut." Every now and then, Mrs. Cho stands up and massages her lower back. She looks over at Ansel seated alone in the window, lifts her hand to him in greeting.

The coffee is warm and sweet. He closes his eyes and drinks it, and when he opens his eyes again, Gail is still there, a presence in the room, the undercurrent of his thoughts.

It is almost seven o'clock. The sun is up, and it pours a warm, golden light across the houses. Last night, he couldn't sleep, and this morning his body feels hollow, a loose string that folds naturally over itself. On the table in front of him, a sheaf of papers: Gail's radiology report, her EKG chart, the pages creased from too much handling. Outside, the branches of the sakura tree flutter in the wind. The tree blooms in March, and by April the blossoms are so heavy all the branches are weighted down. By May, the yard is a snowbank of petals.

Ansel and Gail bought this house ten years ago, in the early-1990s. He had just finished his residency, and Gail was working as a radio producer, making features and documentaries. The house is in Strathcona, the oldest neighbourhood in Vancouver. Even now, the Hastings Mill cabins, where workers lived a century ago, still stand. Past the bustle of Chinatown, the downtown core floats like a picture hung against the North Shore mountains. East, and the mills are visible, Ballentyne Pier, with its brightly coloured stacks of containers, and the tall freight elevators.

Theirs is a restored Queen Anne, gabled windows on the top floors. A solid, unremarkable house. On windy days, he imagines he can feel the wooden beams of the house swaying.

Previous homes together had been small apartments in basements or attics, the two of them tucked in amongst their belongings. Now there are books and records and an old piano. Gail's hand-carved Indonesian box. Ansel's antique microscope; once, they had spent the afternoon looking at odds and ends. He remembers an onion skin, elegant in its simplicity, the cells stacked together like brickwork.

There is the understanding that she is no longer here, that it was sudden and irrevocable, but this understanding is one moment spread over a thousand hours, a continuous thought that tries to forget itself. And then, when that fails, to bargain, to change everything, to fall asleep and go back to another point in time. "Time," Gail had said once, as he fell asleep in her arms, "is the only thing we need."

At Strathcona Elementary School, the Sunday morning tai chi class is already in motion. He can see them through the fence as he walks, grandparents in neon track suits, moving across the pavement in an ensemble, a fluid echo of cause and effect. Bird plucking a leaf from the tree. Hands separating heaven from earth. Gail had listed these off for him. Epic names for the smallest gestures. Together, they step purposefully across the chalk lines for hopscotch and four-square.

Ansel buys his breakfast at the New Town Bakery, where a woman wearing a blank name tag gives him a paper bag filled with warm bread. He continues through Chinatown, past the tanks of melancholy fish. Vegetables spill out from the markets, and the street lamps, recently painted a festive red, glow in the early morning.

After the service, the flowers had followed her across the city, from Hastings Street to 49th Avenue. The houses giving way to Central Park, giving way to the burial grounds. The workers arranged the tall flower stands in concentric circles around her grave, making a perfumed forest. He walked into it and in the centre he found her. Each night the rain knocked them down, the wind scattered the petals across the cemetery, and every day he set them up again. One afternoon, he arrived in the middle of a storm. He raised the flowers up onto their stands, and they collapsed on top of him. He hugged them to his body and lifted them up once more.

Half a year has gone by since then, but this morning, when he walks along the pebbled road beside False Creek, his thoughts return to that small plot of land and the flowers he laid there yesterday. His friend Ed Carney once spent an entire morning giving Ansel his thoughts on passing time. Time's arrow pointing in both directions, the past flying into view as you stumble backwards into the future, Walter Benjamin's angel of history. Ed had mused about scientists who experimented with their circadian rhythms, re-establishing themselves on a twenty-six-hour clock. "Mostly they had the police after them, wondering what trouble they were up to." The conversation had ended there. Ed had gone back to mowing his lawn, and Ansel had continued walking.

Now he sits on the dock at the creek, the moored boats swaying with the current, and he eats his breakfast. Sunday morning and the city is still sleeping, but she is there beside him, running her feet through the water. That is another timeline, the morning of Gail's last birthday, fall and not summer. Their last conversation was a telephone call, long distance. His memories struggle to stay afloat, time moves forward, and Ansel feels the divide in his body. One part of him carrying on, living moment to moment, the other part lost to him on the day she died.

In the afternoon, he walks down the street to Keefer and Princess, to the two-storey that belongs to Gail's parents. Along the way he passes dry lawns, cascading sprinklers, crooked hopscotch drawings, an arrow drawn in chalk, pointing for an instant at his feet, with the words "Typical homo sapiens." When he arrives, Gail's parents are in the kitchen. Matthew is stooped in front of the sink and Clara is at the counter. Ansel leaves his sandals at the kitchen door and enters barefoot. Immediately, the soles of his feet are covered with flour.

"You're early," Clara says, pleased.

The counter is an avalanche of green vegetables. Something that smells sweet and tangy is simmering on the stove. He says, "I've come to help."

Gail's father turns, one hand still holding the cleaver. He looks panicked at the suggestion.

"Wonderful," Clara says. "We still have plenty of time." She gestures him towards the seat across from her.

In the decade that he has been with Gail, this house has not changed in any noticeable way. Even Matthew and Clara are standing at their usual places, the radio is on low, the room drifts in a comfortable quiet. Clara is making dumplings, and watching her, as Gail once said, is like watching a bird build a nest. Nothing much seems to be happening, and then suddenly structure appears.

He does what he can, constructing dumplings from the rounds of dough that dot the counter. Today is the six-month anniversary of Gail's death.

As they work, Clara tells him about the restaurant that her father owned when she was a girl, and they talk about her four sisters, who are now scattered throughout the world. She brushes a strand of greying hair from her forehead, and her fingertips leave a faint trail of flour on her skin. On the fridge behind her, there's a postcard, a snowflake photographed with a wide-angle lens, sent by her third sister, who is visiting St. Petersburg. He tells her that a snowflake is the perfect example of sensitive dependence on initial conditions.

"Sensitive what?" Matthew says, peering down at him through his bifocals.

Ansel says that the shape of a snowflake is the precise

record of all the changing weather conditions it has experienced on its way towards the ground. Things like temperature, humidity, or impurities in the atmosphere. But mostly temperature.

"So," he says, frowning. "People were right all along. No two are ever the same."

Ansel nods, smiling. Each addition to the crystal is dependent on the exact second of its formation, and its place in the atmosphere. Even a difference as small as a breath, or a nudge, will give rise to another shape, another sequence of order and complexity. Matthew stops what he is doing, considering. Clara looks at Ansel now, nodding approval at the dumplings he has folded. "You have no idea how much food we've prepared," she says, dusting flour from her hands. "Gail would have liked it, I think. Knowing we were here, together."

The table is set for eight. Glyn Madden, an old friend and colleague of Gail's at the radio station, sits beside Ansel. Since the funeral, he has seen her only a handful of times, to discuss the documentary that Gail was working on when she died. Opposite them is Ed Carney, whose son Scott is beside Mrs. Cho. Clara and Matthew sit side by side. The empty chair and place setting, intended for spirits departed, is to Ansel's right. The food comes out all at once, a sweet-and-sour fish, spicy coconut soup, peanut noodles, and a half-dozen more dishes, and the table seems to buckle under the weight.

Ansel pours the wine, almost spilling it when Ed announces that he's brought his banjo. "Is there anyone here who might accompany me?" he asks.

"You play the piano, don't you, Glyn?"

"I do, but I've never played a duet with a banjo."

The lenses of Matthew's glasses begin to fog up from the warm food, and he takes them off and lays them, arms open, on the table. As the conversation drifts, Matthew remains silent, but to Ansel he looks relaxed, at ease in this gathering.

"So, Ed, what are you going to play for us?"

"No need to laugh. I have a very good repertoire. It passes the time."

"It's the banjo, Ed. What you need is a cello."

"How about a hurdy gurdy? Not enough people are playing the hurdy gurdy these days."

Arms reach across the table, passing plates, refilling glasses, and outside the sky is a pale and delicate amber. Ansel spoons some spiced beef into a lettuce leaf, drizzles sauce on it, and rolls the leaf into a small package. There are clams tossed in black bean sauce, a dish of prawns and snow peas. The food relaxes the nerves behind Ansel's eyes.

Mrs. Cho is leaning forward with her glass. "So, Glyn, what are you working on now?"

Glyn puts down her chopsticks. "Something that Ed would be very interested in, I think."

"Don't get him started."

"A feature documentary with an intriguing topic. To have a mind, to be a body," she says. "That's the gist of it anyway."

"But," Ed says, "gist is spirit."

Glyn smiles. "Well the idea is to do a history of the mind, or at least what we know about it. Descartes thought there was a very small part of the brain through which the mind travelled into the body." She turns to Ansel. "Ten points, doctor, if you can name it."

"The *glandula pinealis*."

She raises her glass to him in a toast. "Well done. Physics, quantum mechanics, those are often thought of as the frontier of science. But the other frontier might be study into the mind. How neurons and neurotransmitters make thought and feeling and imagination possible. Things that don't seem like they could possibly come from a material thing, a physical entity."

Ed smiles triumphantly. "Then maybe spirit was the right word."

"In a sense."

While the others talk, Gail is here beside him, laughing in delight at the spread of food. She hoists the wine bottle to make sure that every glass is full.

Ed leans back in his chair. "Now correct me if I'm wrong, but one of the reasons we have so much trouble studying the brain is because it's sort of like a big crumpled piece of paper. Lots of surface area in a very small space, tucked away inside folds and such."

"Like the lungs," Ansel says, his attention returning to the table. "There's more surface area there than on a tennis court."

"Then," Clara says, "I would imagine that the most important parts are in the centre. Less liable to damage?"

"Yes and no. Some parts, like the cerebral cortex, are on the surface. Others, like the thalamus or amygdala, are buried. So thought comes from these different regions working together, like a piece of music. Activity sweeps across the brain. Synapses are excited, connections are made. Up comes the lightbulb."

Ed snaps his fingers and says, apropos of nothing, "Did you know, a catfish is basically a swimming tongue and nose?"

"Speaking of synapses," Ansel says, "there's a biologist who coined the phrase 'I link therefore I am.'"

Glyn nods. "That sounds promising. I might have to use that."

Their eyes meet briefly. Ansel says, the words coming before he has time to consider them, "And you're finishing Gail's documentary."

Clara glances up from her plate, watching them.

"Yes, of course, but it was nearly finished. Gail had already written the script." After a moment, she says, "This project meant something to her. She would have wanted it completed."

There's an awkward quiet at the table. Matthew picks up his glasses and gently folds the arms down. Mrs. Cho takes a sip of wine and says, "You're very brave. That girl was such a perfectionist, I'd be afraid to mess it up. She's the type who would come looking for you."

"Spirits again!" says Ed. "Which reminds me, Ansel, I hope you're minding your duties and keeping that plate full." He points over at the place setting beside him.

Scott Carney stands, takes the wine bottle and begins

refilling the glasses. "William Sullivan's diary. That's the documentary you mean?"

Glyn nods.

Clara picks up the serving spoon and begins to ladle more food onto Mrs. Cho's plate. Ansel sees Matthew reach his hand out, rest it against Clara's back, fingertips brushing her dress. Steadying her, or steadying himself, Ansel cannot tell.

Scott keeps pouring, concentrating on the task as he speaks. "The diary belonged to a friend of mine, a woman I had gone to school with, Kathleen Sullivan. All the pages were filled with numbers. She believed it was a diary because this is what her father had told her, decades ago. A diary he had begun in 1942, while serving with the Canadian army in Hong Kong."

Glyn continues the story, telling how Sullivan had continued writing after Hong Kong fell, after he was taken prisoner by the Japanese, when the act of keeping a journal was punishable by summary execution. But by the 1960s, when Sullivan showed the diary to his family, he himself had forgotten the method of decryption. After his death, the diary had been carefully preserved by Kathleen. Eventually, she attempted to have it read, sending it to experts around the world. Gail had forwarded a copy of the book to Harry Jaarsma, a mathematician and a friend from her student days in the Netherlands, in the hope that he would be able to decipher it.

"I still remember telling Gail the story," Scott says, turning to Ansel, "sitting on the front steps of your house."

After the dishes are cleared away, they move out onto the back porch. Ed picks up his banjo and strums a few strings, then father and son do a duet: "Good Night" by the Beatles, but with the rhythm plucked up so they're tapping their feet. The song goes from three minutes to about forty-five seconds. Ed waves off the applause and segues into "Never My Love." Mrs. Cho creaks back and forth on the rocking chair, singing along, "Da da da da, da da. Never, my love." She tells Ed, "I'm so glad you're my age." He puts his soul into the bass walk up.

"I never thought I'd enjoy this on the banjo." Glyn is standing apart from the group, leaning her back against the house.

Scott turns to her. "You'd be surprised how many people say that. The weird thing is, Dad didn't even pick it up until he was in his fifties. It's not something from his childhood, or from his lost country roots. It's a new thing for him."

Ansel leans over the railing. From here, he can see his own house, where he has left the bedroom light on accidentally. In his red wine haze, it makes him think that someone is waiting up for him. That someone is reading in bed, and when he comes home, he will lift the open book off her chest and set it on the table. When he turns around, he sees that Matthew has already gone upstairs to rest. Clara and Mrs. Cho are having a conversation that moves from Cantonese into English and back again. Glyn, Ed and Scott have gone back to talking about the mind. Ed is saying, "At some point, when they've figured everything out, the new kind of human being may have to live without mystery. And I wonder where that will lead us."

Glyn twirls the glass in her hand, then shakes out the last few drops of wine into the air. "That seems to be something that all the scientists can agree on. That the mind was never made to understand itself. Its first job was to collect information from the senses, find some way to unify that knowledge so that the body could escape danger."

Ed shakes his head. "If I could live my life again, I'm not sure what I would do. The world is endlessly fascinating. When you get to my age, that's the main reason for hanging on. Just to find out a little bit more."

"You could join me in radio. The medium of the imagination."

Ed looks at Ansel. "What about you, doctor? If you could start over again, what would you choose?"

He thinks for a short while but comes to no conclusions. There are too many doors and not enough time to open them. He shakes his head. "I've no idea. Some mysteries, I think, were never meant to be solved."

The three of them laugh. Ed plays a decisive chord on the banjo, and the notes hang on the air for a long time before they are carried away down the block, slowly fading. There's a moment when the sound will dissolve past the range of what Ansel is capable of hearing. One moment of separation. He closes his eyes and waits.

That night, after the dishes are done and the house is still, Clara goes into her sewing room. Above her, the skylight frames a handful of stars, a square of night.

On her cutting table, the newspaper is open to an article about the origins of empathy. She read the story this morning, and its contents have remained in her mind, a background to her thoughts. All acts of empathy, of compassion, the article says, arise out of needs of the individual, and, as such, no act is selfless. "Let us try to teach generosity and altruism," says one scientist, "because we are born selfish." Carefully, she clips this article and lays it on the table in front of her. So many things that we do, she thinks, so much in the name of those we love. In her own life, Clara has witnessed acts of selflessness, of empathy, whose motivations she does not doubt. She knows that a single act, a choice, can transform all that came before. Long ago, when she was young, she risked her future on this belief.

Clara stands at the cutting table, smoothing the paper pattern that she drew earlier in the day. She pins the pieces down, examining the weave of the cloth as she works. If she concentrates, she will be able to finish this gown before morning.

Across the hall, she can hear floorboards creaking, and she pictures her husband rising from bed, standing at the curtains, gazing out at this starlit night. When she first met him more than forty years ago, they had been drawn to one another because of their differences. On the surface, they had been north and south, light and dark. Back then, he had carried a hollow within himself, a grief that he could not share. To each other, they had seemed the way out, the path that leads along the river, finally opening on to the sea.

Nearby is the house where her daughter lived. Gail was a runner, and each day she would pass by Clara's window. She would detour through the alley, into the garden, blowing a playful kiss to her mother as she passed. Clara would watch the easy movement of her daughter's body until it disappeared around the corner.

She picks up the chalk, traces the pieces with a steady hand. The halogen lamp flickers and steadies itself again. In the alley, a stray cat walking between the houses sets the security lights off one by one. Lately, the strangest thought has settled in her mind. If she repeats her own actions on the morning that Gail died, she can pass between days, the way a pin passes through this piece of paper, leaving only the faintest trace. Time will bend backwards on itself and Clara will look out the window, see her daughter returning from her run. The way her dark hair sticks to her face, the same determined expression. Prince George, the hotel room, the suitcase of clothes all disintegrating. As clean as the opening of a seam.

She sits down at her sewing machine, replaces the bobbin and threads the needle. She has done this same work almost all her life. Her hands take over when her thoughts retreat.

In the bedroom, Matthew wakes hearing music, a song played on a phonograph, the rustle and scratch of air on the recording. When he opens his eyes, the dream and the music evaporate. The windows are open, and a cool breeze drifts through the room, holding the curtains aloft. Moonlight gleams off the roofs of the houses, and the leaves shift in the trees. He pushes the covers aside and sits up.

When he first arrived in Vancouver, Matthew felt free in this city. The buildings showed no wear, they seemed untouched by the passage of time. Indeed, it seemed as if once they reached a certain age, old buildings came down and new ones replaced them. The mountains, near and distant, the ocean, all these things changed from day to day, never quite the same. During the winters, it rained almost all the time, sheets of water like a brush coating everything, dimming the sounds to a quiet murmur.

When Matthew and his daughter walked together, along Keefer, then Pender, she used to whisper the street names under her breath. Matthew would tell her stories about his childhood before the war, about Sandakan, until he realized that she remembered so much. She wanted to hear every-thing, to know how the story continued. His words ran dry. She was half his height then; the crown of her head reached his waist. He remembers carrying his daughter, her hands clasped around his neck, feeling as if he held a treas-ure in his arms. He held her so tightly, careful of each step he made.

Six months ago, his daughter died suddenly in her sleep. She was away working in the north of the province. It was Matthew who received the phone call, who was the one to tell his wife. He knows that all one's grief cannot stop the present, cannot change the way a life unfolds.

Now, when he walks through this neighbourhood, he loses track of the streets. In his mind, he hears his daughter singing the names to herself, *Keefer, Pender, Adanac*, but his sense of direction has become confused. When he looks around, nothing he sees is familiar. He has lived here for most of his life, but if he picked up a pencil, out of the small islands of memory he could draw the streets of his childhood, the town of Sandakan, Leila Road winding up into the hillside. In the months since his daughter died, things once lost have grown clearer, a flight that takes him from Vancouver to Sandakan, from Sandakan to Jakarta. He remembers how, from the air, the red roofs of the town had disappeared, given way to unbroken jungle, on a journey that began a lifetime ago, and that continues still.

Lately, Matthew's knees have begun to give. A twinge of pain in the ligament, and then an ache centred in the bone. His wife had tenderly rubbed the curve of his knee with her hands. "No more marathons," she had said, a teasing smile lighting her eyes. "Don't despair. You're only sixty-six, and age is a state of mind."

She had learned to alter her pace, move patiently beside his slow shuffle. An old man takes an eternity to walk to the corner store. Their conversations became elongated, paced out from here to there, drawing to a close when they came in sight of the house. All these years, Clara has made most of his clothes. He finds pieces around the house, sleeves opened up on her table, starched collars like overgrown butterflies, one pant leg creased over a chair.

Outside, the stars are shining. Matthew stands at his window, lifts his arms above his head, bends at the waist, feels his body return to him. He remembers the gentleness of his mother's hand in his hair, how when she stepped back from him, the imprint remained, a weight, a memory against his skin.

2

Pieces of Map

SANDAKAN, BRITISH NORTH BORNEO

September, 1945

*W*hen he woke, it was still dark outside. Matthew slipped his foot out from under the sheet and prodded the ground with his toes. Nothing. Two nights ago, running out of the hut, he had lost his shoe. His left foot had lifted out of the grass, into the weightless air. The shoe had disappeared. They had looked for it in the morning, he and Ani, crawling in the grass, but they had found nothing. *Matamu, matamu*, he had whispered. His most important possession, disappeared. She had stood beside him, head tilted like a listening animal while the sun burned down on their necks. Then he and Ani sank back to the ground like fish lowering themselves under water. He had looked up and seen her black hair loose and blowing above the grass. Surely it would give them away. "Stolen," he had whispered to her.

She had nodded, sympathetic, still searching.

Now, inside the hut, he sat up in the dark. A sharp pain rooted itself in his stomach, then flowed through his limbs. Before, when there were chickens, their bickering would wake him up. He would run through the crowd of them, all the way to the outhouse, and they would scatter before his feet, their red combs bobbing.

He blinked, and objects slowly came into focus. The square radio, reaching up a long, thin wire; his father standing on the other side of the hut. As his father listened to the broadcast, he placed both hands on his hips, leaned sideways, then stretched his arms above his head. Matthew focused on his white shirt, a tilting light visible in the room.

His father had been awake for hours. Already, while Matthew slept, he had walked through the aisles of the rubber plantation that had once belonged to their family and now lay under the control of the Japanese army. In the dark, the tappers had been crouched together, heads nearly touching as if they were playing marbles. It was so dark between the trees that only their exhalations, the occasional spitting of betel nut, gave them away. As the sun came up, the workers would set off across the plantation to collect the rubber. The night before, they had tapped the trees, one slash across the bark, a cigarette tin to catch the latex. Now, the latex was to be collected and brought to the storehouse where it would be laid out, then rolled flat. Afterwards, the sheets would be separated and hung to dry in a big closet.

Matthew heard the sound of a vehicle on the road outside. His father quickly replaced the radio in its hiding place in the floor, then pushed a cabinet over top. The door opened and shut, letting in a stream of light, and his father was gone. The hut finally stirred.

There was no *ubi kayu* to eat, no morning meal. Matthew saw two cigarettes on the table. His mother said, distractedly, "I'm going to visit your uncle this afternoon. Promise me you won't go to Leila Road today." She turned for a moment to glance towards the door.

"Yes, mother," he said. Quickly, he rolled the cigarettes into his hand and dropped them into his pocket.

Outside, walking along the road, he found Ani sitting on the ground, waiting for him.

She smiled when she saw him, getting to her feet. He followed her gaze down the hillside. The sun had left an orange shadow on the water, but up here the fog still clung to the ground, and the air was cool and misty.

Slowly, they began to walk uphill, keeping close to Leila Road, but staying hidden by a line of tall trees. Above them, the blossoms of yellow flowers opened like tiny birds. Their centres, a blush of red, reminded him of a bag of circassian beans he had once owned. His father had watched him scattering them across the table. "Don't put those in your mouth," he had warned Matthew. "Before you know it, a suga tree will take root in your body." Now, Matthew reached his hand up, pressed his fingers against the back of his head, feeling for any sign of unusual growth. "Can a seed grow from the top of your head, if you'd swallowed it first?"

"No," she said, thinking, "or else everybody would have done it by now."

"If you could, what seeds would you eat?"

She thought for a second, and then said, "Bananas."

"Good choice." They walked from tree to tree. Above their heads, the branches disappeared into mist. Higher still, the branches re-emerged, floating in the sky.

"What about you?"

"Chickens."

"A chicken tree?" She laughed. When she did, the mist seemed to break apart, separating like heavy milk on a cup of coffee. "Well, maybe we can find some eggs today."

Ani was ten years old, five months older than Matthew, but already she was several inches taller. She wore a pale sarong, fastened by a square knot. The colour had faded from sun and dirt, so now the fabric was a colour he couldn't name. A noon sky on a hot day, a fading white. Her hair was gathered in a long braid that swung against her back. Some days, when they were both too hungry to walk, they would hide themselves in one of the craters left behind by British bombs at the top of the hill. They would warm their feet in the shafts of sunlight that fell between the leaves, but still he found himself shivering, even on the hottest days.

She told him once about a game played in town on the *padang*, the green pitch, with wooden sticks and heavy balls. The field no longer existed, but in a time that Ani could still remember, ladies once stood on the lawns, drinking tea from delicate cups. The cups had handles like a child's ear. "You were there," she told him, trying to prod his memories. "I saw you walking with your mother."

He tried hard to remember it.

At the start of the war, the English women had gone away on a boat. Ani had stood on Jalan Satu, at the white fence beside the eyeglass shop. "You know the one?"

He nodded.

Waves of heat had moved on the water, blurring the women in their long dresses, who waved to their husbands from the steamboat. Even in the heat, they wore gloves. "They sounded like birds crying." She had been seven years old when the war came to Sandakan. Before their surrender, the British had set the oil tanks and bridges on fire, black smoke rising in columns to the sky. "Remember? All the coins were thrown into the sea, and the tanks were still burning when the Japanese came. They were so angry, they opened fire on the air."

Before the war, Matthew had lived in a fine house on Jalan Campbell, in the centre of Sandakan town. He remembered the tabletop radio, its big grill and squeaky knobs. There was a sofa made of soft material, shelves of Chinese books. His father's business partners drank tea and then cognac in the dining room, speaking Hakka or English peppered with Malay. He and Ani had sat beside one another in St. Michael's Church mission school, tracing the map of British North Borneo into their notebooks. He imagined he was looking down on Sandakan from above, at the town perched on the curve of the Sulu Sea, following the coast south to Tawau, where his mother was born, at the border between the British protectorate and the Dutch East Indies.

At the start of the occupation, three years ago, the Japanese had taken over the schools. He and Ani had learned to sing Japanese songs, and also the anthem, the *Kimigayo*. "*May the reign of the Emperor continue for a thousand, nay, eight thousand generations.*" The schools had operated for almost a year before closing down again. Radios were made illegal, though his father kept one hidden away. In the dark, his father would push the cabinet aside, set up the wire, bring the floating voices into their small hut.

It was getting warmer.

Ani stood up, circling around to a *bunga kubur* tree whose blossoms were beginning to fall. The flowers were the size of his father's open hand. She held one now, her hand gone, her wrist ending in a burst of petals. Ani walked along the row of trees, her arm outstretched, the flower held aloft. Around them, the mist was lifting. They were fully visible, no longer hidden from the road. He saw something in the leaves, a piece of clothing, bloodied, the shape of body.

"Ani," he said, his voice more frightened than he intended.

She knelt down beside a sandalwood tree and placed the flower in the hollow between two roots. "Everyone says the fighting is done." When she turned to face him, her eyes, so wistful, stilled his heart. "And I wanted to leave something for my parents, now that the war is over."

One morning when he is twenty-eight years old, Matthew wakes in his home in Vancouver to the sound of a child crying. Beside him, his wife, Clara, is fast asleep. She shifts uneasily, turning her head, as if the crying of the child has entered her dreams.

He finds his slippers, then walks carefully across the room and out into the hallway, where, from the nursery doorway, he sees his tiny daughter sobbing. Her hands are confused in the blanket, twisting the fabric into a tangled knot. Her eyes are pressed tight, as if concentrating on a sound that only she can hear. She is almost a year old. "It's okay," he says. "It's all right." Her arms reach out to his voice. Only then does he step through the doorway and enter the room. At her crib, he places his hand on her head and finds that her soft, dark hair is damp with sweat.

He withdraws his hand, unsure what to do. It is Clara their daughter always turns to. Gail falls asleep gripping her mother's body, her face barely visible, her body curled like a little animal against her mother's chest.

Gail, he whispers, leaning over her, pushing the hair back from her face. *Little Gail*. He puts his hand against her forehead to comfort her, but she does not stop crying.

Standing there, he has a memory of Ani as she was when they were children, and the image of her is startlingly vivid. "Even in the heat they wore gloves," she says, describing the British women leaving Sandakan, the steamboat that vanished into the blue of the sea. He is sitting with her on the fringe of the jungle, not wanting to move. His eyes are closed so everything else will fall away and her voice will become the entire world.

He lifts his daughter out of the crib and sits down on the carpeted floor. He rocks the child in his arms. Matthew sees that she is struggling to wake herself, so he whispers to her to give her something to hold on to, a voice to follow out of her own consciousness. Eventually, she opens her eyes, blinking, but she does not seem surprised to find him there. He continues to hold her, saying whatever comes to mind. That her mother will be here soon, that it is morning now, and this day will progress in its usual way. Breakfast, and afterwards they will go to the park. Perhaps, later on, a ride in the car through the city.

And miraculously, his daughter seems to be listening. After a few moments, her breathing calms. Her eyes are still wet with tears, but she is looking through them, focused now on his face. The words keep coming, about lunch and dinner, about a warm bath when the sun goes down. He tells her how his mother used to bathe him outside, under the orange lamp of the sun. How he could hear the songs of kingfishers in the trees and imagined that they were laughing at him, the naked boy playing in a round tub of water. They threw seeds and nuts down at him, and then they spread their wings and lifted up into the white sky.

She does not fall asleep again, and he keeps on talking until Clara wakes and finds them there.

That night, he dreams of a road that leads away from Sandakan harbour, and then of a tunnel under the ground. He sees his father, weeping, thrown from a boat into the sea.

Matthew dives in after him. He finds that he can breathe easily, air flows into and out of his lungs. As he descends, the water grows bright, as if lit from a source far below. For a long time he swims in this place, looking neither forward nor back, carried safely, effortlessly, by a current within the sea. By the time he realizes that his lungs are empty, it is too late, his thoughts are already torn, losing substance. The surface is no longer visible.

In January 1945, when the British bombs exploded on Sandakan, all the people ran to the hillside.

Matthew had been asleep in his bed in the house on Jalan Campbell. The noise of the planes stunned him awake, and then he was half-carried, half-dragged, across the floor, down the stairs and out of the house. Panic seized his chest, a pebble in his lungs. His mother was holding jewellery in her hands, gold chains tangled together. A wedding photograph. He heard voices, someone screaming, sirens, and then the first bomb fell, the explosion deafening him. The air began to burn. His mother grabbed him, he did not know where his father was, and they began to run uphill, through the thick smoke, ash raining on their skin, away from Leila Road and into the jungle. He stumbled over a body, its eyes open, heard a man crying. In the sky, flares exploded, opening windows of light on them, exposing the bellies of planes falling on Sandakan. A stickiness ran from his ears, staining his fingers dark when he touched the place. He saw the necklaces snap, coming out of his mother's hands, and then the bombs dropping, slow and heavy, as if they might be carried past by the wind. The town exploded in a wash of flames.

More people ran up the hill, and around him the jungle seemed to move and shift. Pictures ran through his mind, an egg, a bag of marbles. He wanted to close his eyes, float his body up to where it could not be harmed. His mother tried to cover him, pushing his face against the bark of a tree. Everything smelled of flowers, a sweet, cloying perfume filling his lungs. A plane seemed to stall above them, and in place of its engine he heard the sound of a whistle. The fall began and he counted the seconds, the noise so piercing he could not hear himself speak the last number before the explosion. A tree cracked, swaying towards them. They became nothing. The whistles did not stop. A flare lit up the dead around him, burning pictures in his eyes. The pebble of fear in his chest exploded, and the fragments flooded his body.

After the planes left, they did not move. The town glimmered, a red haze that burned continuously as he fell in and out of sleep. Morning came and he breathed only smoke. On Jalan Campbell, they found his father standing in rubble where the front wall of their house lay crumpled. There was blood on his clothes. He, too, had slept in the jungle. He said that these bombs were meant to save them, to strike the Japanese, to ease the Allied entry into Sandakan and the liberation of the town.

Every night for three weeks, the bombs came and they ran into the dark. But after the planes turned back, no Allied soldiers came.

In the jungle and on the hillside, people built temporary shelters, crowding themselves together. This was where Ani lived with her father. There was no food, and each day she scavenged for jungle fern and sweet potatoes. The dead were buried everywhere.

Matthew and Ani walked through what remained of Sandakan town, through the rubble and glass, through wood heaved at odd angles as if the entire street were still in the act of collapsing. In all this, they found porcelain bowls, undamaged. A half-dozen pairs of spectacles, a rattan chair. He thought he saw people suspended, the shape of a hand. Touch them, and they crumbled to dirt. On Jalan Campbell, where his house once stood, and Jalan Satu, where Ani and her father had lived, nothing but beams, twisted and black, remained.

Matthew and his parents found their way to an abandoned hut at the edge of their former plantation. Before the war, he remembered, his father had taken him to watch the tapping of the rubber trees; at night, lamps ringed with oil were used to ward away the moths. The aisles had been hallways of light, tunnels that led to mysterious destinations. Now, with the shortage in kerosene, the lamps remained unlit. When he looked out at the darkness, his chest seemed to fill with water, submerging his lungs. Each night he woke to the sound of army trucks rumbling past. He knew that the Japanese police, the *kempeitai*, came after curfew, sweeping the huts for guerillas and taking away any person, any family, they suspected. In his dreams, the road became a part of his body, gravel crumbling through his bloodstream, catching in his throat. He was afraid of the unlit plantation, of the decaying huts farther down the hillside. The dwellings were not safe. At any moment, a person could be pulled from his home, away from his family, and executed in the glare of a torch.

Sometimes, in the night, Matthew saw his father rise from bed, sleepless, a shadow among shadows in the room. Outside, there were gunshots, voices shouting. The war, his father once said, would be no more than a drop of rain on their long lives. If they were smart, if they were careful, they could compromise in order to survive. His father made promises that he could not keep. He said the war would pass, and life as they remembered it would return, as inevitably as one season followed another.

He and Ani now stood on Leila Road, a path that led along the coast, through the ruined town, and up to the top of the hill. When the ridge turned east, they could see the bay stretching out before them, the chalk hills of Berhala Island glowing red against the sparkling water. Farther up along the road, there was a marker for Mile 8, where the prisoner-of-war camps and airfield had been built. The ghost road, people had begun to call it, the point at which the path became grown over and impassable, finally giving way to jungle.

Some days, walking here, they would see Japanese soldiers, and they would run to the side of the road, drop their eyes and bow at the waist. Panic gripped his body, holding him still. He would stare at the black millipedes, the shiny backs of the beetles climbing over his feet. He saw the darkened skin of the soldiers' hands, the rifles swinging casually against their legs.

Ani would sing the *Kimigayo*, her voice lingering over the long notes. He heard a strange and unfamiliar sadness in her voice. "*Koke no musu made.*" "*And for the eternity that it takes for small stones to grow into a great rock and become covered with moss.*" The soldiers sang along with her. They showed her photographs of their loved ones, their mothers, gazing into the flash of the camera. Ani's face was still and expressionless. They rewarded her with handkerchiefs filled with balls of rice, or sometimes an egg.

What if they were seen? But Ani had no choice. The schools had been closed long ago, her parents were gone, and she had only herself to depend on.

Afterwards, Ani would divide the reward into equal halves. They did not linger over the food. The eggs swelled her cheeks into a wide smile, and she would lie back on the dirt, letting the sun warm her skin, savouring that brief moment when the pain of hunger retreated.

Once, angry, not knowing if what they were doing was right, he had refused the egg she offered him.

She did not answer for a long time. "Your family isn't starving," she said, her voice low as if afraid to injure him. "Not like the others."

At Ani's words, he wanted to lie on the grass, close his eyes, and give his shame up and everything with it. He saw his father rising in the morning, reaching his arms into the sky. This was the best time of the day, when the house was still and he saw his father at peace, unhurried, alone in the half-light.

In the years before the war reached Sandakan, his parents had planted the seeds for a garden, hidden in the jungle. They grew *padi*, eggplant and yams, enough to feed themselves through the coming turmoil. But they had been unlucky. Two years ago, an informer had gone to the Japanese and the garden was discovered. One morning, soldiers had burst into the house. He remembered his father, still wearing his housecoat, the first blow knocking him to the floor. The soldiers said that it was treason to withhold supplies from the occupying force. They went through the rooms, calmly shattering the glass cabinets, opening his father's desk, spilling papers on the ground. He thought his father had been shot, the way the rifle was pointed, how the bayonet wavered beside his head as he lay on the floor. His mother's scream-ing had faded to nothing, colour had drained from the world. Only later, when the gun was lowered, did Matthew's senses return, piece by piece, sound by sound.

In the days that followed, it seemed they had been for-tunate. His father began to spend time at the Japanese offices. Sometimes he came home with an extra ration of rice, eggs or a tin of milk. In the mornings, he walked away from the house, his head held high, towards town.

He and Ani walked farther uphill. Below, the debris of the town shone, bleached by the sun, the odd post or beam still standing above the wreckage. Even now, in the chaos of the flattened buildings, the grid of streets was still visible.

"Who told you the war was over?" he said suddenly.

"Lohkman's brother heard it on the radio. The Emperor himself, he said the war is over." She paused, looking out at the sea. "But that was more than a month ago, near the beginning of August."

They walked in silence, bare feet crackling the leaves on the ground.

She gestured towards the harbour. She told him that when the British came back, there would be tables full of food, of English cakes and tea. Boats would arrive again, from Australia and Singapore.

Today, no soldiers appeared on the road. When Ani and Matthew reached the crater, their hands were empty. Ani slid down the crater wall, and he followed behind her. Inside, protected, he thought of them as goldfish, resting in the centre of the bowl. The edges of the trees were sharp against the light.

The Japanese would soon give up Sandakan. Even his mother, who always kept her words to herself, had said the same. One morning in August, a strange and terrible bomb had fallen on Japan. What kind of bomb? he had wondered, but no one knew. Only that behind it, a lasting emptiness remained. The guns and bayonets, the soldiers in their brown uniforms, the cities, had turned to air.

They sat in the crater, back-to-back, and listened to a round of gunfire. The sound was close, behind the hill, but not enough to worry. Sitting like this, the heaviness of her head against his own would tilt his forward. Matthew pulled his knees up to his chest and clasped his arms around them. In the hollow of his back, Ani's shoulder blades felt like two small wings.

Inside the crater, no wind blew. Outside, on solid ground, there were strips of shade and light, but in here the light turned strange, almost liquid. There were no plants, nothing that grew. The bottom of the crater curved up like a boat, a hollow in which he and Ani could rest. In here, he, too, became something else, his body so insubstantial it seemed a memory of itself. Only by removing himself completely from the crater, by climbing carefully back over the lip, could he become whole once more.

He watched a gust of wind stir the branches of the trees. Leaves and flowers spun slowly down, twisting in slow and intricate spirals.

Unlike Ani, who tried to remember everything, Matthew had kept only a handful of memories from before the war. These stood out from his thoughts, shining like coins in a bowl of water.

When he told this to Ani, she asked, "What is the very first thing that you remember?"

His mother washing him in a round tin bucket. This was long ago, when they had lived in a small house beside the rubber plantation. His mother would set the tub on the ground outside, and she would fill it with cool water. Then, kneeling in front of him, she would unwrap him from his clothes, lift him up and set him down in the tub. The cold water shocked his skin, and the surprise mingled with the yelling of the rubber tappers, the flash of bulbuls and kingfishers above him. In the background, he heard warning shouts, coconuts knock-knocking to the ground. With fingers spread wide, one of his mother's hands spanned Matthew's back. She poured water from a cup, and the liquid sheeted down his skin. If he lay flat, bending only his knees, he could rest his head on the bottom of the bucket. His mother's voice blurred and became a metallic echo in the water. Matthew remembered watching their shadows on the ground, his flowing into his mother's, then coming apart.

"And what else?" Ani loosened her hair from its braid and it opened up in waves.

His mother planting vegetables, in preparation for the war. The garden was hidden in a cleared area in the jungle. In the mornings, she would bundle him up and place him inside a large basket, along with a canteen of water. The basket was attached to one end of a pole. A second basket, filled with food, was attached to the other end. She then picked up the pole and, balancing it across her shoulders, began walking up the road. The fronds of the basket were itchy against his skin, and they smelled of wood husk. Matthew, lying back and looking at the sky, could see his mother pass in, then out, of sight.

At some point, they would come to a bridge. He heard it long before he saw it, a roar in his ears that grew louder, so loud that it flooded his vision. His mother would adjust the pole along one shoulder, causing the basket to dip and sway. He would look out and see the river, a deep blue field. Fear made him lie still. If he fell, he would not be able reach out, open his arms and catch himself. From moment to moment, he swung like a pendulum, his body handed from the sky to the water and back again.

Nearby to that garden in the jungle, he remembered, his father had buried sheets of rubber from the plantation, so that his fortune would not fall into Japanese hands.

Ani's memories had always been different. She had walked with her parents from the Dutch East Indies over the hills into Tawau, then north across the spine of the island and into Sandakan. She remembered passing the volcanoes of Semporna, the smooth cones that encircled the city.

"It took a whole season," she told him now, lying back in the crater. "I was too small to walk the entire way, so sometimes my mother tied me to her back and carried me. The cloth was bound so tight, I felt as if I was a part of her body." She closed her eyes as she spoke. "We had no map. My father knew his way along the jungle tracks. Some days we went by river and some days through the jungle."

Near the start of the war, her mother had given birth to a baby girl. It had been during the rainy season in Sandakan, and the baby was very small. Sometimes the baby would cry, but her cry was muffled, as if she had a painful throat. Later, when she cried, no sound came out at all. The baby died in her mother's arms, but even then the baby could not let go. She tried to pull her mother after her, into the place where she was going. "Because my sister was so small," Ani said, "and she was frightened of going alone."

Her mother's body had become feverish. When she held her mother's hand, Ani could feel the pulse beating fast, as if she were running away. The indent of Ani's fingers remained, the skin like a piece of fruit left too long in the field. "Saira," her father said, repeating the name, calling her back. "This is your home." Night after night, Ani and her father stayed beside her, listening as her breathing slowed and slowed, slipping free. She died while they slept, and by morning her body was already cool.

The Japanese ordered her father to work on the airfield at Mile 8. The workers had no tools, no *changkul* or axes or machetes. Sometimes, when her father returned to the house on Jalan Satu, so weary he could not lift his arms, he would nudge a small potato from his pocket and lay it in her hands.

Each day, she walked along the fringe of the jungle looking for fern tips, swamp cabbage and yams. Perhaps, she said, she could learn to live off the air, the way the plants transformed sunshine into food. It was true. Sometimes, when she lay down in the hot grass, the sun soaking into all of her limbs, she felt a round and perfect fullness settling in her body. "We used to roast wild boar outside over coals," she said. "The meat was so soft it melted on your tongue, it slid like sugar into your stomach. At night now, I have dreams about it."

Before she died, her mother had told her that she might find other family in Tarakan, in the Dutch East Indies, after the war. She asked Ani to promise her that she would go back one day, if she could. There were uncles, aunts and crowds of cousins. Ani said that she imagined a row of houses, each one opening to welcome her, each face a reminder of her mother's. When the war was truly over here in Sandakan, she would keep her promise and travel back to her family; she would walk back over the ridges of Borneo and into the Dutch East Indies, high above the little islands and the glowing blue sea. In the hills, she remembered, there were wildflowers. There were flowers whose cups were the length of a child's body. One could sleep inside, she thought, if the rains came. Folded up in a smell.

He said they could go together. The town of Sandakan was gone, but he still remembered where all the buildings once stood, the Sandakan Hotel, the eyeglass shop, the clattering racket of the tin makers and the cloth banners that beat in the wind. The Japanese soldiers had stolen everything, and then the British planes had set it all on fire. Thick black smoke had overrun the sky. All their possessions, his father's books, Matthew's bag of red circassian beans, no longer part of the world.

When two elephants fight, what does it have to do with us? This is what the men in town had said before the war, when Britain and Japan seemed far away.

The ground was rubble, strange twisted shapes. If you touched them, pieces came off in your hands. Once, he and Ani had come across a coconut plantation that no longer bore fruit, and he asked her now if she remembered where it stood. The trees, thin and silvery, had been sawed off at the top so that nothing grew from the crown. A pale forest with no canopy, hundreds of slender lines, as if they had been surprised and then somehow ambushed.

"Near to the ghost road," she said. "But nobody goes there at night."

Matthew had heard rumours about this place, Mile 8, the prisoner-of-war camps. There, prisoners were cursed to walk forever. They said only, *jalan jalan*, carrying other soldiers on their backs. Men lay in the mud and begged for food, but they disappeared when you reached out to help them. Ani said that if you walked there, you might cross the line unknowingly and find yourself unable to return to the place of the living.

"Do you think it hurts?"

"No," she said. "It happens too fast." Her eyes were closed, and when she spoke again, her voice was clear, as if bracing itself. "I think people don't realize they're dying, they feel no pain. It comes too quickly, when their thoughts are turned the other way."

He moved his fingers along the ground, tracing a series of lines in the dirt. Sometimes his thoughts felt like a moving stream, a flickering light. He missed his shoes. He remembered the feel of them, how they rubbed against his heels, reminding him all the time of their presence. He and Ani were sitting up on the edge of the crater now, in the shade of candlenut trees. Ani placed her hands one over the other, making the shadow of a swan on the ground. She set the swan down on his knee. When it touched his skin, the hands flew apart, the illusion vanished. "Don't be afraid," she said, so softly that the words seemed a part of his own thoughts. "We'll always take care of each other, no matter where we go."

She laid her head against his shoulder, and he closed his eyes for a time.

Ani had told Matthew how, three days after her father disappeared, she had walked the Leila Road to Mile 8. It was early in the morning, still dark; only the rubber tappers had started the day. The night before, rumours of mass killings had spread to the huts. She had followed the rumours there, to the airfield, where she saw pieces of clothing, stained, and then she recognized her father's body. Bullets had opened his chest. She stood a few feet away, unable to move closer, to touch him. The nightjars and the cicadas crowded her ears with their sound. She cried without hearing herself; for how long, she didn't know. By the time she looked up, the sky had grown pale. She had to leave. The road that she walked on led past the prisoner-of-war camps. Someone in the dark reached through the fence, took hold of her hand. *Tolong*, he said. *Help me.* He pressed money into her palm, a few words in broken Malay, a name. He wanted her to take a message to someone who lived on the hillside. She could smell him, the prisoner, blood and sweat and urine.

Ani grasped the money in her hand and turned, running, her bare feet sinking into the mud. She expected to hear a voice, a gunshot, but nothing followed after her. The road curved down along the hill, and, in the dawn light, the sea was a burning blue. It reminded her of the chrome on a car she had seen once. Before. Long ago. When cars had first appeared in Sandakan, rolling off the steamers.

She saw the mangrove trees, vividly green, curving away from the shore. Her thoughts spun loose. There was no way for her to bury her father. Before, a gravestone would be made and there would be ceremonies, the same as they had carried

out for her mother, the doors of the house kept open for three
nights to mark the passing of her mother's soul into the land
of the dead. In the dark, she and her father had stayed awake,
naming the birds by their sounds, each nudging the other if
one of them began to drift to sleep. "She has a great distance
to travel," her father had said. "Much farther than when we
walked from Tarakan. In the afterlife, she lives in a village just
like the one she was born in. She will cook and clean and help
with the planting. But it is like our world turned upside-
down. Plenty of food and happiness, and no one knows
suffering. But sometimes souls get lost and are unable to find
their way. That's why we must stay awake and make sure that
she is sent away properly. It is our most important task."

Her father had been lying on the airfield for three days.
Too late, already, to help him; his soul had departed, though
he did not know the way. Ani imagined that the line of dead
was long, a single-file line, and he could follow the trail that
had been left by others. That, in itself, was a blessing.

On the road, the money clutched in her hand, she could
see the islands off the coast, round turtle backs floating on
the sea. Beside her, bellflowers hung suspended upside down.
She imagined holding a gun in her arms, she saw a lost child,
a dead girl, standing where she stood, feet sinking in the
mud. The sun was rising. She looked through the sights, her
hand poised in the instant before firing. Their spirits were so
far from home, the landscape was so changed, so ruined, they
would never find their way back.

Ani left that girl standing there, the air still shattering
around her. She walked in the direction of the mud huts,

keeping to the right of the path, in case a soldier came suddenly onto the road before her.

⁓

There are mornings when Matthew wakes and he forgets that he is old. He thinks that he is seven, perhaps ten years old, but then it is like being on a hilltop in the fog. He cannot see five feet ahead or five feet back.

When he thinks of those years, there is a particular place that he sees, Leila Road, before it was paved and renamed, before the new developments began to crowd the hillside. It was a dirt track in the 1940s, and he had walked it many times, sometimes alone, sometimes with Ani. He remembers something that she told him once. They had been playing *main lering*, a game with a stick and a hoop. "If you dream about a hoop, it means that you have come to the end of your troubles and that only abundant happiness will follow."

Almost sixty years have passed since then, and he lives here, in Canada, a country that considers itself young. Where he comes from was broken, reborn, North Borneo, now East Malaysia, reshaped and growing. He has seen the country recently in photographs, the glittering cities, the twin towers in Kuala Lumpur rising above the skyline, eighty-eight storeys high. In speeches reported by the international press, the prime minister of Malaysia speaks of a multimedia super corridor, a futuristic business centre in the heart of the nation, taking the place of the palm oil, rubber and coconut plantations that he remembers so well.

When the war finally ended in September of 1945, Matthew and his mother fled Sandakan alone, fearful in the night. In the decades that followed, he returned only twice, both times thinking that he could find a reason, a person who could bind him together, contain his memories, finally. The first time he returned, he was eighteen years old. The town had changed greatly, and he could not recognize the buildings. One day, he came to the end of Leila Road and stepped into the jungle. The trees closed behind him, and he felt a curtain come down between him and the life that he knew, the solid houses, the rubber plantation. All the yearning that he carried – for change, to be afraid no longer – began to quiet. He saw that the grief that overwhelmed him might be set aside. It was possible, if only he were strong enough. He could leave Sandakan, let Ani go, create for himself a different life, separate from the future he had once imagined.

Here, in Canada, the roads are clean and straight, and the landscape, familiar now, steadies him. His memory, which has weakened throughout the years, sometimes causes him to doubt himself. The dead slip through his hands, leaving only a wash of silence. "What are you thinking?" his wife will ask him, seeing that he is lost. He is trying to hold on to his father's voice, the face of his child, the days that marked the end of the war. Even now, too late, he imagines finding the way out. In his nightmares, he tries to tell his father that another path exists, that the centre of his self, the goodness that makes him whole, once lost, can never be recovered. But the words that Matthew speaks carry no sound, they are a rustling on the air.

During those long hours when he cannot sleep, he tries to piece together every detail. He remembers a night when Japanese soldiers came to the hut, how he tried to make himself invisible. He pictures the basket in which his mother carried him, how he had swung, safe, above the rising water. The voices of the Japanese soldiers fell around him. "Are you hungry?" they asked him, teasingly. "*Makan makan?*" His mother had warned him not speak, not to show any emotion. He could only nod his head, his body motionless before them. They could kick him aside or let him be.

The Japanese soldiers held a sheaf of forms, a list of the requisitions to be made. Not only crops and livestock, but also fishing boats and nets, the means to earn a living. His father signed page after page while the soldiers nodded, smiling. They said that they were anxious to involve the local population, they declared that Japan would be a guiding hand, a light, for Asia. His father accepted the reward, pieces of meat or dried fish, tins of vegetables, cigarettes.

When the soldiers left the hut, his father's face was calm. Ink smudges marked his fingers and the edge of his right hand. At dinner, he took almost nothing for himself, only a bit of millet or an extra ball of rice. As Matthew and his mother ate, he studied them, watching closely, as if he took comfort in their movements, as if the familiarity of their presence could convince him that nothing had been lost.

Only once did Matthew hear his mother's despair. She begged his father to come to his senses. She said that they would find a way to make do, somehow. *We can go to Tawau.*

We can stay with my family. Matthew's father had wept. *The war is everywhere.* She said that when the British returned, there would be no safe place for him. His father had closed his eyes, blocking her out. People are calling you a collaborator, she said. A murderer.

Lying on his cot, watching, Matthew had felt his body cramp with fear and hunger. To drown out the words, he thought of food, meat cooked in sugar, and it started a rumbling of pain so clean he no longer heard silence or sound. He knew that only his father's actions protected them. Rumours, descriptions from nearby towns had trickled in. *Sook ching*, the killings were called, a cleansing. Entire households, villages, destroyed. Day and night, these killings entered his dreams.

Before the war, when men from the British North Borneo Company had roamed the streets, and the red flag with the Union Jack and the lion had fluttered above the harbour, his father had worked beside those British men. On Friday evenings, they would drink cognac on the *padang*, laughing easily in English and Malay. Matthew still remembers the postcards addressed to his father that lined the shelves of the old house, showing photographs or paintings of distant cities, London, Singapore, Berlin. When his father was Matthew's age, he had travelled alone, by ship, from China to Malaya, and onwards to North Borneo. He said that when Matthew was older, they would travel together back to his village in China. They would pack their trunks with gifts, and no one would recognize the frightened boy who had been sent away some twenty years before. He had changed, his father said, remade himself. He had become a man who could be at home in any place in the world.

When the British surrender began, his father had gone methodically through the drawers, discarding the remnants of their previous lives, evidence of his work for the British North Borneo Company. When he came to the postcards, he ripped them up; at first, one at time, then in handfuls, the pieces scattering on the carpet. His face was expressionless. Only after he left the house did Matthew's mother kneel down, sweeping the pieces up with her hands, leaving no evidence.

The face that Matthew remembers now, more than fifty years later, is indistinct. He sees his father as if through a layer of dust, a tall man walking, his back held straight, towards the road. When he turns to look at Matthew, his eyes are empty, the light hollowed out. He tells Matthew that it is too late, that understanding cannot save him, the home, the town that lies in ruins. *Go back the way you came*, he says. *You cannot know, cannot imagine, all that has led up to this moment.*

The last time they climbed up this far, to the end of Leila Road, they had heard rifle shots shattering the air. He and Ani had run into the jungle, crouching together in the mud. More shots were fired, and then they heard a troop of men approaching. Soon, a group of prisoners appeared on the road, half naked, dirt clinging to their skin, their bodies cavernous. They walked on legs that were like cherry stems, threatening to break. Japanese soldiers surrounded the prisoners, a fence of brown uniforms, of guns and bayonets. Some of the men were ill; it was clear they would not survive much longer. They stumbled uphill, away from Sandakan and the camp, following the road to where it ended, becoming only mud and jungle. They continued, into the trees.

Matthew closed his eyes. Eventually, he felt Ani taking hold of his hand, pulling him up. The road was deserted once more, and she led him to a small river where they could wash the mud from their clothes. She had walked in wearing her sarong, hiding her face under the water, and he could not see her expression. He had watched her hair rising to the surface, floating like a sheet of silk.

Later, they heard that the British and Australian prisoners had been sent on a long march through the jungle to Ranau, a town more than 250 kilometres away. Those who could not walk had been killed, at the outset or during the journey, and their bodies left unburied.

Now, from the crater where they sat, he and Ani could see smoke, thick and dark, rising from the airfield and the prisoner-of-war camps. Flames suddenly became visible, flickering above the trees. Without speaking, they got to their feet, hearing a truck, an engine idling somewhere nearby. Half-running, half-walking, they went back along Leila Road in the direction of Ani's hut.

It was on the hillside, one in a row of similar structures, built from discarded wood and topped with a tin roof, now rusted. Inside, it was empty except for a few items of clothing folded neatly on the ground. Everything else had been sold or traded. They lay back on the mud floor, flies hovering around them, but he was too tired to brush them away. Rain began, millions of tiny hammers on the roof.

"I brought these for you." He reached into his pocket and retrieved the two slightly crushed cigarettes. He knew they could be used to buy food on the black market, that cigarettes had become more valuable than the Japanese imperial money that everyone carried.

She smiled, holding them up, turning them round and round, then she laid them on her stomach. He saw the first tear trickle out of one of her eyes, slide into her hair, and disappear.

For a moment he was stunned silent. Then he said, hesitantly, "When the British return, the shops will open again, and we'll go down to the market to buy rice, and also flowers to decorate the table."

Ani nodded, listening, and he went on. He said that the mission school would reopen, and they would each be assigned their own desk, with its sliding drawer for pencils and paper and textbooks wrapped in brown paper. At lunchtime, they would play football on the *padang*. The field would be watered each evening so that, under the noon sun, the grass was a brilliant green.

He remembered the ringing of the St. Michael's Church bell on Sundays, how all the men stood together in their crisp, white shirts, and the women, in their sarongs and brightly coloured dresses, laughed together under the shade of the trees.

He and Ani lay in silence, and he reached out and held her hand. When sleep began to brush at the edges of his thoughts, he heard her voice beside him. "Once," she said, "a long time ago, there was a man who was very poor and desperate. His wife had died, and then each of his children." For many years, he had wandered the island, but the land was not plentiful as it once had been, and all the plantations were owned by only a handful of wealthy men. One night, as he slept beneath the open sky, he was surprised by thieves, and these men took from him all that he had. Even this was not enough to appease their anger, and the men beat him and threw his body into a canal and ran away into the night.

Matthew nodded and sighed; in his mind, he cradled the bleeding man and wiped the blood from his wounds.

Ani spoke quietly, her voice a whisper, leading him through the story. When the man opened his eyes, she said, it was daylight. He crawled out of the canal and found himself in the centre of a vast *padi* field that had not yet been planted. In all his years of wandering, he had never come across a field like this; from east to west, from north to south, he knew, the land was jealously guarded. In the distance was a simple house, and the man began to walk in that direction, hoping to be granted work that would see him through the coming season. His knock at the door was answered by an old woman. When the man offered his labour, she asked if he would take one-fifth of the crop in lieu of payment, and the man joyfully accepted.

The man laboured in the *padi* fields, trying to remember all the skills he had learned. Month after month, he poured his knowledge into the field. The soil was rich and fertile, and the rains arrived and watered his crop. When it neared the time for harvest, he opened one pod but found it was empty. Each night he opened another, and each night he found it empty.

This was where Matthew began to drift to sleep, breathing in the dry muddy smell of the hut, Ani's calm, low voice blanketing him. The afternoon rainfall began to ease. He thought he lived inside a cupboard, then, some place warm and safe that housed only he and Ani.

"Every day, the old woman asked him, 'When shall we harvest?' And he said, 'Tomorrow.' The man was so ashamed that he decided he had to run away.

"On the day he was to leave, he decided to look one last time. When he opened a pod, he saw that it was filled with gold. He opened another and another, and each pod spilled tiny pieces of gold into his open hand."

The first time he stepped onto an airplane, it was 1953. He was eighteen years old and he was heartbroken. From the air, he had gazed down at Sandakan, the tidy rooftops, the vast plantations and, surrounding everything, jungle. In the years after the war, people in North Borneo had grieved their dead, laying stones and burning incense, tending the graves of their loved ones. But a collaborator is someone forever apart. His father had no grave in Sandakan, and his spirit floated untended, unmourned, except in Matthew's thoughts, and in those of his mother. As the airplane rose higher, the thread that connected Matthew to the town grew taut, stretching, until it finally gave way. When the plane turned towards Australia, he looked down and saw the island of Borneo, so grand and beautiful in his imagination, diminish to a speck on the wide sea.

That memory merges into another, of his daughter, standing in the departure lounge of the Vancouver airport. He watches as his daughter embraces his wife. They are at ease with one another, they have always been, their attachment visible for all to see. She is twenty-four years old, full of hopes, expectations, on her way to study in Europe. This is her first journey away from them.

The fluorescent lights press against his eyes. He is brought back by his daughter's touch. She has turned towards him, and in Matthew's arms now she is slender and fragile. She has Clara's face, open and generous, always perceptive. The airport, brightly lit, full of noise and chaos, falls away from them. For a moment, he is a child again, sitting on his father's shoulders, far above the ground. This is a time before the war, the leaves in the rubber plantation are a canopy high above them, and he listens to the sound of his father's footsteps. But the lamps go out and he is alone in the trees. The question haunts him still: To what lengths would he go to keep his child safe? How much of himself would he sacrifice? When she was young, Gail had followed him everywhere. All these years, he has tried to understand how their relationship changed. He has failed her in some way, he thinks, closed himself off in order to protect her, to protect them both. Whenever she asked about his childhood, about her grandparents and the life he lived in East Malaysia, he smiled, looked away, or brushed her questions aside. In this new country, he told himself, there would be no need to reach back into the past for consolation. He has long accepted that some questions will find no meaningful answers, some stories cannot bear repeating.

Don't leave, he wants to say, holding her. *How can I help you to understand?*

Instead, he keeps his peace. And his daughter, so full of life, so young, kisses him gently on the cheek. Then she turns and walks away, disappearing through the gate.

Inside the hut, the absence of noise wakes him. Matthew sits up, cross-legged, waiting patiently to get his bearings. Outside, the rain has stopped, and the doorway is edged in faint light. Ani is still asleep, her mouth slightly open. A jade pendant, once worn by her mother, lies beside her on a square of cloth.

He touches her shoulder to say goodbye. One of her hands clutches the fabric of her sarong. She does not stir.

Outside the hut, he sees the last of the sunset, a sliver of turquoise light against the curve of the hill. He follows the road, where the thin trunks of the rubber trees leave a shadow, barely perceptible. At the side of the track, almost hidden by the grass, he notices a bicycle wheel lying abandoned and he goes to examine it. Lifting the wheel in his hands, he remembers a game of *main lering* played on Jalan Campbell on a hot, dusty day, how the rains started and the wheel was forgotten. Someone found fruit on the ground, a fresh coconut, and the children broke the shell open and shared the liquid between them.

There were other games, too. *Congkak*, played on a wooden board pitted with eight holes. Its bottom curved like a boat, one end rising up in the shape of a magical bird. To play, they'd used shells, seeds or stones, whatever was at hand. The loser would have to place the *congkak* board on his head and walk up the road and back again, the other children laughing alongside him.

Matthew finds a branch at the side of the road and sets the wheel upright, then pauses, listening. It is a busy time of evening, yet the road is empty. Where are the trucks, the labourers returning from the plantations, people hurrying home before curfew?

He puts the wheel in motion, using the branch to keep it steady. As he quickens his pace, the sky changes to red, to purple. The colours appear so solid, he feels that he could reach up and pull the sky down, settle it over him like a vast curtain.

Eventually he comes to a place where the trees part, and he has a clear view down to the harbour. Below, smoke is rising from the Japanese administration buildings, the wind carrying it towards the water, where it hangs, suspended, in the twilight. There is a bonfire, soldiers gathered around. Fragments, pieces of paper, float in the air above them.

Even after the heavy rain, the road is dusty once more. He continues walking, and the bicycle wheel rolls quietly beside him.

The hut comes into sight, his father standing in the doorway. Matthew is suddenly aware of the dust on his skin, the layer of dirt on his clothes. He hesitates, not wanting to disturb his father's thoughts, not wanting to be seen, and the wheel, steadied by his hand, glides to a standstill beside him.

His father is looking in the other direction, down the road. Then he turns, sees Matthew, and motions him forward with his hand. "Come, Matthew," he says. "There is something I need you to do."

Matthew lays the bicycle wheel against the side of the hut, then follows his father inside. His mother is nowhere to be seen; she must still be visiting her brother on the far side of the plantation. His father pushes the cabinet aside and brings out the radio, but he doesn't switch it on. Instead, while Matthew watches, his father kneels down again. When he straightens, he is holding a large glass jar filled with coins and bills.

"Look at me." His father's eyes are clear, his shoulders relaxed. "This is British currency," he says, placing one hand lightly on Matthew's arm. "This will be valuable again after the war is over. Do you understand?"

Matthew nods.

"I want you to go into the plantation. You must be very careful and you must make sure that no one sees you. No one at all. Not the Japanese, not the workers, nor any children hanging about." His father puts his cigarette to his lips, draws, then exhales, studying Matthew. "Count out the rows. At the thirtieth row, go to the thirtieth tree. I want you to bury this jar in that exact place. Do you understand?"

"Yes, father."

"Good." His father stands up. He puts the jar into an old rice sack. "Take it now. Make sure that you are not seen."

Matthew nods, his stomach tightening.

"Now," his father repeats, his voice firm. "Go quickly."

Matthew takes hold of the sack. He is surprised by its weight, but he swings it carefully over his shoulder.

"When you return," his father says, almost as an afterthought, "stay inside the hut. Keep the door closed and wait for your mother. Everything will turn out for the best."

The last of the day's light is gone, but already he can see the moon, low in the sky. Matthew shifts the weight on his shoulders. He walks forward a few steps, then glances back. His father is outside, leaning against the hut, head bowed, and he reaches into his shirt pocket, withdrawing a handkerchief. He wipes his face and hands, then straightens his body and steps slowly, resolutely, away from the wall.

Matthew begins to run. When he reaches the edge of the plantation, he is breathing fast. Behind him, a truck rumbles along the road, and when he stops and turns he sees that the truck has come to rest in front of the hut and two Japanese soldiers are climbing out. His father goes to meet them. Matthew stands motionless. The leaves of the rubber trees shift in the wind and a light breeze cools his sweating body. He lowers his arm, lets the sack rest on the ground. The sounds twist around him, a bird or an animal crying, and from somewhere nearby, the acrid smell of smoke.

In the distance, he sees three distinct flares as cigarettes are lit; the embers are visible, though small as fireflies. Beside him, the plantation seems immense, unfathomable without the light from the kerosene lamps. He has never gone into it alone, and never when the lamps were unlit.

He walks into the plantation and the light of the moon dims. Beneath the canopy of trees, the darkness seems to press against his eyes, a blindfold, a weight. He walks on and on, touching each tree as he passes it. Something on the ground catches his feet, and he stumbles forward. There is a smell of vomit, of decay. When he puts his hands down, trying to steady himself, they are in water, something wet. His heart collapses inside his chest. He has lost count. Terrified of making a mistake, he retraces his steps. He finds his way back to the road, beyond the trees where the moon is once again visible.

Far away, the three embers glimmer in the dark. His legs, trembling, give way and he crouches on the ground. His entire body is shaking now, and he wishes that his mother would return, that she would light the last candle-end. A tiny flame glowing inside the hut to bring him home.

He does not want to disappoint his father, but he cannot step back into the trees. Breathing heavily, he lifts the sack onto his shoulder and stands. He walks in the direction of the hut.

As he draws near, he begins to hear their voices, softer than usual. A few seconds later, he is close enough to make out their words, but he stays hidden in the dense brush beside the road. They are speaking in broken Malay, sometimes changing to Japanese. He stops and kneels on the ground, almost behind the hut, hugging the sack to his chest.

The Japanese lieutenant is standing beside his father. Matthew recognizes him immediately, a man taller than all the rest, who, when he comes to the hut, brings meat and cigarettes. The lieutenant is speaking. He says that Australian soldiers have landed in the west of Borneo.

In his hands, his father is holding another jar, also filled with money.

"It's over," the lieutenant continues. "I don't have a choice any more."

His father's voice is quiet, strained. "And the others who worked with me. I went into town. The offices are abandoned."

"The others?" The lieutenant pauses, exhales a plume of smoke. He says, angrily, "What do you think happened to the others?"

The second Japanese soldier walks a few paces back, glancing into the open door of the hut. Matthew quiets his breathing, wills his body to become a part of the darkness. The moon traces the faintest light on the ground.

His father turns to face the soldier. "Come," he says, his voice almost a whisper. "Take this money."

The soldier laughs. "You see, we know you. That's just what I expected you to say."

"I thought you would have tried to leave Sandakan." The lieutenant's voice is casual. "I thought you understood;

the most dangerous time is when war is over." He drops his cigarette-end on the ground and puts it out with his boot. Reaching into his pocket, he takes out a box, opens it, and offers it to Matthew's father. Two more cigarettes are lit.

The ember of his father's cigarette wavers in the air, and for a moment his father gazes into the trees as if searching for something, an opening, a way to escape. His eyes rest on the patch of ground directly in front of Matthew. His father lifts his eyes, and Matthew knows that he has been seen. He wants to stand up and go to him. He begins to push himself up from the ground, but the expression on his father's face, surprise, but something more, grief, incomprehension, stops him. His father closes his eyes, and when he opens them again, they seem to burrow into Matthew's body, holding him still. The lieutenant says quietly, "Where are your wife and son?"

His father does not answer at once. "My wife is with her brother," he says finally. "I do not know where my son is."

Time passes, and his father holds the lieutenant's gaze.

The lieutenant looks towards the hut. He walks to the doorway, steps in, and disappears.

"Please," his father says. "Take this money."

The lieutenant re-emerges. He approaches Matthew's father, taking the jar thoughtfully in his hands. His eyes drift over the trees. Matthew's legs, frozen in a kneeling position, begin to tingle, and a wave of sickness causes him bow his head, eyes watering. The lieutenant taps his cigarette and the ashes fall to the ground. "From what I hear, all of Tokyo is burning. There isn't a building standing. It's tragic, but this is the nature of war, and you and I, we are both on the losing side." He pauses, looks down at the jar in his hand. "Maybe you don't believe it, but I pity you. I'm offering you a choice. Come with us now. Let's not do this here in the open."

His father's voice is low. "Everyone knows what happened here, this will not change the things that matter —"

The other soldier, standing by the door of the hut, has come forward. With a heavy movement, he swings his rifle into Matthew's father's back. His father is taken by surprise. He cries out in pain, falling forward on his hands and knees.

The lieutenant says something to the soldier, but Matthew cannot understand the words. His father crawls forward a little, then stumbles to his feet.

"I have done everything you asked. I'm begging you. I have a family —"

"I cannot help you any more."

His father lurches forward and begins to run blindly towards the road. The soldier catches him easily and he swings his rifle up, where it remains for a second before he brings it forcefully down. His father crumples. His arms reach up to shield his head and Matthew can no longer see his face.

The lieutenant's left hand, holding his cigarette, draws a line in the dark, and stops. The soldier sets his rifle casually on the ground. In his hand there is now a pistol. He puts the pistol against Matthew's father's head. His father starts to say something, three or four words, but Matthew hears only "*Tolong, tolong*. Please," before the first shot is fired. His father's body shudders and falls forward. He hits the ground chest-first, both arms outstretched, the hands open. Matthew scrabbles at the grass as if he might crawl towards his father, but his fingers close around air. The world empties before the second and third shots. While the sounds are still audible, the first soldier drops his left hand and lets his cigarette fall to the dirt.

The other man is picking up his rifle. They are speaking to one another in low voices, and then his father is lifted off the ground, swung and tossed into the back of the truck. The two men climb into the cab, the lieutenant carrying the jar of money. The engine starts, the headlights sweep the road. The truck reverses, bearing down on Matthew, the lights freezing him. The gears sound and the truck begins to roll forward. The truck turns down the road and drives away.

Matthew lies in the dark, unmoving. The sound of his breathing lifts away from him. The truck's wheels have raised a cloud of dust and he can taste the road in his mouth, in the back of his throat.

His legs ache with the effort, but he pushes himself to standing. In the dark, he fumbles for the bag and pulls it over his shoulder. Then, turning, he walks slowly in the direction of the plantation.

All his thoughts are clear. He goes first to the storehouse where sheets of rubber hang to dry, and there he finds a small shovel. Then he goes back and begins to count out the rows. His eyes have now adjusted to the darkness. In front of the thirtieth tree of the thirtieth row, Matthew sets down the sack. There are notches in the wood, thin diagonal lines where the rubber has been tapped. All around him, he hears the itching sound of cicadas, a bird, unidentifiable night sounds.

In his mind, his father says again, *Make sure no one sees you*. Matthew stares into the darkness, then kneels on the ground. He traces an outline in the dirt, making a circle, then he begins to dig with the shovel. His father comes towards him. *Please*, he says to Matthew, *go quickly*. This is the place where he will plant the money. It will be like the seeds that his father warned him not to swallow, a strange plant growing from an unexpected place. After a few minutes, Matthew has made a small opening in the ground. Not enough. It has to be so deep that he can stand in it, with only his fingertips brushing the air.

His father gets to his feet. *Take the money*, he tells the men. He gestures towards Matthew, and Matthew steps out from his hiding place and onto the road. He goes to stand beside his father. His father places his hand on Matthew's shoulder.

Minutes pass, perhaps hours. The plantation falls away, and he returns to the house on Jalan Campbell. High on a shelf, there is a wooden box whose contents he cannot see. All he hears is the scratch of a record, then a woman's voice. Through a doorway, he glimpses his parents standing together, his mother holding a jacket open, his father sliding his arms into the sleeves. She runs her hands across his back. He turns to face her. Matthew climbs down into the hole that he has made. There are places so narrow that he has to use his body to widen the opening. When he is standing at the bottom, he reaches his hands up and turns his face towards the fresh air. The dirt surrounding him radiates heat, and he realizes that his entire body is sweating, he can feel the drops running from his hair, down his face and neck. Gripping the surface, he braces his knees against the walls of the hole and forces himself out. He feels no pain and no fatigue. His arms lift him out of the ground and he does not feel the effort.

Lying on his stomach, he lowers the sack as far as he can, then lets it go, hearing it strike at the bottom of the hole. The glass jar does not seem to break. Slowly, he replaces the dirt until the hole is completely filled. He packs the earth down carefully, using his hands and feet to remove any signs of disturbance.

As he does this, he listens for men or trucks, but even the cicadas have stopped their singing and the air is still. Again and again, his thoughts return to the burning embers, the rifle on the ground and the pistol in the soldier's hand, but he pushes these images away. He has swallowed something wrong. Inside his skin, something that he cannot contain is pulsing and breathing, but there is no way to let it out.

Walking back, he sees a dull light flickering inside the hut and realizes that his mother has returned before him. He lingers outside, staring at the faint candlelight. Dirt is caked to his skin, and he stands in the grass, crumbling the pieces off with his hands. He has lost his shirt, but he does not remember how or when. There are no sounds of planes or gunfire; the night is extraordinarily calm, peaceful. Matthew gathers himself together and walks forward. Alongside the hut, he sees, as if from another time, the bicycle wheel and the stick lying beside it. He pushes open the door.

On the table, a low candle wavers. He stands motionless, looking into the shadows. The hut is empty.

There are two plates of food, rice and meat. The food smells so fragrant, so good, a dizziness comes over him, but he cannot bring himself to eat. One of the settings, he realizes, is meant for his father. A third dish, his mother's, is sitting empty but unwashed on the other side of the table. His mother has been here, but now she has gone, and this realization makes him pause, eyes stinging. Did the Japanese soldiers return? But there is nothing out of place in the hut.

Shaking, Matthew walks to the other side of the table. Beside his parents' bed, the metal tub has been filled with water; it is a still lake in the half-darkened room. He touches the surface, the water is warm. He can smell his mother's soap, the small perfumed square that she keeps wrapped in paper. When he has taken off his clothes, he climbs into the bath. The panic begins to subside, and he slides down until only his mouth and nose remain above the surface, the dirt from the plantation dissolving off his skin. He keeps his eyes open as the room moves in waves above him.

Go now. Quickly. The soldiers in the truck drive away, and their lights sweep across his father, who stands on the steps watching them leave.

Matthew closes his eyes. His father falls backward. His legs dangle loosely from the soldiers' arms.

Much later, a caravan of vehicles passes by on the road outside. The walls shake, and small ripples start to form in the water, expanding out, moving against his body. Matthew climbs out of the tub, dries his body with a sarong, and sits on his bed. He is waiting for his mother; she is getting ready for Sunday mass in a time before the war. She has a pearl necklace that rests in a cushioned box. When she puts it on, she turns first one way and then another, admiring the play of light along its length. In St. Michael's Church, she sits on the bench beside him, and he leans his face against her body, the fabric of her dress shifting against his cheek.

Ani says, The boy buried his treasure in a hidden place. In this place, all the trees were silver, and fruit fell from the trees and lined the ground. For months and months, the boy cared for his secret. He nourished the soil and watered the dirt. One day, the first leaves appeared. The stems grew strong and the leaves became bountiful.

This is the treasure that allows the boy to return to the other side. For when he opens the leaves, pieces of gold fall into his hands. He has been trapped here for many, many years. As many years as it takes for a boy to grow into an old man.

He falls asleep to the sound of more trucks on the road, and he returns to the bridge his mother carried him over, the basket that rocked him back and forth, the sound of rushing water taking hold of him. This memory floods his vision. He opens his mouth and finds he can breathe it in, finds that the water miraculously pours out of his body, out of his skin.

Sometime in the middle of the night, he wakes hearing the door opening. His mother is there beside him, her hand smoothing his hair, smoothing the sarong that covers his body. She says that she has been down to the harbour. She has seen the Australian soldiers arrive in Sandakan. He looks up at her face, so beautiful to him, and he does not know if she is crying out of joy or sadness. She tells him that she has searched all night for his father. "I wasn't here," she says, her voice catching, tearing. She repeats the words, trying again. He tries to speak but no sounds come. She cups her hand against his head, as if to hold his thoughts, as if to stop them from sliding loose, and eventually sleep takes over once more.

He wakes expecting to see his father. Matthew opens his eyes, already picturing a day like every other: the radio in the room, the wire reaching up, his father concentrating on the sound. Instead, the room is still. He realizes that he has slept far longer than usual; the sun has risen, and he can see the light filtering in through the slats of the hut.

On the far side of the room, his mother is brushing her hair. It falls past her shoulders, down her back, and she gathers it up in her hands, slowly twisting it into a complicated knot. Her arms are too thin, too fragile. She is not yet aware of him. She faces the wall, as if imagining a mirror there, and brushes the stray hairs back from her face.

His mother turns and crosses the room. He tries to tell her that the one they love is not dead, that he is only hidden away, safe. Her eyes are dark and swollen. When she puts her fingertips to his cheek, her hands are trembling. She tells him that all the Japanese have gone away, they have given up Sandakan. Under cover of night, they abandoned the town and then disappeared. "Rest now," she says, putting her lips to his hair, holding on to him. Without realizing it, she repeats his father's words. "Everything will turn out for the best."

Because he cannot bear to see her sadness, he closes his eyes, tries to find sleep again.

He lies still, the sarong covering his body. His heart is beating fast, and his mouth tastes of a bitter, metallic dust. When the war is truly over, he imagines that the cities will be empty places, that all the trees and shops and houses will be tidied away, swept clean like the bowl of a crater. Sleep comes, and in his dream, which is bright with colour and very clear, people move through the open space, a film of dust clinging to their bodies. The cities are like Sandakan. He walks the abandoned streets, remembering where each building stood, the tin maker, the eyeglass shop, everybody remembers, but no buildings will grow there again.

When he steps outside in the afternoon, the sky is white. His mother remains inside, and he closes the door behind him. When he kneels on the ground, brushing his hand over the loose dirt, he finds no cigarette ends, no boot marks, no stray bullets.

He begins to walk downhill, towards the harbour. There are people gathered beside their huts, listening to a radio that cuts in and out with static. Some have almost no clothes, they sit in the shade of the trees, or pace the grass. Two small boys hurry past him, almost running.

His father says, *You must pay attention. Always pay attention.*

Up in the sky, an airplane is coming nearer. Matthew watches small pebbles shiver across the ground. The plane descends through the clouds. The two boys are calling to each other. The younger one starts to scream. The plane is too close, flying so low, the trees in its path are bending away. Out of the belly of the plane, something falls. Matthew does not flinch or try to escape. He says, *I'm sorry. I wasn't paying attention. I can't remember what day this is.* A parachute opens, he watches the cloth open and snap. It passes by him, carrying a box, sailing down to earth. The box hits a tree, the parachute buckles, the lines fall down, and the silk blooms down around the tree, as if to protect it. A woman runs towards the box, dragging a child behind her.

He can feel his thoughts dissolving to liquid. Is it the heat? Which day was yesterday? Part of him tries to focus that picture in his mind, a hand opening to reveal a pistol. He sits down in the dust. At the tree, the woman with the small girl is lifting out cans of food. She is putting something into her pocket. Matthew watches her, and in his mind he hears gunshots. One shot, a pause, and then another. But the woman does not fall down. She laughs and smiles and pulls a blanket out of the box. Nobody reacts to the gunfire. But Matthew has thrown his body onto the road. He lies there, his hands gripping the dirt.

Some time later, a man lifts him up off the ground, and Matthew feels as if the weight of his own body has been left behind on the road. The soldier wears a brimmed, floppy hat and he has light-coloured eyes and he asks Matthew if he has eaten. The soldier tells him, in broken Malay, that the war is finished now, that he has nothing to be afraid of any more.

3

A New Geometry

Each morning, Ansel commutes to work on his bicycle. Today, the rain is steady, clinging to the buildings, tipping down the leaves of the trees. In Vancouver, there are many varieties of rain, but the most common, he believes, is the kind that tries to convince you it isn't there, the kind that is so thin it makes the windshield wipers squeak. He has walked for hours in this kind of rain, without an umbrella, and still emerged reasonably dry.

After years of leaving umbrellas in assorted places – buses, of course, but also elevators, take-out coffee windows, public washrooms – Gail had given up carrying them. She wore jackets with hoods, and kept her distance from small gadgets: mobile phones, Palm Pilots, USB keys. "Give me things that announce their presence," she said. "Did you know we used to have the world's largest hockey stick in Vancouver? It came with its own puck." In the evenings they used to walk along False Creek, and sometimes the rain would condense over the water, fog lifting into the dark.

By 8:00 a.m., when Ansel arrives at the clinic, there are already people leaning against the entrance, waiting to be let in. He opens the door for them despite foreseeing the grumbles of the reception staff, not quite ready for the morning intake. The patients quietly descend the stairs. This morning, there's a family with three young daughters, two yawning med students, and a middle-aged woman. The woman is pale and trembling, and Ansel stays beside her and she uses his arm as a bannister. "It's the arthritis," she says, not looking at him.

"Just a few more steps now."

He takes them to the waiting room, shows the girls where the crayons and drawing paper are, then goes on to his office. He flicks the light switches as he walks, and the fluorescent lights buzz on around him, throwing down a blue shadow before settling into a wavering glow. At the end of the corridor, Ansel unlocks his office door, hangs his jacket and helmet on the coat stand, and sits down at his desk. He has a few minutes before the first patient, not quite enough time to deal with the stack of referrals, emails and lab results left over from the day before.

In Ansel's basement office, there are three high windows, just inches above the ground outside. They frame blades of grass, dandelions in the summer, a few small stones. The light falls in three rectangular shafts along his desk. The offices have always reminded him of a warren, the hallways that merge together, leading towards a tunnel that connects to

Vancouver General Hospital. He has worked here, at the provincial tuberculosis clinic, for almost five years as a clinician and researcher, and each day has a familiar routine. The first half-dozen appointments of the morning, along with files and chest X-rays, are waiting in his in-tray. There's a photocopied abstract on the relationship between AIDS and syphilis, and, underneath, two faxes. One is from his father, about an upcoming medical conference in Chicago. The other is from the hospital in Prince George, where Gail, ill, had gone the day before she died. The hospital writes that they have concluded their review of the case and now consider the file closed. A pain branches out from behind his eyes, a dull pulsing, and he stares at the page for a moment, until the lines begin to run together. Ansel pushes the correspondence aside and opens his Thermos of coffee.

His work is a comfort to him. Even as a child, he never considered a career outside of medicine. Both of his parents were doctors, his father a heart surgeon, and his mother a GP. Night after night, his father came home at dawn, an overcoat on top of his rumpled greens. If the surgery had gone well, his father would put a record on, Ella Fitzgerald or Muddy Waters, the music rising like smoke through the house. From bed, Ansel could hear the murmur of his parents' conversation, his father's low voice taking pleasure in relaying the details of the surgery. Even before Ansel learned to read, his mother had taught him how to use a stethoscope, how to listen for opacities, crackles and echoes in the lungs, how to track the beating of a heart. By the time he turned four, he had practised on both his parents, as well as his older sister.

He remembers warming the diaphragm between his hands then setting it against their skin, astonished each time by the familiar sound, the reliable *lub dub* of their hearts.

It was Ansel and not his sister, Lydia, who got to go on rounds with their father. While Lydia played guitar in her bedroom, Ansel would concentrate on his father's rumbling voice relating Mrs. B.'s myocardial infarction followed by congestive failure and arrhythmia, elaborating on her EKG and digitalis treatment. "Are you following this, Ansel?" To which all the residents and interns would laugh. When he was twelve, he read his father's copy of *The Microbe Hunters*, then he saved his allowance for a year and bought a microscope. That year, he made a list of his top one hundred scientists. The obvious ones, Galileo, Einstein, Newton. And then, depending on the month, or what he was reading, Tesla, Koch, Curie, Salk, Leeuwenhoek, Darwin and Wallace. And always Louis Pasteur.

"Ah," his father had said once, examining the names. "The beer makers are fond of him."

Lydia shook her head. "What is it with men and lists?"

For a time, Ansel had strayed towards cardiology, interning for half a year at St. Paul's Hospital. In surgery, he waited while people slid away from him into the wash of anesthesia, their presence literally fading from the room. Dr. Biring, his mentor, would sing while he worked, rock ballads, folk songs, anything. The words, Biring said, were like a ladder he could climb down, and thus descend into his memory. Sometimes, in the operating room, humming along with

Biring, Ansel was surprised to look up and see the patient's face, framed by a green plastic cap. Their minds had been disconnected from the organs that he worked on. Retractors held the chest wall back, exposing the heart; every few seconds, the heart pumped out of the skin. There were tiny cameras that he could swim through a person's body, a tool to magnify his own sight, a device to reach where his hands couldn't.

From surgery, he went to a one-month placement in the Burn Unit. This was where he had met Gail, almost ten years ago. She was working as a reporter then, covering a crash that had happened at the airport, a Cessna that had stalled in mid-air.

He had to come out of the hospital every hour just to breathe, to escape the pain, the bodies, rotated, covered in Silvadene. It was the middle of the night, and Gail was rooted outside, along with the other journalists, waiting for a break in the story. By 4:00 a.m., she was the only one left, still sipping her coffee. "You don't have to stay here all night, do you?"

"No." She had smiled, embarrassed. "You must think I'm eager or something."

"If you leave me a number, I can call you if there's more to report."

"Actually, I don't have an apartment yet. I just got back to Vancouver a few days ago."

He asked where she had been, and Gail said, "In the Arctic Circle, but only for a month. I was living in Prague before that." When he asked what she did there, she told him, "This and that. I make radio features, soundscapes. I'm not the sharpest interviewer, but I like to listen."

After morning sign-in, they ate breakfast in the cafeteria. Her eyes kept wandering over to a group of doctors in wrinkled greens, surgical masks dangling from their necks and covers on their shoes. She was twenty-nine, dressed in jeans and a cotton T-shirt. She leaned towards him, long dark hair falling forward, a triangle of buttered toast dangling from her fingertips, and asked him what kind of medicine he hoped to practise. He told her that, initially, he had wanted to be a surgeon.

She paused, studying him. "You don't seem the type," she said at last. "I picture the surgeon as someone who parachutes in, gets the job done, then waves airily as he goes home to bed. You strike me as a more long-haul kind of person."

He laughed and cut a piece of jam from its packet. "I haven't decided what I want to be yet. I guess I'm leaning towards internal medicine."

He had his bicycle there, but she loaded it into the back of her van and drove him home. At his front door, she said, "You can see the hospital from your house."

Ansel looked behind him. The Centennial Pavilion, built in the shape of a star, little windows in neat rows like a line of type, hovered over them. When he turned back, he saw that her eyes were ringed and dark. "Where are you staying?" he said.

"In my van until I find a place."

He fumbled for the right words. "You're welcome, if you want, to stay here."

She laughed, suddenly hugging him. "Thanks. Maybe when we get to know each other a bit better."

In the examining room, the family is seated, waiting for him. Two of the girls are working on crayon drawings, and the third, the youngest one, has drawn a picture of an imposing man in a white coat, stethoscope around his neck. The man has dark hair, like Ansel, and his expression is moody, sober. The figure reminds Ansel of the way he had once pictured his own father, larger than life, replete with answers.

As he enters, the family gathers around him. He seats the girls, one, two, three, on the examining table, and motions the parents to take the chairs. "Dr. Ressing," the father says immediately, "we were on an airplane. Somebody from the health region called us. They said we had to get tested right away, the entire family."

He tells them how a young woman on their flight had contracted tuberculosis on her travels. "You're being screened as a preventative measure. Most people's defences are strong enough to prevent the TB from causing disease. We'll do a skin test on each of you, and then in three days we need you to come back for the second part of the procedure." He tests them one at a time, starting with the father.

The youngest girl is crying and whispering, "No needles, please, no needles," over and over, and by the time Ansel has sat down beside her, she has buried her head against her mother's stomach. He takes her right arm and rubs a bit of alcohol on it. The mother is clucking at her, saying something in Pakistani, then smiling indulgently. She holds the girl's arm steady, and Ansel inserts the point. The girl screams pitifully, pressing her body into her mother's side. The fluid pools below the surface of her skin.

"That's it."

The girl blinks, cautiously eyeing her wound, then gazes up at him, tear trails on her cheeks. Startling everyone, she lifts her arm and grabs hold of his stethoscope. He is yanked forward.

Her parents exclaim in surprise, shaking their heads, apologizing, but Ansel doesn't move. He is nose to nose with the little girl. "Will you let me have your drawing?" he asks, pointing at the sheet of paper in her hand. She agrees to the trade.

He fits the earpieces on her ears, pushes his lab coat aside and sets the stethoscope against his chest.

After that first meeting in the hospital, he had sought her out, calling the telephone number she had given him, the number at her parents' house. On his days off, he accompanied Gail as she travelled the city, interviewing people for her work at CBC-Radio. She had begun working on a piece about memorials. She had been introduced to a thirty-year-old man whose fiancée had died eight years ago. In the first year after her death, he had poured his grief and loss into his garden. As the years passed, the garden had become a memorial to her, and a permanent part of his life. "This is the blue season," he told them. He wore a microphone affixed to a coat hanger that Gail had widened, then placed around his neck. The contraption rested firmly on his chest. A trick she had learned, she told him, from a producer in Prague, in the hope that the microphone would be forgotten by the speaker. It would became a part of his or her own body.

Ansel, who knew nothing about plants, looked around. Blue flowers, blue blossoms in all shapes and sizes. Delphiniums, bellflowers. There was a ghostly sadness to it. Latin names spilled off the tongue of the young man.

Gail was wearing a blue skirt and top, and she merged seamlessly into the palette of the garden. Her hair hung loose, reaching the small of her back, and a woven hat shaded her face from the sun. She held the young man's gaze as he spoke, adjusting the recording levels with her right hand. A thin line of wire ran between them, from the microphone to the recorder, and then to the headphones that Gail wore. Watching her, it had seemed to Ansel as if he stood at the edge of a doorway. The world that she inhabited was full of stories, of questions. That expression, her face relaxed, yet held in concentration as she listened, is the one that remains with him now.

"This one is my favourite, and the one I've grown the most," the young man told Gail. The flower was sky blue with a creamy yellow eye. He extended his hand as if presenting something. "A large slope of them, beginning somehow at waist level, trembling in the wind, would be quite a statement."

The next day, she visited a woman who balanced stones, one on top of the other, in her garden, an imitation of the inukshuk scattered on the shores of English Bay. The Inuit word *inukshuk*, Gail told Ansel over dinner, means "likeness of a person." The direction of a leg or an arm may be used for navigation, or might signal the presence of fish in a nearby lake. The middle-aged woman, an immigrant from Scotland, had lost her twin sister to cancer. She said that she balanced the stones on hot summer days when she and her four children sat in the backyard. They had seen these structures while walking around Stanley Park, and the image had stayed in their minds.

While Ansel sat in the living room copying out his rotation notes, Gail played him parts of the interview. She told him that Inuit tradition forbids the destruction of an inukshuk. The woman said, "I suppose the wind and rain will take them down one day. But there's a tradition that says dismantling them would be a desecration. And I understand that." She paused and then said, barely audibly, "Yes, a desecration. I saw it that way. Even though I knew, my sister knew, it would happen one day."

Gail was sitting cross-legged on the floor. "I have all these outtakes," she told him. "These reels and reels. Just tapes of people talking, but I can't throw them away. Sometimes, people remember things they haven't thought about in years, a private memory, a story. You know that feeling when you're moving house, going through boxes, and you find something unexpected? That's what I feel is happening to them. Inside their minds, they open the box, and there it is right in front of them, almost as if they're seeing it for the first time."

He told her that memory is a tricky thing. "Sometimes, we forget, because the right cues, a word, a face, never arise. Until someone reminds us, we forget that the box is there. Sometimes there's disassociation. The memories splinter into different worlds."

"It's Nietzsche. The ability to forget is what brings us peace."

"He was on to something in a biochemical way, too. If there's a trauma, or a difficult memory, sometimes that severs the links. The memories themselves don't disappear, but you can't find your way back to them, because the glue that connects the different streams is somehow dissolved. That's the idea, anyway."

"And can you tell me, dear doctor, where I go after I die, or when the world ends, and if there's a magnanimous god in the heavens? Or, more pressingly, why giraffes don't faint when they lower their heads to the ground?"

"Ah, let me see. I'm sure that's in my notes somewhere."

When she came down with the flu, he moved her out of her van and into the house. Set her up like a hospital patient. Brought meals to her three times a day. She demanded a bedpan. He ignored her and took her vital signs, writing them down on a notepad that he kept at her bedside, on top of a copy of *The Hitchhiker's Guide to the Galaxy*. At night, lying in bed, he read aloud to her, beginning with his favourite section on the oblivious Rain God, the miserable truck driver adored by clouds everywhere.

"You nutter," she said, drowsily, her words slurring into his pillow. "Why don't you find some healthy people to hang out with?"

He began to yearn for winter. At the first frost, she had said, she would move out of her van and into his apartment.

If he could have seen into the future, he would not have believed the affair possible. And yet it had happened, one year ago now, the relationship brief, intense. On the night he told Gail, she had stood with her back to him, as if to separate the image of him from the words she was hearing. In the days that followed, she did not go up to the bedroom. Instead, she slept in her office downstairs, some nights leaving the house entirely, taking the car, disappearing. He listened to the sound of the door closing, tires on the gravel. Those nights are still vivid, a rift, a heartbreak, dismantling everything that had come before. But settling them, finally, on a different ground.

Even before she caught her flight to Prince George, she had been fatigued, coughing. He no longer tries to push these thoughts away. She had picked up a cold, a virus, that persisted. He had wanted her to cancel the trip, to stay with him, but she said that this interview with Nathan Sullivan, Kathleen's older brother, was necessary. His words were the last remaining piece. Nathan would be in the country for only a few days, and she might not have the chance again.

On the phone from Prince George, she told him that she had woken two days ago with a tightness in her chest. When, that morning, even breathing had become painful, she had gone to the hospital. The emergency room physician had diagnosed pneumonia and prescribed antibiotics.

He had wanted to drop everything and go to her. Her voice remains in his memory, surprised. Moved by his concern. "It's just a glorified cold," she had said, laughing. "Stop fussing." She said that she would sleep the illness off, and tomorrow evening she would catch her flight home, as scheduled. But he had persuaded her otherwise, telling her that she should stay there until she was fully recovered.

The pace at which Gail disappears from his life has slowed, a loss that is spread out over time, bits and pieces that break down and gradually disintegrate. He recalls mornings when, waking first, he would see the room take shape around him and turn to find her curled away, her hair sweeping up across the pillows, away from her neck. He would place his lips there, her skin smelling of the sheets, of warmth.

Every Sunday, he drives to the cemetery. Often, he sees Clara. On his most recent visit, he had lain his own small offering down, then he had taken a cloth and cleaned the dirt and grass from the marker. He told her passing things, the grocery list, jokes, ramblings. Quotidian details that they have always shared. He heard her voice, Did you sleep well?, Did you dream?, What shall we do today?, And then, my love, what then?

At 10:30, Ansel has an appointment with a new patient, Alistair Cameron. A nurse at the AIDS outreach clinic has referred him here. According to the file, he has already been hit three times with pneumonia, once with Kaposi's and once with CMV retinitis. "Symptoms suggestive of TB infection. No previous BCG vaccination." Ansel reads the history closely, seeing an immune-compromised patient with probable tuberculosis, a diagnosis that he has no wish to give.

Thirty minutes go by and Alistair Cameron does not arrive.

Sitting in his office, he turns to the cassette player he keeps beside his desk. After a moment, he picks up the headphones and slides them on. He rests one finger on the controls, hesitating, but he cannot help himself. All he wants is to hear her voice. He hits Play, and a young man begins to speak, reading from the letters of Franz Kafka. "I shall never get well again. Just because what we are dealing with here is not tuberculosis that can be nursed back to health in a sanatorium deckchair but a weapon that remains indispensable as long as I live. It and I cannot go on living together – or apart from each other."

A slight pause, then a voice reading from a "Dispensary Instruction Sheet," an artifact from the 1930s. "No fondling or kissing of other members of the family, particularly not of children. Married Partners to sleep in separate beds preferably separated by a partition. Most important: Family members must immediately notify the dispensary of the death of the patient."

"The history of tuberculosis, the white death, is deeply embedded in the history of the modern world." Gail's radio voice is much the same as her usual voice. Only here the pauses are more deliberate, her tone intimate. "Influenza, the Black Plague, syphilis and AIDS – these diseases, like tuberculosis, have their own personalities in much the same way that nations have historic periods. Tuberculosis rose with the Industrial Revolution, in a time of poverty and cramped living conditions, among the child labourers of the nineteenth century and in the inhabitants of bohemia on the Left Bank. It came to prominence again between the two world wars, and reappears now in developing nations and in the urban ghettoes of North America. Tuberculosis, as the saying goes, is the perfect expression of an imperfect civilization."

A year after they met, Gail had begun working on this documentary. Since its completion, he has kept a copy in his office, lending it to students, colleagues or interested patients. Now, occasionally, he plays it to hear her voice, preserved and distinct, as if she is in the room there with him. He closes his eyes, bows his head under the weight of the headphones, and the sound runs over him.

Canned music starts up, and then a man's voice reminiscent of the late 1950s. "The beginning of the end came in 1943, when Selman Abraham Waksman observed that certain bacteria and micro-organisms in the soil could inhibit others. These inhibitors made use of certain chemical substances, known to us now as antibiotics." The commentator goes on to describe the case of Patricia S., a twenty-one-year-old woman in the terminal stages of pulmonary and disseminated TB. "She responded to Waksman's inhibitor at once. Like a fairy tale, she got up and left the hospital, completely cured."

The music slides to silence, and Gail's voice returns to the forefront. "The tuberculosis bacillus, discovered by Robert Koch in 1882, became famous to doctors and even the general public. A slender, elegantly curved rod, so small that a dozen or more could fit inside a medium-sized tissue cell."

"My name is John de Vreede. I'm the director of New York City Tuberculosis Control. On August 30, 1991, the United States Centre for Disease Control reported four small outbreaks of tuberculosis. Three of the outbreaks occurred here, in New York City. Almost all the patients were HIV-positive, drug users or alcoholics. We knew, at that time, that there were as many as seven million cases in the developing world. But here in America, tuberculosis, consumption – in the public perception this disease was gone. Eradicated. It was a character in a folk memory."

When they first met, Gail had been using a portable DAT machine. Interviewing Ansel for this piece, she had listened to his voice using a set of headphones, saying that his voice was being funnelled directly into her ears, through the canals of her brain, woven into her thoughts forever.

"Dr. Ressing."

"To counter the possibility of drug resistance, we now treat each patient with four different drugs: isoniazad, rifampicin, pyrazinamide and ethambutol. If they don't respond, if they are multi-drug resistant, then we have nothing. No medical treatment for the disease. We're back to the eighteen hundreds."

Ansel has his eyes open, but he can see Gail listening. He can see her glancing down at her notes, at the needle on the recorder. There was something in her manner that Ansel recognized early on, something that others were always drawn to in her. You believed you could trust her – whatever you said, whatever you confided – that she would hold that trust as something sacred.

The intercom buzzes, startling him. When he touches the button, Pauline's voice comes through in a crackle of static. "Your 10:30 just checked in. Room Three."

He thanks her, then stands, shrugging on his lab coat. He starts down the corridor, the file flipped open, reading as he goes.

Inside the room, a young man sits on the examining table. He is wearing a frayed windbreaker over a thin T-shirt and jeans. There is a ball cap in his right hand. His face has the inquisitiveness of a young boy, though he is pale and clearly ill. "Hi, Alistair, I'm Dr. Ressing."

"Al is okay."

"Call me Ansel."

"You look young, Doctor, if you don't mind me saying it."

"Thirty-eight." Ansel opens the file and looks at it again. "We were born in the same year."

Alistair Cameron nods. "The similarities end there, I think."

"You're from Alaska?"

"Juneau. And you?"

"Vancouver."

"Lucky you."

Ansel wheels a chair out and sits across from Al Cameron. He orders his thoughts, unclips the pen from his lab coat, and begins to take a case history. Born in 1961, parents came up from Nebraska. High school education. Came to Vancouver when he was thirty-six. HIV positive for three years. Full blown AIDS since last September. His only family is a younger sister who lives in Victoria. Al spills it out like something memorized a long time ago. "There it is," he says, shrugging. He lifts his right hand and turns it over as if looking for dust. "This time? Tuberculosis, hopefully not drug-resistant. Picked up in one of the shelters probably. It travels through the air, could be dangerous for someone like me." He pauses and touches the side of his neck. "Lymph nodes swollen and sore. Definitely a bad sign."

Ansel places his hand against the man's neck. He does a thorough physical. Febrile to 103, and his pulse is high. Through his stethoscope, Ansel can hear the faintest of crackles in the upper part of the left lung. He does the tuberculin test, and Alistair looks away as the liquid is injected just below the surface of the skin. A reaction develops almost immediately.

"It takes two or three days to be sure of the results. There might be some swelling or itching, but try to leave it alone." He looks down at the chart, to the notes he has made. He has seen so many young men and women like Alistair, who have come to him at the end of their lives. For a moment, Gail is standing beside him, she is resting her head against his arm. "I'm going to admit you," he says.

Al lifts his shoulders, then lets them fall. "I figured you might."

Ansel walks him to his office, then takes the paperwork

over to Pauline. He orders a chest X-ray and a blood test, and Pauline phones over for a bed.

He returns to the office with two mugs of coffee. Al is sitting at his desk, facing the computer screen. He is peering at Ansel's photograph of Gail.

"Your girlfriend?"

Ansel nods.

Al sets the photo back down on the desk. "This morning, instead of coming here, I walked over to Trout Lake. You know where that is?"

Ansel nods at the picture. "Gail is a runner." He catches himself, but then he continues anyway. "Sometimes she goes there. It's only a few kilometres from our house."

"A lake in the middle of the city. Families and kids playing in the water. Lots of people running on the trails. Maybe I've even seen your girlfriend. And then me, just sitting on the sand like I own the place. Someone was playing the cello." He laughs and shakes his head. "There was no way I was going to get up, leave that behind, and come here."

"I'm glad you came."

"Well. It started to rain."

The bed comes through in half an hour. Ansel drops what he's doing and goes to find Al Cameron, who is making his way through a stack of magazines in the waiting room. Together they walk through the underground corridors towards the hospital reception.

Al trails his hand along the wall as he walks. "What next, then?"

"If it is TB, we'll get you started on a course of drugs. It's difficult, because we don't want to interfere with the meds you're currently on. If it's not TB, then it's something else. You've got some time with the radiologist this afternoon. We'll see."

Al pats his pocket. "Thank God for health coverage," he says. "There are thousands of dollars of good drugs pouring through this body."

At noon, Ansel goes outside and stands on the front steps of the clinic. Beside him, there's a young man and woman, cigarettes moving from hand to mouth in a circling, fluid gesture. The man breathes out rings of smoke, small and perfect, expanding as they float away from him. The woman smiles. "What luck," she says, leaning her head against him. He puts his arm tenderly around her waist.

The nerves around Ansel's eyes begin to tense, and he finds that he has to look away. Lately, all displays of affection have caused this response in him, whether between lovers, between parents and children, or children and grandparents.

Neither he nor Gail had wanted to hang up the phone, and so they continued talking, though her voice seemed to fade in and out, a thread he kept losing.

In a dream that recurs, Ansel catches a plane that night, he arrives in time.

He knows it is impossible, irrational, but he is lifted away from the present, set down in a different timeline. The details of their lives, all the habitual acts, the cherished conversations, continue to accumulate, day after day, into the future.

By the time he arrived in Prince George with Gail's parents, it was too late to change what had occurred. When he closes his eyes, the city, her body, is blocked out, he turns his memory away from the room in the hospital basement where they'd brought him and Gail's parents. Instead, he is in the airplane, flying over the Cascade Mountains, looking down on the snow and fog. When the mountains fall away, highways emerge, thin lines moving across the land, unravelling from the towns.

Everything after, the funeral, the interment, blurs into a single moment. He has gone on, returning to work, doing all that is required of him. One part of him moves ahead, the other is lost, and each passing day widens this breach, a knife edge in his body.

He has copies of the coroner's findings, the radiology report, EKG charts, the hospital records. She had contracted a bacterial infection, a sudden devastating pneumonia. This, the coroner believed, had depleted the oxygen in her bloodstream, triggering a stroke. The paramedics had said that she was peaceful, there was no sign of pain. Night after night, he studies the test results, trying to find the gaps, the detail that might have saved her. He suspects an underlying medical condition, one that would have made her more susceptible, cardiomyopathy or channelopathy, undiagnosed. The charts and details hold a power over him, as if they will shed light not only on her illness but on Gail herself, who she was, everything she once hoped for, what she believed at the end. He has written to the hospital, met with the attending physician, tried to draw a line from the hour she died, back through the night, to the previous day. Lives change in an instant, he knows this. He knows one can never be prepared. But his desire to make sense of her death will not subside. If she had not been released from the hospital, if he had gone to her, if the diary had never fallen into her hands, if someone had found her sooner, if it had not been winter. At night, the avalanche of possibilities comes to him, a weight collapsing against his body, he cannot breathe, cannot weep for all the exits he seeks to find.

After he closes his files that afternoon, he bicycles home. Clouds have moved in, and the rain, hesitant at first, quickly loses its inhibitions and becomes a downpour. He stops briefly at the side of the bike path and switches his generator on. When he begins pedalling, the sound of the machine washes out behind him and his headlight beams into the rain. He and Gail had come across this generator at the second-hand cycle shop on Dunbar Street, attached to an inexpensive bike. She had waxed poetic on the bicycles of Prague and Amsterdam, on the cleverness of using kinetic energy to power headlights, and the wastefulness of batteries. Ansel had buckled under the eloquence of her argument, or so he told her, and shelled out ten bucks for the old wreck that the generator was attached to. They had ridden it home, Gail perched on the back of the bicycle. She had been belting out

a song while he pedalled. What song? U2, "Beautiful Day."
Tone deaf, as usual. Afterwards, on the front lawn, they had
surgically removed the generator and attached the wires to
his own bicycle. *Voilà*, a bit of Amsterdam in Vancouver.

The bicycle ride home is what saves him. A decade of
the same route, down Heather Street, his body swaying past
the roundabouts, down the sloping hill to the sea. Even the
cars seem to scatter around him.

On Keefer Street, the lights from Chinatown shine a red
and yellow river across the wet pavement. Rivulets soak into
his shoes, and he feels as if his ankles are underwater. He
continues on, past the line of seniors' homes, towards the
high roofs of Strathcona.

When he arrives home, he carries his bicycle up the
front stairs. The house is quiet, and it smells of old coffee.
Inside the house, Ansel peels off his wet clothes and steps
into the shower. The steam hits his lungs and his body fills
with warmth.

Gail has her hand on the small of his back. She says,
"Pull yourself together, Ans." He lifts his face towards the
streaming water, and she circles her arms around his waist.

"With the kind of day I've had?"

She laughs. "You'll have to prescribe your own drug
regimen."

The air is all fog and heat. She says, "I spent the day in my
pyjamas. Reading. Mainlining coffee. Listening to music."

"There was a man my age. He's coming to the end."

After he turns the shower off, he remains standing there,
watching the steam whirling up into the overhead fan.

In the living room he puts on a CD, a bluegrass compilation she brought home one day and then played incessantly. Gail, the sous-chef: "My one talent," she says. "I can chop onions without shedding a tear." Ansel views cooking as a kind of construction game, a sort of Lego with food. A casserole built floor by floor, a skylight of potatoes. Six months later, he has not got himself out of the habit of cooking for two. To compensate, he now cooks every other day; slow, elaborate meals. The sun goes down as he whips up the potatoes, dices the onions and leeks.

By the time everything is ready, the rain has stopped, so he carries his dinner out onto the front porch. The sky above is a soothing light, warm colours crowding the horizon. Ansel can see Ed Carney sitting on his porch, and he lifts his hand in greeting. Watching Ed stand up, take the steps one at time and hobble down the sidewalk towards him, is like watching bread rise. So Ansel goes into the house, gets a second helping of casserole for his friend, and another glass of wine, and by the time he returns with a tray, Ed has reached his front yard.

Ed makes himself comfortable, and the two sit eating quietly while the occasional car grumbles by along Keefer.

Ed describes the coyote he saw earlier, sprinting down the middle of the street. Across the road, Mrs. Cho is visible in her window, reading the newspaper. She looks up and sees them sitting there, beams a smile to them, then closes the blinds.

To Ansel, Ed still has the build of a mailman, lean and reedy, with eyes that have a tendency to mist up as he loses himself in one train of thought or another. He retired just a year ago, after forty years at Canada Post. Because Gail used to work at home, she would stop by his house during the day for coffee and conversation. She told Ansel once that Ed spent the day making pinhole cameras, reading *Nature*, and writing letters to his grandchildren about the biologist Alfred Russel Wallace. He told his grandchildren that evolution was still the defining idea of modern times, just as it had been when he was a child. "Stem cells, Dolly, robotics, theories of everything, he and Darwin are the bedrock," he said. "And to think people still refuse to teach him. It's downright madness." In the evenings, the three of them used to while away the hours while Ed peppered them with snippets of esoterica. Mathematical equations for the distribution of seeds on a sunflower head, and so on.

This evening, he has launched into a story about the first open heart transplant. Hamilton Naki was a gardener, Ed tells Ansel. As a young man, he had apprenticed to a doctor at the University of Cape Town who needed help with his laboratory animals. It was 1950s South Africa, so Naki, who was black, kept his designation as gardener, even while he was learning to transplant organs in animals. "He worked on giraffes," Ed says. "Imagine that. What kind of operating table would you use? And in what room?"

"You have to operate when they're standing upright," Ansel says. "Giraffes have high blood pressure, so it's best if they don't lie down. So, no operating table. Just a scaffold."

Ed nods, pleased. "When Barnaard performed his famous surgery," he continues, "Naki was the man who led the first team, the one that removed the heart from a twenty-five-year-old donor, a woman who had been hit by a car. She had stopped to buy a cake. It's sadder than a Raymond Carver story." It was 1967, and Naki's contribution was carefully hidden. Naki was at the press conference announcing the success of the surgery, but identified himself as a gardener who worked at the research institute. "Until this year," Ed says, "no one knew. Not even his neighbours. He retired with a gardener's pension."

They both shake their heads in wonder. Ansel remembers the first time he saw an exposed heart pumping. The way it leapt out of the cavity had shocked him, made him put his gloved hand to his own chest.

"Which part of this man's life was fiction?" Ed is saying.

"For him, none of it. Which means, I suppose, it depends on where you're standing."

Ed sets his plate down on the floor. "If you're in an airplane," he says, "a cloud ten feet away looks just the same as one ten thousand feet away. Clouds, they're every bit as fractal as broccoli or cauliflower. A very small part of a cloud, the way it looks up close, is the same shape as one in its entirety."

Ansel smiles. "Does that console you, Ed?"

"You know, the strange thing is, sometimes it really does."

"Because of the pattern?"

Ed shakes his head.

"Because it's mysterious?"

He takes a sip of wine, then slowly twirls the glass by its stem. "That's part of it. We're here for just a speck of time, and my greatest regret is that I don't know more. I'm like those sci-fi kids that want to peer into the future. Just let me read ahead a bit. Let me stay up another hour, flashlight under the covers. That's my comfort."

When the rain starts again, they're on to the second bottle of wine. "Ed," Ansel says, "what kind of rain would you say this is?"

Ed peers into the night. "It's like water out of a salad spinner."

"Who invented the salad spinner?"

He shakes his head, laughing. "Can't say, can't say."

Ansel can hear a siren coming down Hastings Street, and a short while later, several more. The sound is carried away, into the night. Ed says, "People told me I should start again after Patricia died. They said the house was too big for an old man, too many things to remind me."

Ansel listens in silence, watching the glimmering light of a plane up above, disappearing as the clouds sweep slowly across it. Behind them, music from the CD player drifts out of the house. Their home is still very much how she left it. Her clothes, her belongings. All the rolls of reel-to-reel, the DAT and Mini Discs. Touch a button, and her voice fills the room.

"I've got a picture of you two sitting right here," Ed says. He takes a sip of wine, wipes his mouth with the back of his hand.

Ansel's favourite song is playing on the CD now. Dom Turner's "Down by the Riverbed." He can hear the accordion and harmonica, the bluesy guitar.

Gail is singing, "I've got a case of Anselitis." She has a glass of wine in her right hand, and she's swaying down the front steps.

"I've thought about leaving, too, Ed. But everything I have is in this house."

"She was young. Thirty-nine is young." Ed's eyes are red and watery. "What am I saying? Seventy is young."

In the months after Patricia died, before Scott Carney moved back into the house to be with his father, Gail used to pack a dinner for Ed and walk it over to him. Ansel could see her from this very chair, standing in the doorway. Ed Carney talking her ear off about fertility clinics, or a new super skin being developed by the U.S. Army, about Marconi and the telegraph: "The man that signalled the death of the carrier pigeon." He filled his mind with so much in order to keep it aloft, like a balloon setting sail from the grief in his body.

"I don't need to think up ideas for radio projects," Gail had said, part-laughing, part-crying, when she came home again. "I have an Ed."

Now, Ed pushes himself up to standing. He looks across the street to his own house, where the front light burns in the dark. "She was like a daughter to me. And my boy, Scott, he thought of her as family, too. The way they laughed together, the way they argued. He was always trying to pitch ideas to her. He finally got to her with that coded diary; it was just the type of thing that would spark her imagination."

"Ed," Ansel says. When he looks up at his friend, the stars seem to blur behind the clouds. "Do you think there's a biological purpose to grieving? An evolutionary purpose."

Ed puts his hands in his pockets. "I guess it's to keep us alive somehow."

Ansel looks at him expectantly.

"Grief is the time when you ask all the questions. If you don't find some way to answer them, you won't go on living. You won't think about having children. Maybe it's an evolutionary imperative to find a way to accept death, your own and others. We forget that it's a possibility. People die and we're surprised. It always seems so unlikely. That's a trick of the mind." He pauses, and then looks back towards his house. "It's like what you were saying about perspective. From far away, I can accept everything. I can see the things that repeat themselves, the patterns and so on. I accept that the universe is thirteen billion years old. But up close, right here, is where you feel pain, grief. Right here, there are some things that I can never be at peace with." He shakes his head. "What helps me is when I fall asleep and dream of her, dream of my Patricia, and she says, There's nothing to worry about. Relax. Let it go." He shakes his head. "But that doesn't happen nearly enough, not enough at all."

That night, Ansel wakes up in the dark, the covers off him, a street lamp pouring light into the room. He says her name, but the word that remains in the air is a sound, a word that is beginning to lose its meaning, because it receives no answer.

Downstairs, he puts the kettle on. Sleeping, he thinks, is over for Ansel Ressing. This is a new era. Last week, he had gone walking each night, crossing the invisible boundary between Strathcona and the Downtown Eastside, walking to Main and Hastings, where crowds of people were still awake, milling about. The crowds made him think of Gail's description of the Arctic in the winter, people living their waking lives in the dark.

Tonight, he takes his glass of tea and goes into Gail's office. He turns the lights on and then dims them, because she says, authoritatively, "You can't hear as well when the lights are bright."

All her equipment is here, everything dusty. There is a shelf crammed with reels of tape, grease pencils, razor blades and splicing tape. What is he ever going to do with all of this? The CBC has already collected and archived some of her work, but the rest – features and documentaries, unfinished fragments, all the scattered interviews and soundscapes that she always thought she'd organize – remains here.

He turns on her computer and waits while the icons flash up one by one. When the screen settles, he opens the sound-editing program, moves the cursor through the files and chooses one at random. A slightly accented voice comes up from the console: Harry Jaarsma's. "Cryptography is a kind of protection. Think of the Sullivan diary as a message from the past, but one that has been buried beneath many layers.

"Every language leaves its own unique footprint. Cryptography, you know, is a complicated profession. You are given something in code, someone says, 'Break this,' and then it becomes a game, a chase. Of course, you assume that there is something to be pursued, some meaning to be unravelled.

It is exactly the kind of thing that can destroy a person. It is like a scent it is so strong, but there is no physical proof of it. What if you cannot, despite all efforts, find the way in? We have a saying in Dutch. *I hear the bell toll, but I know not where the hands of the clock lie.*"

The fragment of interview ends, the sound waves on the screen become a straight line, and the room falls quiet.

Outside the house, Ansel can hear people walking by, a man and a woman speaking in jocular, teasing voices. It is late, a quarter after three. He clicks on the icon for Gail's inbox, and the email program opens up onto the screen.

Even now, all these months later, new correspondence occasionally arrives for her – queries from overseas, notes from people she has worked with or interviewed. He opens an email from Harry Jaarsma, one that he has read before. *I know of course that you're gone, but your account is still open. These emails don't bounce back. I miss you in very many small ways.* This email is accompanied by a series of JPEGs, magnified images of the Mandelbrot Set. Before she saw these images, Gail said, she had never been able to picture the idea of infinity.

The pictures open up slowly, each one magnifying a small part of the preceding image. The shapes remain elusively familiar, scorpion tails and chains of spirals, evolving across generations.

One of the new messages catches Ansel's eye. He opens it without thinking.

Lieve Gail, I haven't heard from you in many months. I hope all is well. I have been thinking about you. Do write soon. Yours, Sipke.

The name is familiar, but in his fatigue, he cannot place it. Ansel writes back, telling him that he is sorry. He gives him, as briefly as possible, the details of what has happened.

He hits Send and leans back, closing his eyes.

Gail says, "In radio, sounds might be translated into microwave signals and then shot at a satellite floating in space. People say it's like shooting the eye out of a squirrel from a ten-mile range." She laughs, wrinkling her eyes as if she is picturing that very image. "These signals are then broadcast back to us, but some parts always escape. Some parts turn their back on the Earth, and maybe they keep travelling forever."

His affair with Mariana happened last summer, when Gail's work had taken her to Toronto. One night after working the evening shift at the clinic, he and Mariana had gone out for a drink. They were surrounded by a group of people, other doctors and friends, and then, a short time later, he looked up to find that everyone else had gone home. Yet he and Mariana had lingered on.

She was a respirologist, and was at the clinic covering for another doctor who was on leave. He found himself drawn to the way she sat at a table, legs crossed, chin resting on her hands. She was warm and serious and she was married, so, at first, he believed that there was no risk, no potential for the affair that later occurred. His own feelings he had dismissed as harmless, unremarkable.

The bar grew noisy, and they moved to a corner table. She said that her father had been a doctor, too, and she had never doubted that she, herself, would study medicine. Yet the more time passed, the more she had second thoughts. It was a career that set one apart, she said, made one solitary in ways she would not have chosen. Each encounter was so intimate, and yet professional. Always, doctors had to close a part of themselves off, from their patients, from their loved ones.

At some point, he had taken her hand and leaned across to kiss her. For a single, brief second, she pulled back, and then she did not. He remembered, still, the taste of her lips, of citrus, of the bitterness of the wine. She said that her husband and son were away on a camping trip. They left the bar and wandered out into the warm summer night. There were streams of traffic moving down Cambie Street, people flowing out of the local cinema, into coffee shops and bars. He and Mariana were holding hands, and they turned into a quiet residential street towards her home. He remembers all this now as if he is recalling the details of someone else's life, once told to him.

Sometimes, the things that should be difficult occur so easily, to undress someone else, to put your lips to theirs, to breathe in the scent of their skin and forget what came before. He can pinpoint this moment, isolate, study every detail. The second before he leaned across the table to kiss her, the second before his hand reached out, taking hers.

Mariana unlocked the door to her house. She switched all the lights on as they went, and his eyes half-closed against the brightness. The layout was familiar to him from some childhood remembrance, the hallway leading from the living room, past the kitchen, the thick carpet beneath his feet. There had been a birthday recently, and cards were displayed on the coffee table. Framed photographs hung neatly on the walls. They passed the open door of the child's room, a lone airplane suspended from the ceiling.

In the afternoons that followed, he and Mariana had walked the three blocks from the clinic to her house. They would let themselves in and walk through the quiet rooms. Lying beside her, he told himself he had crossed into a different country, another place, separate from his relationship with Gail. As if the affair was an event happening to him, as if every moment were not a choice, deliberated over, settled on.

Once, in his office at work, Mariana had set a scan against the light box showing him the clouding of a patient's lungs. She had described the patient's history and present condition. While she spoke, Ansel wondered what would happen now a device had been invented that, with the use of light, allowed one to see through the human body. He knew the shape and weight of a heart, the density of a human rib, the mysterious and beautiful branching of the ventricles. He knew that at a time of grief, the body was flooded with chemicals, and these chemicals were the groundwork for the emotions that people felt, responses mapped in the body like ink flooding the bloodstream. Mariana had told him once that there was a time when they might have found happiness together but that perhaps the moment had already passed. By the time they met, they had moved on to other possibilities, they had begun to live out other lives. We always choose in blindness, she said. We always choose looking backwards.

As the weeks passed, his life seemed to split in two, the affair that he had begun, and his relationship with Gail, whom he loved. Two parts that could not touch, because they told something very different about the man he was and the person that he wished to be. In September, he had ended the affair and told Gail everything. She had listened in silence, then she tried to escape him, agitated, going from room to room. He followed after her, terrified that if he closed his eyes, she would disappear. Her pain is still vivid to him, the lines on her face. What did he want from her? she had asked. What did he want her to say?

He wanted her to be angry with him, to accuse him. To tell him why she found it so easy to leave for months at a time, to commit herself so wholeheartedly to her work. To admit the truth to herself if she had now, finally, fallen out of love with him.

She was incensed. How dare he turn the blame around? Her anger seemed to shimmer around them, and then it simply dissolved, evaporating into the air. Her acceptance was, to him, worse than any other response. She said she felt as if they had been struggling for so long, and now they had finally reached the end.

In that moment, so much between them was clear, all the barriers and edges, the failure to grasp something unnamed that they both wanted. They saw that they could step back, lower their hands, let this something fall.

He told her that he wanted to continue on, to try to find a way from this place. But their days and nights entered a kind of limbo. They existed in the house, side by side, the ritual of their years together shielding them from a growing distance. Several weeks later, on Gail's thirty-ninth birthday, they had walked together along the creek. On the water, white sails opened like handkerchiefs.

"Are you happy, Ans?"

Gail had asked him this out of the blue, her gaze turned away from him so that he could not see her eyes.

Yes, he told her. This was where he wanted to be. But her hurt was visible, almost a pallor on her skin. He felt he could not reach her, as if some part of her, below the surface, had turned irrevocably away from him.

Late in the fall, Gail went to Amsterdam to see Harry Jaarsma. When she returned, she was full of life, impassioned. She seemed to want change, within herself, between them, and she believed all things were possible. She said that the past is not static, our memories fold and bend, we change with every step taken into the future. As the weeks passed, they had found a way to begin again. In February, she had gone to Prince George.

There is so much that he yearns to remember – everything that she ever said to him, the way she walked, her face when she woke, her singing voice.

He is still sitting at the computer, dawn beginning to move in through the windows, when the response comes back.

How? Sipke Vermeulen has written. How could something like this happen?

He had forgotten the name, but he remembers now that Gail had met Sipke Vermeulen when she went to the Netherlands that last fall. He had known her parents, after the war. She told him about a place where they had gone, an island that was now a part of the continent, a place she would one day return to, with Ansel. For a long time he sits in front of the screen, hands resting on the keyboard. But he does not know how to answer. Eventually, he closes the window and shuts the computer down.

Outside, he hears voices again. People who cannot go home, who haunt the streets of the Downtown Eastside.

She says, "Come to bed, Ans. My feet are cold."

"Yes," he answers. "Gail."

And when he closes his eyes and finds her, she rests her feet against his calves. He holds on to her, and the heat of both their bodies realigns, and comes to an equilibrium.

The next day, Ansel wakes up, his throat dry and his mind clear. He's overslept. He knows this by the amount of sunshine coming into the room. Downstairs, someone is singing. The CD that he put on last night is still going, looping endlessly on itself.

He stumbles into the bathroom, throws cold water on his face and pats his hair down. He looks longingly at the coffee pot, but there isn't enough time. In five minutes, he's out the door and circling False Creek. Little birds fleck the water and boats are moored in the August sunshine. He doesn't recognize any of the commuters. This is the 9:00 a.m.

set, somewhat more laid back. They wear wraparound sun-glasses. He pedals fast, speeds around the blind corners, hearing the lap of water on the moorings.

At the clinic, Pauline hands him a sheaf of papers. "Your first appointment never showed. But Alistair Cameron has results." She shrugs. "It feels like chaos, but it isn't. It's a state of being, really."

Alone, in his office, Ansel reads the radiology report on Al Cameron. The X-rays confirm active pulmonary tuberculosis.

His eyes are drawn to the photograph that Al had noticed the day before, and he reaches across the desk, picks up the frame. She had been home from Amsterdam for only a week by then, and they had decided to travel to the southwest coast of Vancouver Island to see friends. On the morning he'd taken this photograph, they had walked along the shore of the Pacific Ocean, stopping to explore the tide pools, to admire red starfish and tightly wound snails. Gail is wearing jeans and a windbreaker, and her hair, now shoulder length, blows lightly around her face. He remembers standing on the rocks, framing her in the camera's lens, the gentleness of her expression when she looked up to see him.

He has often wondered what dreams she had, if any, what last image accompanied her at the end, away from life, away from consciousness. When he tries to imagine that passage, the ground gives way, he falls with her.

Before he goes home that afternoon, Ansel stops at the ward to pay Al Cameron a visit.

He is lying in bed, IV tubes feeding his veins. His green-stockinged feet poke out from the hospital blankets and his eyes appear listless.

Ansel stands at his bedside reading the chart for several minutes before either man speaks.

"Streptomycin is out."

"Yes, in your case, streptomycin is out."

"What have you got for me then?"

"I don't know, Al. Let's wait for the tests to come back."

"TB is consumption, right?"

"That's right."

"It's an old disease. Strange to think of yourself as a modern person saddled with an old disease."

Ansel tries to remember the exact lines from Gail's documentary. Kafka, diagnosed with consumption, had imagined a dialogue between his brain and his lungs. He tells the story to Al, the words returning to him as he speaks. "'The brain found itself in a position where it could no longer sustain its burden of pain and affliction. It said, "I give up, but if there is still anyone here who cares at all for the preservation of the whole, let him then lessen my burden, and I'll be able to carry on for a while yet." At that point, the lung came forward; it didn't have much to lose.'"

Al smiles, a lovely ghost of a smile, of something remembered. He shifts his arms, then pushes himself to sitting.

"Do you have kids, Ansel?"

"No."

"Do you want some?"

"Yes."

"Am I prying too much?"

Ansel puts the chart down beside the bed. A feeling comes, like a pressure against his skin, then slowly, inexplicably, gives way. "No, you're not prying."

Al pulls the sheets up against his body. He says, "I think that I've accepted it, that I've come to terms with everything. But when I wake up the next day, that peace vanishes like it was never there, or as if it were all an illusion. That's what I find so difficult. I just want to accept it and be at rest. No more questions, no more doubt."

Ansel nods, unable to speak. He feels that he could put his hand out, reach her, hold on for one moment. Don't go, he thinks. She doesn't say anything, because they both know how it ends, they always knew they could not change it. *Gail.* He stands half turned away from Al, afraid of his emotion.

"Am I allowed a phone call? This isn't like jail, is it?"

Ansel hands him his phone. "You know the number?"

Al nods.

"Okay. This one's on the clinic." He returns Al's chart to the foot of the bed.

When Ansel leaves the room, Al Cameron is lying on his side, the covers up over his body.

"I'm here," he is saying. "I'm here." He and the phone inside a small cave of stillness.

4

Aloft

Clara sits beneath the skylight of her sewing room, a square of light falling through the window, marking a border around her. It is early morning, still but for the occasional birdsong, and an animal, a squirrel, she thinks, scurrying across the roof. The day is open in front of her, a pocket of space to fill. She will finish her sewing this morning, and then, later on, she will gather flowers from the garden and take them to the cemetery for her daughter.

She runs her hand across the newspaper, blinking the sleep from her eyes. The article she is reading tells how scientists in Austria have measured the shortest interval of time ever observed, one hundred attoseconds, or a quintillionth of a second. *To imagine how long this is*, the article says, *if 100 attoseconds is stretched so long it lasts one second, one second would last 300 million years on the same scale*. Time, Clara believes, is the great mystery. Since Einstein, physicists have argued that time is merely a convention, that only the speed of light is constant everywhere in the universe. If one travelled fast enough, time would bend, and one person's past could theoretically become another person's future.

In her workroom, a dozen costumes hang from a clothes rail. The show, a children's production of *The Nutcracker*, is scheduled for September, completely out of season, but the children from the dance school don't seem to mind. Over the last few weeks, they have trooped in for their fittings, girls in frothy tutus skipping down the hallway, the Snow Queen waiting, aloof, hands on her hips, in a sequined dress. Clara is putting the finishing touches on a giant head for King Rat. On her table is a stack of pipe cleaners which she plans to shape into whiskers.

From her window, she can see Matthew standing in the garden. He looks up at the August sky, the low sweep of clouds, then lowers his head, surveying the last of the summer flowers. Because of the arthritis in his knees, her husband walks slowly, with the aid of a cane. She is tempted to put down her coffee, to join him outside, but work cannot wait. The garden has always been Matthew's domain. There, he loses track of himself and the hours. He can coax the most stubborn flowers into bloom.

In another hour or so, he will come back inside the house. Each morning is the same. They will put the kettle on for tea, prepare a light breakfast. Every act, every routine, helps, the way sitting in a car travelling along the highway can seem a comfort, a motion to fall back on, to keep their thoughts contained as they move into another place.

She had grown up in her father's restaurant in Kowloon, and the Hong Kong that Clara remembers is cramped and vibrant, a city heated by the press of bodies. On Reclamation Street, where they lived, the buildings, crowded shoulder to shoulder, seemed to jostle for space. Laundry shook in the wind, people overflowed onto balconies, onto the sidewalks.

After school, during the dinner hour, she would work the floor of the restaurant, greeting customers as they stepped through the shuttered doors: elderly men, newspapers tucked under their arms, young women in shifts and trousers towing a line of children. In the kitchen, behind glass, cooks appeared and disappeared in the steamy air. "Ching Yun," her father would say proudly, calling her by her Chinese name. "Hurry and bring this gentleman a glass of tea." Always, she had felt at ease in the ebb and flow of the restaurant, chopsticks clicking against porcelain bowls, the clatter of her father's abacus. She balanced a half-dozen plates in her arms, listening sympathetically when a customer complained about the state of the world, his children or simply the weather. Leftover food she carried to the back door, where the very old and the very young would congregate, carrying tin plates.

Behind the kitchen, faded linoleum stairs led up to their living space. She and her four younger sisters lived in one room, one on top of the other, sharing their clothes, their hairbrushes and slippers. Her sisters spent their days working in the restaurant, but Clara, as the eldest, had been enrolled at St. Mary's School. In the evenings, while her sisters finished their chores, she sat at the dining table, writing essays or laboratory notes, or helping her mother with the sewing. She worked quickly, impatient to join her father in the sitting room, where each night he would open a novel and step away from the world. She gathered what lay discarded at his feet, reading, in English or Chinese, *Father Goriot*, *A Tale of Two Cities*, *Journey to the West*. Hours later, while the rest of the household slept, she remained awake, reading by candlelight. Her sisters sighed in their sleep, breathed in unison, while she, turning pages, shuddered or wept or shook with laughter.

In *Journey to the West*, the young monk Xuanzang is called by the Bodhisattva on a pilgrimage to India. He is joined on his travels by three disciples who have each been given the task of accompanying him in order to atone for past mistakes. To make amends. The stories that make up *Journey to the West* are enshrined in countless Chinese operas. On Sundays, she and her father would take the bus to the theatre, a converted temple, where they bought their tickets from an old whiskered man who slept in the booth with one eye open. Like a dolphin, her father said once, awake just enough to stay afloat. In the open auditorium that day, Clara made her way to the front, past the grandmothers seated on stools, drinking tea, littering the ground with sunflower seeds. She stood so close to the stage that the sound of the gongs exploded in her ears, tingling up her spine; she could see the stitching of the Monkey King's yellow robes as he somersaulted across the stage. All the while, her father, beside her, followed the undercurrent of the story. The quest for enlightenment, the spiritual journey that remained at the core.

She was twelve years old the day, the moment, the city became altered for her. When she herself suddenly became clear.

The evening of the accident, her father had the radio on. From where she stood, sweeping the entrance to the restaurant, she heard the first chiming notes, a clang of symbols. Inside the restaurant, an elderly man, his voice scratchy with age, began to sing. The diners clapped, calling encouragement, joining their voices with his.

It was twilight. She stood outside listening, the broom in her hand. A crowd of people had gathered on the sidewalk, looking up at the apartment building across the street. When she craned her neck back and lifted her eyes, she saw a boy pacing back and forth on the flat roof. A flash of colour slid across the sky, a kite high above him. The wind picked it up and twisted it round, a dragon with a long and flickering tail, spiralling.

She saw the edge of the roof, the boy walking without seeing it. Her throat caught.

It happened in the space of a second. The boy, head tilted up, watched the progress of his kite. He stepped backwards into air. Someone beside her screamed, and then she heard only silence. For a moment as he fell, his body unfurled, hands darting out, legs kicking away.

The crowd surged forward, and she began to run, reaching her arms out as if she could catch him. A few steps away, in front of her, the boy hit the sidewalk.

Voices cried out, a screaming that rose in volume, the sound travelling over her. The side of his head was badly crushed, his legs twisted grotesquely beneath him. The boy's eyes were open, but she did not think he could see. People moved towards him, stopping when they saw blood staining the ground.

Seconds passed. Around her, nobody moved.

The air was thick. She had to push against it, fighting the sickness that rose in her chest. She forced herself to go and kneel beside him. Gently, she placed one hand on his forehead, and then carefully she took his hand.

Behind her, someone asked, "Is he still breathing?"

Clara nodded but she didn't look up. "Call an ambulance."

Footsteps hurried away. She heard a girl sobbing, calling for her parents, but nobody answered. The parents were not there, someone said, they had gone this morning to Hong Kong Island. At the sound of the girl's voice, something changed in the boy's expression, and Clara knew that he was looking at her, seeing her face. He was younger than she, perhaps ten years old. She held his hand tighter. "Don't be afraid," she said. His hair was matted and glistening, the blood still running out. She told him that this was only the beginning of a long walk, an important journey. He blinked up at her, seeming to understand, seeming to trust her. She said that she would stay with him for as long as she could.

The noise of the siren came to her then, a sound enveloping her like heat. The medics, a blur of white, surged forward. She saw them remove the boy's hand from hers, and then someone placed their hands on her shoulders, pulling her gradually away.

When the ambulance had disappeared, she found herself alone, the bystanders gaping at the pool of blood, her stained clothes. She saw her father, the panicked expression on his face, as he made his way to where she stood. She began to walk in the direction that the ambulance had gone, but her father reached out, caught her hand, held her still.

Two nights later, he sat with her in a corner of the restaurant. He told her that the boy, in the presence of his parents and his sister, had died a few hours ago.

She nodded but said nothing.

"What are you thinking, Ching Yun?"

Around them, chairs scraped, voices rose and fell. "We all stood and watched it happen," she said, at last. "If I had thought to call out to him, I could have stopped it. If I had only tried to reach him."

He stared at her for a moment, saying nothing. Then he said that what she believed was false. The boy had been too far up, he had been lost in a world of his own.

She shook her head and pushed her chair back, standing up. Her father let her go. She went outside into the cool evening air. On the sidewalk, she smelled tobacco smoke and looked up to see the mechanics next door sitting on crates, cigarettes pinched between their lips. Fluorescent signs arced over the street, glowing bridges of colour. From the dwellings above, raucous laughter tumbled down. She heard the clatter of mahjong tiles, a chorus of radios.

She kept walking, across the street, up the stairs of the apartment building, until, finally, she reached the rooftop. This morning, she had learned from the boy's sister that this had been his favourite place. He always wanted to be alone, his sister said, flying his kites, and when he was older, he wanted to find work on the merchant ships, to travel from port to port, seeing the world.

Below, the ground was neon, an electric river. In the distance, Kowloon Harbour was a series of tiny lights surrounded by a flood of dark, a breath away from Hong Kong Island. In her mind, she could fill in the emptiness, temples clouded by the smoke of burning joss sticks, streets reaching up like ladders, composed entirely of stone steps. At the summit, she imagined children setting their kites aloft.

Farther away were countries she had never set foot in, but which filtered through her imagination. Britain and China, India and America. For the first time in her life, she wanted to be anywhere but where she stood. She wanted to come to all things with the clarity in which she had seen the boy, and in which she had been seen by him.

When Clara was nineteen years old, her father took her aside to that same table. He set an envelope in front of her, the letter that she had been waiting for, an answer from the University of Melbourne. Her hands shook as she read the lines, then handed the sheet of paper back to him. Her father leapt to his feet, shouting the news to everyone in the restaurant. The cooks came out from behind the glass, her mother and sisters rushed to embrace her.

On that day, she gave herself an English name, as many young women were choosing to do, on their departure from Hong Kong. Leung Ching Yun, Clearest Spring, the name of her childhood slipped away from her, into the past. She wrote her new name out in the letter she sent to the University of Melbourne. *Clara Leung.*

As a young woman, when describing Matthew to friends, she would often speak of fate, of how she and Matthew had crossed paths on the narrow, snow-covered walkways of the university, of their chance meetings as they hurried from one class to another. They had the same group of friends, expatriate Asians in Melbourne, from as far away as Malaya, North Borneo, Thailand and Hong Kong.

She and Matthew had stood out from the group – the men mostly enrolled in science programs, the women taking classes at the secretarial college. She studied literature, hoping one day to be a schoolteacher. Matthew had started a degree in civil engineering, but a year shy of completion, he had given in to his longing and transferred to the history department.

She can still see him as he was then, a young man of twenty-three, his hair carefully combed, his expression serious. The first time Matthew came to the boarding house where she lived, he carried a bouquet of flowers in each hand. *I couldn't decide*, he had told her, his eyes pensive. *I couldn't choose.* He was wearing his usual clothes, slacks, a white shirt and a sports jacket. They spent the day in the kitchen, trying to recreate the dishes of their childhoods: laksas, dumplings, fragrant breads. Eleanor Henley, Clara's landlady, was in charge of the turntable. She played Elvis and Slim Dusty, "A Pub with No Beer." Eleanor watching Clara and Matthew with a knowing, motherly smile.

Standing over the stove, he asked about her family, about Kowloon. Clara described the restaurant, the crowded rooms where she and her sisters had amused themselves, dressing up in their parents' finery. Each week, her mother would light sticks of incense and pour wine into tiny porcelain cups. She held whispered conversations with the ancestors, urging them to drink freely, to live well.

From the time of her adolescence, she told Matthew, she had known she would leave Hong Kong, she would go into the world beyond. *Too many books*, her mother had said, chiding her, *too many idle dreams*. And yet her parents had not tried to dissuade her.

At one point, when Eleanor turned her back, he whispered in her ear. Would she follow him anywhere, to Malaya, to Britain, to Canada? He looked at her as if afraid she might vanish from the room, vanish into thin air.

"Just ask," she said, teasing. "Ask and you'll know."

The night she saw her first snowfall, they were sitting together in a restaurant, winter coats buttoned up against the chill. She and Matthew watched the twirl of snowflakes through the plate glass windows, sparks of white carried sideways by the wind. He began to tell Clara about his father.

During the war, he said, his father had worked for the Japanese occupation forces, and in September of 1945 he had been murdered by the men he worked with. Hidden in the trees, he had seen his father's death, watched as the body was thrown inside a truck, and the truck driven away. He spoke quickly, as if fearing the words themselves could cut him, as if he were hurrying along a narrow ledge.

The blurred lights of the passing cars slipped across their table. "And afterwards," she said, softly. "How did you go on?"

"We left Sandakan, my mother and I. We took the steamer to Tawau, in the south. It was sudden. There was no time even to find his body, to bury it properly. Later on, in Tawau, my mother remarried. Her new husband had children of his own. She went on." There was fatigue in his voice, but no anger.

"Sandakan was all that I had known. Everything I loved was there. The year I turned eighteen, I went back by myself. But people remembered my father. They knew what he had done during the war. They remembered things I hadn't known at the time. I came to see that there was no place for me there, that what I wanted had disappeared long ago."

His words trailed off, and he looked up at her, his eyes blank, as if he had lost his place. There was a cup of coffee on the table in front of him and he reached for it, holding it in his hands.

"So you left Sandakan," she said, wanting to help him, to prod him forward. "And you came here."

In his eyes, she saw uncertainty, and then a decision slowly taking shape. She waited, saying nothing.

"There was someone I had known there from that earlier time. A girl, Ani. Her parents had died during the war, but she still lived there, in Sandakan. We saw each other again."

His voice changed when he spoke her name, a detachment that Clara heard as something more. For a time, he said, he had believed he would remain there, with her. But this was not to be. Instead, he left, coming here, to Melbourne. "That was five years ago." His voice was distant, as if a lifetime lay between the heartbreak he had experienced and the man he was now. "After a while, I wrote to her, but there was no response. It was as if she had disappeared." Finally, from his uncle in Sandakan, he learned that she was living in Jakarta. She had a child now.

His hands lay on the table, and he pressed them together, as if to contain some other question, to hold his memories still.

"There are things in my life that I hoped would turn out differently. Things that I thought I was capable of changing. But isn't it this way for everyone?" He met her eyes. "The war was a rift, a scar. Going back only opened up the memory, but there was no solace. I only saw the terrible waste of it, the things I couldn't change." He said that when they graduated the following spring, he would not return to North Borneo. Australia was closed to Asian immigrants, but he had decided to apply to Canada. After graduation, would she marry him? Would she go with him to Canada?

She was twenty-one years old, and in her mind the choice was clear; she must commit herself, or pass by this opening forever. "Yes," she said, believing herself strong enough, in love enough, to ground him and keep him safe.

Around them, the restaurant dimmed and flickered, the passing cars, the snow. His childhood in Sandakan twisted like a wire in his body, but when she took his hand, it was a gesture that held a promise. I will take a share of your grief. If you trust me, I will carry it within my own heart.

In the cemetery, the leaves shimmer in the noon heat. On the far side of the grounds, an interment is taking place. A gathering of people, a gathering of flowers. A bulldozer sits a few metres away, waiting to compact the earth.

When she arrives at the marker, Ansel is there before her. He is leaning against the stone, his hands in his pockets. He talks to Gail, to himself. This conversation that never ceases.

She shows him the book she has brought with her, *Journey to the West*, the pages yellowed and brittle. For a little while, they reminisce about childhood belongings, and as they talk he turns the pages, studying the rows of Chinese characters. "It's a puzzle," he says. "Like standing on the lawn in front of someone's house and wondering what it's like inside."

She is reminded of their first conversation after Gail died, when he came to her, distraught, saying that Gail had telephoned him, that he should have gone to her in Prince George. She thought then, as she does now, that the deepest pain comes from knowing that you are powerless, incapable of protecting the ones you love. A sudden death leaves so few answers. She and Matthew and Ansel are clutching at air, they are suspended in time. Her daughter was in the midst of life, she had so much more to ask, to say. Clara thinks of Ansel as a son. One day, he will meet someone else, he will fall in love and marry, it is inevitable. And what of her daughter? Gail will fade into the past, a memory, a ghost in his mind. There is no other way. One cannot live in the past.

He begins to walk among the headstones, stepping into a garden planted nearby, giving her some time alone.

From the bag she has brought with her, Clara takes out a small stack of paper squares, each one decorated at the centre with a piece of gold foil. These joss sheets are part of an old Chinese ritual, one her parents practised, and their parents before them. When she was a child, she would watch the women gathered together, their hands deftly rolling each sheet into a cylinder, puffing it out slightly with a breath of air, then tucking the ends together. These paper objects, shaped like small boats, represent pieces of gold and silver, precious ingots once used in Old China. One or two women, the most skilled, created more complex objects, a two-dimensional dress, a house, a wristwatch, even shoes, folded to lie flat. When the women set the offerings alight, the rising smoke would carry their gifts into the afterlife, where their ancestors, penniless, would gather them up and use these riches to pay their way through the land of the dead.

The ritual occupies her hands as she releases her mind, sets it down beside the idea of her daughter. The remembrance of her presence in the room, her heart beating quietly and in its own solitude – the physical form of the girl that she misses.

Occasionally, Matthew accompanies her here. He tends the flowers that he planted, in defiance of cemetery regulations. Now stonecrop and aster form a border around the marker, a brush of mauve and blue. Unlike Clara, her husband finds no comfort in being here. Since Gail's death, his whole body has begun to curve forward, his gait has slowed to a shuffle. In six months, he has aged a decade. She knows that he is still looking for some other form of consolation. All his life, he has struggled to accept what cannot be changed, to hold fast to a core truth within himself. Judgment, goodness. The thread that would bind the two, and show him the way forward.

When they married in 1960, the wedding was lavish, a banquet thrown by her father in a fine hotel in Hong Kong. Clara's parents gave them an antique wedding chest, made from rosewood, carved with a scene of ladies seated under cherry blossoms. Matthew's mother had sent them a gift of money and a letter saying that she could not come, that her husband had been ill and she had to remain in Tawau to look after work in the plantation.

At night, when everyone had gone to sleep, Clara remained awake beside the rosewood chest, running her hands along the grooves in the wood. Her feelings for Matthew seemed to her like a fever, a lightness in her body. A lifetime, she had told herself. In front of us stretches a lifetime.

While they waited for their application to be assessed by the Canadian embassy, they lived with her parents, Matthew helping her father in the restaurant while Clara worked as a teacher's assistant in the school where she herself had once studied. Two years later, their immigration papers were finally approved. That night, they had closed the door to their bedroom, lain down beside one another. "I was afraid to get my hopes up," he said. Weeks later, in the lounge at Kai Tek airport, her parents and sisters gathered around and embraced her. She remembers, still, the scent of their hair, their perfume. To them, Melbourne had seemed the end of the world. Canada was unimaginable.

The morning she and Matthew arrived in Vancouver, the sky was overcast, the light diffused. Their plane descended towards the coastline, lowering through the clouds. The Pacific Ocean gave way to little islands, ribbons of land before the continent appeared before them. Clara was eight weeks pregnant and she had named her baby already – Gail, a gale wind, a strong wind – certain that she was carrying a daughter. She stared out the window, amazed at the blanket of trees, the city perched on the shelf of land.

They found an apartment near Main Street, a tiny one-bedroom overlooking East Broadway. While they waited for their furniture to arrive by steamer from Hong Kong, they slept on a thin piece of foam. Matthew would put his ear to her stomach, listening for movements of their child. He touched her stomach as if it were a precious glass, fragile and mysterious.

At first, the change in their lives, the adventure, carried

them through the months. They used all their savings for the down payment on a home, a two-storey on Keefer Street. She felt as if they were adding details to a picture, bringing home a chesterfield one day, a second-hand coffee table the next. They measured the windows for curtains, which she sewed and embroidered by hand. At the second-hand shops downtown, she bought books and lined the shelves with them, adding them to the ones they had brought with them from Melbourne and Hong Kong.

She could find no work as a schoolteacher and so started her own business as a seamstress. All through Chinatown, she posted handwritten signs, and there was steady work mending shirts and coats, the occasional wedding gown. Together, she and Matthew painted the walls of her workroom, built cabinets for notions and patterns. A year passed. Still Matthew was out of work. To meet their mortgage payments, he took a job in a restaurant. Eventually, he apprenticed as a cook.

After Gail was born, he began to withdraw into himself, sleeping less or not at all. Day by day, he faltered. Clara could not put her finger on the event that caused this change in him. Perhaps it was only the winter. It rained and rained, flooding the streets, and the city seemed to melt away, leaving a poverty around them that they had not expected. Two blocks down, people lived in cardboard boxes. There were prostitutes in the back alleys, needles hidden in the grass. On overcast days, the mountains and water disappeared, indistinguishable behind the mist. Clara and Matthew wrapped themselves up in sweaters found at the Salvation Army, unable to adjust to the cold and damp. He could not sleep, and began to disappear from the house at night. When he came home, exhausted, ill, he said that he wanted to return to Australia, to Malaysia, that he had underestimated how different this country would be. He had been mistaken, he said, to believe he could start over, leave Sandakan and all that happened there behind.

His father lived on in his mind, a presence that shaped his thoughts. The way, when he rose from bed in the morning, his confidence seemed to make the house full. In the darkness, his father would walk the aisles of the rubber plantation, he and the workers wearing headlamps or carrying torches, a stream of light illuminating the track ahead of them. How beautiful their home had been, on Jalan Campbell. There had been cabinets full of glass figurines and trinkets, pottery from China, painted fans. He remembered his parents dancing, the phonograph on the high shelf, music like a tent around them. Now Matthew was twenty-eight years old, the same age his father had been when he died. He said that he was losing his bearings, he did not know how to see into the future, how to become the man he wished to be.

At night, she listened to his dreams, and in the day, when he stared listlessly at the newspaper, she ran her hands over his back, searching for the knots of tension, easing them with her fingers. In the dining room was a chandelier, laden with crystal beads. She had found it, abandoned, in the attic of the house. Each week, while Gail, only a year old, slept in a sling against her body, she unhooked the pieces and, one by one, cleaned them to a shine. She focused her thoughts on the task, imagining the moment when she reassembled the chandelier. A hundred lights burning. Darkness receding like fog on the water.

It was Clara who encouraged him to write to his mother in Tawau, to his uncle who still lived in Sandakan. It was she who took those letters to the post office and sent them away, thinking that it was the disconnection, the act of immigration, that was breaking her husband apart.

But when the letters came back, the unexpected happened. Whatever had been supporting her husband seemed to collapse. He came apart like a string unravelling. She did not know, then, what it was that she had set into motion.

The grounds are busy today, and Clara cannot help but watch the other people gathered here, some in groups, talking together, others crouched on the ground, alone, their faces hidden. Here, she stands among the other bereaved, outside of time, in a landscape devoted only to memory.

Nearby is a tall metal container, one of many that the cemetery distributes through the grounds. The bottom is lined with ashes, remnants of previous offerings. She lights the first folded sheet, and a thin strand of smoke rises into the air, then she touches the sheet to another, and then another. Inside the container, the flames flicker and twist. When all of the pieces are burning, she picks up the book again and begins to remove the pages. The air around her is warm and heavy. The pages turn to fire, to ashes, a transmutation that she cannot see, the book becoming filaments in the air.

In the afterlife that she imagines, the pieces fall around Gail, so numerous they cover her like a blanket, a protection against the cold.

"Zuang Zi dreamed that he was a butterfly," her father used to say, beginning the famous story. "When he awoke, he wondered whether he was a man dreaming he was a butterfly. Or if, perhaps, he was a butterfly dreaming that he was a man." This life is illusory, her father said. It has the quality, the importance, of a dream.

She had argued with him, remembering the boy as he lay on the sidewalk, the kite lifting away from him. In life, she said, one feels both exultation and suffering. The emotions, intense though fragmentary, are real. They exist. Her father had nodded, taken aback by her insistence. He said there were consequences to one's actions. She must choose for herself what to put into this world.

All those years ago, Matthew had written to Sandakan, and from his uncle he had learned Ani's whereabouts. He had written to her, and, eventually, a letter came back from Jakarta. He laid it on the table between them, overwhelmed, unable to hide his distress. So much had been left unfinished. He told her there were things he needed to know.

She had felt as if a part of herself were dying, coming to an end.

He said that he had a nightmare in which he was an old man. He walked in the dirt but left no marks. He went into the water thinking it could hold him up, but the water just passed through him.

She wondered if was possible to cross back in time, cross borders and nations, begin again, if this was what he needed. The thought had come to her suddenly: *If you go, you will not return.* She believes in the present moment, that a decision made now can shift the balance, that every act realigns the past. Imagine it this way, she had told Matthew. It is like walking across a vast field as the sun rises, burns, and slowly falls. The shadows around us change depending on which direction we walk, what steps we choose to take.

"Look at me," she said.

He met her eyes, and she did not allow herself to falter.

She told him to leave, to travel to Jakarta, to find what he needed to know. Come back, she said, only if you intend to stay.

5

The Bird Feather

JAKARTA

1957

*I*n the heat of the afternoon, Ani's son sleeps peacefully in her arms. Through the half-shuttered windows, she can hear the sound of the city drifting by, bicycle bells, the nervous rattling of mopeds and *bemo*s. The vendors call out their wares, singing the words above the traffic. On Ani's stomach, Wideh's breaths are deep and easy. He presses his mouth against her chin, opens and closes his lips as if he is chewing, dreaming once more about food. She loops her arms around his warm and sweating body, keeps time by the rhythm of his breathing.

In the kitchen, she can hear the muted brushing of Saskia's slippers on the tiled floor as she sets a pot of water to boil. Saskia's daughter, Tash, is whispering, *I'm hungry, Ibu*, as she rummages in the cupboard for cookies. Ani closes her eyes and the apartment falls away, her few belongings, a

divan, cot and a small charcoal brazier, the thin blue curtain
that divides the room.

Four years ago, she had left Sandakan, boarding the
steamer for Tarakan. There, she had met her mother's eldest
brother, Bashir, who was ill, and from there she had gone to
Ujung Padang, then Pontianak, continuing on to Jakarta. It
was on the boat from Pontianak that she had met Saskia,
born in the same year as Ani. Saskia and her family had wel-
comed her into their lives, helping her to find her place here.
In this city of three million people, she feels as if she has disappeared, slipped into the outline she has made for herself: a
twenty-two-year-old woman, known as a widow, alone in
the world except for her small son.

A canal runs along the far side of Jalan Kamboja. Lying
on the divan, she can hear the watery murmur of people
bathing, the high, laughing voices of women and children.
They sit on the stone steps, or crouch low, scrubbing their
clothes. She imagines the colours of their sarongs turning
bright when they emerge from the canal, the children holding
their noses and submerging their faces as they balance in
precarious handstands. They take turns leaping into the
warm water.

Tomorrow morning, she will go to Saskia's house in
Kebajoran and they will run through the list one last time,
complete all the necessary preparations for Saskia's departure
at the end of the week. The notice had come just forty-eight
hours ago, with the news that her family had secured a place
on the next boat leaving for Holland. Since early January,
more than ten thousand Dutch and Indonesians have been

repatriated, families starting over in another country, now that the Dutch East Indies have ceased to exist.

"From the time I was a little girl," Saskia had said, "I thought I would always live here, that I would be buried beside my parents, and that I would live for eternity with the spirits from ages past."

"You might come back one day. Nobody knows what the future brings."

"*Tempo dulu*. Those times are gone now."

"If it were possible, would you change something in your life?"

"It's like a Dutch sentence, twists and turns and finally, at the very end, the verb that you've been waiting for. You can't really say anything about the sentence until it's finished." She laughed. "Quite a trick, if you ask me."

Over the past few days, Ani has helped fill her trunk with woolen sweaters and socks, with neatly packaged spices, heirlooms and photographs. Weary, they collapsed in Saskia's sitting room, household goods scattered around them, their children circling on tiptoe.

Saskia's husband, Siem Dertik, teaches engineering at the technical school in Jakarta. He reminds Ani of her father, and this resemblance both pains and steadies her. Their family is a mirror of Ani's own, the mother and father whom Ani carries in her memory, the little girl who was once so treasured.

Siem is patient and endlessly curious. Like Ani's father, he takes pleasure in knowing the names of things, in explaining their origin. He reads books in Indonesian, Dutch,

French and English, the languages of his mixed background. In the evenings, while the children listen raptly, he tells them about space in the universe, how it stretches, collapses and folds. He writes equations for the way objects fall through space, following the trajectory of force and gravity. The trajectory of the object, he explains, can be plotted, point by point, a graph revealing the past, the present and the anticipated future.

Once, in the kitchen, she had seen Wideh standing beside Siem, imitating the movements of his hands as he prepared the evening meal. Wearing identical slippers, he imitated Siem's walk, a quick shuffle, as he moved in the small room.

Here, in Jakarta, nothing holds to a steady state. Electricity and water can't be depended upon, and the military parades in Freedom Square now spill onto the streets, taking over the roads. Only in Wideh can she recognize the passing time. Ani puts her nose to his hair, she smells the sweetness of his skin, talc and sweat. When she looks at him, she is moved by his resemblance to his father, the high cheekbones, the searching eyes. He is an echo of the boy she knew long ago. She wraps one of her hands around his, and it reminds her of Chinese boxes, one disappearing completely within the other. *Ibu*, he says, half waking, and Ani whispers his name, *Wideh*. He sighs, gazing at her for a moment, then returns to his dreams.

There was a time when she could find her way in Sandakan without seeing the landmarks, the sea or even the horizon. This was 1953, and in the mornings, at first light, she folded her sarong between her legs, climbed onto her bicycle, pedalled hard until gravity pulled her down the slope of the hill. In the fog, nothing was visible. People on the road could hear her coming. They ran from her, the baskets on their backs toppling, root vegetables spilling onto the ground as she sped past, missing them by inches. *Murderous child!* She only heard *murder* – before she left them behind.

The bicycle, an Australian-made Malvern Star, was painted blue, and the frame felt almost weightless. When she leaned her body forward, the wheels seemed to lift off the ground. She skittered over the rocks, the pedals throwing her feet off, and then steadied again. The road curved downhill, towards the market and the sea. Ani steered with her hips. *Beware, beware*, and children ran. She was more than Ani, then. She was unpredictable, a piece of light streaking across the ground.

The market gardeners laid their offerings on straw mats. A yellow pyramid of bananas, hillocks of red and green chili peppers, everything neat as the stones in a *congkak* game. Under a pink umbrella, her neighbour Eika crouched on the ground, chattering about the ginger bulbs and lemongrass. Beside her, watermelons and spiny jackfruit, Hooi-joo smoking, exhaling with her face lifted towards the sky. They took turns jingling their pockets, shouting out, "Sister, sister, take a look here."

This morning, the market was full of old women. The older they were, the more they pushed. But Ani would have none of it. She shoved right back, sticking her elbow into someone's arm, then propelling herself forward. "You'll make a fine old maid," someone snapped, and Ani turned her body, shoved the woman aside. Eika pressed something into her hand, a paper bag filled with seeds. "Take this to Lohkman for me?" she asked, blushing when she said his name. Ani took it from her hand, smiling, and then she was carried past by the crowd. At the fish market, Lohkman was bargaining with a dealer, both men seated cross-legged on a tarpaulin. "At thirty, I won't give," he said.

"Give me your basement price then."

"Thirty-five."

"Lohkman, my friend, speak decently. A little lower perhaps?"

He ignored the dealer, turning to Ani. *Kelah* and black pomfret, lines of shiny blue wandering beneath the fishes' skin, were stacked neatly at his feet. "Will you have coffee tonight?" she asked him.

He faked a yawn, stretched his arms into the sky. "Not with the money they're offering me."

She laughed and handed him the paper bag from Eika. "From an admirer."

"Not another one."

"Are we fishing tonight?"

Lohkman nodded. "My brother says the sea is too choppy for *dorab*. We can use the casting nets." As she turned to go, he said, "Don't be late, Ani. If you are, I'll make you swim for the boat."

The dealer, half teasing, laid his head-cloth on top of the fish, put his head on it and pretended to go to sleep. "Should I bid?" he said, in a tragic voice. "I don't know. The seller ignores me."

Riding home, loaded down with vegetables, was when she felt the worth of her Malvern Star and its never-before-seen-in-Sandakan metal carrier. She balanced on the pedals, the bicycle shifting side to side with her weight. Ani passed women who walked tilted over, bamboo poles heavy across their backs. When she looked over her shoulder, they were only shadows on the ground, swaying with the trees. From the ridge, she could see Sandakan harbour, a stroke of blue beneath the mist. The town was two straight lines of *atap* roofs and a swirl of people.

In the last year, concrete and glass had come to Sandakan. There were new British administration buildings south of the market, and the *padang* was busy again with picnics and cricket games. Each night, families spread woven mats on the grass. They turned their faces towards the west, hushed in reverence as the sun fell behind the hills.

In her room, there is a calendar on the wall, and each morning she tears off the previous day and unveils the new one. She has the sense that the days are precise and ordered, free from overlap or confusion. Her life now with Mas's family, in the house on the hillside with a view of Sandakan town, is more than she dared to imagine. But even now she wonders what it would be like to leave here, finally, to travel to Tarakan, and keep the promise she made to her mother so many years ago.

In what remained of the buildings taken over by the Japanese during the war, the British had set up temporary offices and also an orphanage. Ani had stayed there for a month until Mas, a cousin to Ani's mother, had found her. Before the war, Halim and Mas's had been a family of six, now they were four. All of the children had been boys. The eldest had died early on. But if the war had ended sooner, Mas once said, a few weeks or a month, perhaps her youngest might have survived. She said this and half-smiled, her eyes pained, knowing that it was not useful to wish for a different present.

Ani had been ten years old when she came to live with them, a small, thin girl, and Halim used to joke that even her shadow was malnourished. It traipsed behind her, finally disappearing when she dove into the water to swim with Lohkman and her friends. One morning, she had woken to the call of the muezzin, a sound she had not heard since before the war. The lone voice travelled across the hillside, calling the faithful to prayer, his words lingering above the houses. She had lain awake remembering the long journey she made with her parents from the Dutch East Indies to Sandakan. They had walked barefoot along a mud track, where the flowers were taller than she was. She remembered her father's hand against the back of her head, the sound of her mother's feet always behind her. They ate mangoes from the nearby trees. In her memories, she fell asleep eating, the sweetness coating her tongue and lips, her limbs exhausted, warm air settling down on her.

Mas believes in spirits. They live in shapes and in the air; sometimes they are the souls of those who have not yet found their way to the land of the dead. Without them, she says, the world would be too bleak. But for Ani it is different. She knows that her parents are gone, that they do not remain in the air around her, they are not embodied by the sunlight or the curve of the Earth. She doesn't dare say it aloud, and yet Mas knows.

So many in Sandakan cannot speak about the war at all. To them, it is something left at the wayside, best forgotten. Sometimes, that is why she prefers to be with Lohkman. He is eighteen, the same age as she is, and they have both completed their studies at the mission school. She feels at ease with him, because they believe the same things; what happened in the past is there, unaltered by spirits or wishes. It will never disappear.

Ani changed out of the sarong she had worn to the market and replaced it with a clean one, smoothing the material against her body. On the dresser was her mother's jade pendant, carved in the shape of a bird. She had kept it safe all these years. Closing her eyes briefly, she ran one finger over the delicate stone. Tomorrow morning, she would see Matthew; they had arranged to meet near the harbour, after the night fishing was done. Since the end of the war, he had been living in Tawau with his mother, returning to Sandakan only a few weeks ago. When she looked up again, she barely recognized herself, a young woman in the mirror, the happiness that she possessed.

In the outdoor kitchen, Mas sighed and puttered, moving around the fire as if in conversation with it. Ani reached over Mas's shoulder, stirring the mixture of coconut and warm water. The two boys ran circles around them, hollering, then screamed back inside the house. Mas waved her arm meditatively across the food to push the flies away. On the edge of the road, Halim was deep in conversation with a neighbour. People passed by, on bicycle, going to work or the market, and they lifted their hands towards Halim, sounding their bells in greeting.

When breakfast was done, Ani cleared the dishes, stacking them neatly on the sideboard. Halim was the first to leave, setting off for town, where he worked as a clerk for the Hong Kong Bank. A few minutes later, Mas hurried out of the house, the boys running to keep up with her, towards the school, where she taught the Form Three class.

Sandakan, after the war, was not so different from the way Ani imagined it would be. The harbour was crowded with boats again, with *prahu*s and steamers; on windy nights, their hulls knocked together like a great wooden chime. When she was fourteen, the British North Borneo Company had organized a dance, setting up a phonograph on the new *padang*. Men and women twirled gracefully in one another's arms, the pattern of the women's dresses blurring together, colours fading as the field turned slowly to darkness. Each time they moved past her, she felt a breeze on her skin, ethereal and cool. She could look up and find her parents there beside her. Later, they would carry her back to the house on Jalan Satu. Minutes passed, and she stood at the edge of the field, her heart pounding, afraid to step onto the grass and break the spell.

On the hillside overlooking Sandakan, there had once been hundreds of crosses and markers to remember the dead. Later, these graves were cleared to make room for the new houses. People said that on the ocean floor there were Allied planes shot from the skies, lying side by side with Japanese battleships, the twisted metal still holding their crew. The sea would always keep them.

In the reopened school, she had learned how to chart the course of the rainy season. During the monsoons, the skies cloud over at a precise moment and the mangroves sink a little farther into the sea. The roads wash away. In the new Sandakan, steamers round the northern tip of Borneo, and new roads link the coast to the interior towns. Commercial flights land at the aerodrome, lifting off to Kota Kinabalu, to Singapore and Hong Kong. She would sit at her desk in the schoolroom, holding her worn textbooks for English and Mathematics, staring at the letters and numbers until her eyes grew tired and the meaning slid from her grasp. The words edged themselves into her thoughts, set their roots down inside her memory, trying to ease out the old words that still remained.

Well past midnight, she rose in the dark and dressed quickly, then walked down to the harbour, where she found Lohkman and his brother gathering nets into the boat.

They spoke for a few minutes about the night's work, then they pushed the boat away from shore, climbing deftly in. Lohkman pulled the cord, the engine stuttered to life, and they slid over the glassy water. From the bay, she could see the town for what it was, a small opening in the jungle, the cloth of the Union Jack moving to and fro above the neat white buildings and the green *padang*. To her right, stilt houses crowded out from the land, a water village balanced on floating docks. On every side, the green repetition of the trees, the *kendilong*, closed in on them.

Lohkman came from a family of fishermen. During the war, his family's boats had been confiscated and they had hidden in the jungle. When the war ended, only Lohkman, his brother, Tajuddin, and Tajuddin's wife remained, and they had built a small dwelling in the water village.

Lohkman cut the engine and the boat drifted. His brother crouched at the stern of the boat, slowly murmuring a prayer. Tajuddin was in his thirties, and his hair, already white, stirred in the wind. Tajuddin extended his leg over the side, touched his bare foot to the water. "There is but one God," he said, his voice dissipating on the wind. Still wearing his clothes, he let his body fall overboard.

The sound of the water opening eventually turned into a hush and then silence. Ani watched the hand that still held tight to the gunwale, the rest of the body invisible beneath the surface. Lohkman kept the boat steady. Underneath the water, Tajuddin was listening for the shoals of fish. Each species had a distinctive sound, and if he waited and listened, he could recognize them and follow the sound to where they lay. Years ago, he had taught Lohkman all he knew of fish-craft, about the wind and currents, how to handle the boat and make use of the many types of nets. Lohkman had told Ani that for six months he had studied the art of listening for the fish. At first, he could not distinguish them from the sound of the sea and the waves, but over time the skill had come to him.

They heard his brother before they saw him, a ripple of water, and then his face, silver hair falling across his eyes. He climbed up into the boat, ignoring Lohkman's outstretched hand, started the engine, and steered the boat west.

At the appointed place, she gathered the *jala*, a circular net weighted with metal rings. Turning her body, Ani opened her arms and cast the net. It bloomed in the air, unfurling in the shape of a bell, falling smooth and flat. The swaying movements of her arms swept the fish into the folds. Lohkman's brother had taught her how to throw the casting net when she was only thirteen. She had a talent for it, and a love of the water, and so, even though girls rarely went out with the men, he had given her a place on his boat. Two or three nights each week, depending on the season and the tides, they went out together.

Once, Lohkman had taken her underwater. He had shown her how to release the air from her lungs, a stream of bubbles trailing from their lips, their weight sinking them to the sea floor. Schools of fish brushed their bodies, circling them in a well of colour. Below, weeds unfurled to touch them. When they came up for air, he told her how to listen for the sound of the *ikan selar kuning*, with its deep-yellow stripe, which made a noise like the wind. He touched the small of her back, bringing her attention to the waving sea life, the colours so bright it sent a slow thrill along the length of her body.

Taking turns now, moving from one side of the boat to the other, they cast their nets out, speaking little. They poured their catch into the hold beneath the floorboards of the boat. Occasionally, Tajuddin would dive again, surfacing to direct the boat to a different location.

In the quiet, she thought of Matthew, of that morning, last month, when she came off the boat at dawn and saw him standing on the shoreline. His bicycle leaned against his hip, his eyes searching the returning boats, the crowd of people, finally coming to rest on her. Later, she learned that when he had asked for news of her, people told him to come here, saying that it would be easy to find her on Tajuddin's boat, with its red phoenix painted on the hull. She was carrying her take-home bundle of fish and prawns, and she held the bundle in the crook of one arm, awkwardly, surprise holding her still. He had been a child when she last saw him. Changed, she thought, yet utterly familiar. She stood on the sand, the tide running over her feet, and another lifetime flooded her memory.

Later that day, in the evening, they had walked along Leila Road, and then into the rubber plantation that had once been owned by Matthew's father and now belonged to his uncle. It was why he had returned to Sandakan, Matthew said, to help his uncle manage the plantation. In four months, he would leave for Australia to begin university. The end of the war was still so vivid to them both, the day on which the Australian soldiers arrived, when the Japanese surrendered the town. She remembered that night, on the shore, when Matthew had described to her the burning cigarettes, his father running blindly, then pushed to his knees and shot. His face had seemed to her like a mask then, vacant, frightening to see. She had feared that if she reached out to touch him, he would splinter in her hands. And then, suddenly, he had disappeared from her life. Two days after his father's murder, Matthew and his mother had fled Sandakan. They had taken the first steamer they could arrange passage on.

She told him about the orphanage, where her life had faded into a kind of stillness, an endless grieving, with all those that she loved disappeared. "There was a story that I told myself," she said. "In my imagination, you had found a way into Sandakan, the way it once was. When the adults around me spoke of an afterlife, of wandering souls, this was the place I imagined. Not something in the future, but something known from before. A place that I, myself, had once seen."

Behind them, the sun set, illuminating the ridges of the hills, trailing darkness behind it. The plantation lamps were lit, row by row, and she felt as if she were walking the corridors of an infinite house.

He described Tawau to her, his mother's extended family, and the stilt house where they lived for three years. Then, the year he turned twelve, his mother had remarried, and the photographs of his father, the letters and writing pens, had been put into boxes and packed away. His mother, he said, needed to go on with her life, to leave the stigma of her first marriage behind. "But sometimes, at night," Matthew said, "even now, my mother leaves the back door propped open with a stone. After the war, everything was left unfinished. We never found my father's body and she never had the chance to bury him. He's gone, of course. She knows this. And yet some part of her still believes he'll come back again."

He said that he remembered watching Ani sing the *Kimigayo*, the way she once traded stolen cigarettes for food. He could describe the sarong that she wore, the long braid of her hair. He remembered her when she had lived through the worst of her solitude.

They had walked between the rows of trees, stopping every now and then to catch their breath, to look up through the high leaves and thereby slow the passing of time. They talked about Mas and Halim, about the fishing boats and the peaceful routine of each day. In Sandakan, she had seen new buildings rise from the ground – the hospital and Magistrate's Court, the administration offices – all the while unable to forget what had lain there before, the rubble and waste, and even further back, like something imagined, the old town.

In the plantation, that first kiss had surprised them both. She remembered the rush in her body, a trembling that grew, second by second, causing a pain that she didn't recognize. The kiss lengthened, drew itself out, began again, the pain beginning to diminish, replaced by some greater feeling, hope, release.

Now, coming back to the shore, the sun was already free from the horizon. The engine hummed, and the boat sped through the water, carried by the tide. Tajuddin was murmuring a prayer, eyes half-closed, giving thanks for their nets full of scabbard fish, of mackerel and prawns. She listened to the noise of the hull, low and rumbling, like a ghost voice that could not speak above the water. From the shore, she could see the day boats heading out. A fleet of five *buatan barat*, painted a brilliant red, their sails taut against the wind. When Lohkman slid the boat against the sand, she looked immediately towards the road, searching for a glimpse of Matthew. "Dear Ani," Lohkman said, as he helped her ashore. "Be careful."

She took his hand gratefully, jumping into the shallow water.

On Jalan Satu, Matthew was waiting for her, his bicycle leaning against the fence. When she came up to him, he put away the magazine he had been reading and they began to walk together, past the stores and restaurants where the long shutters were being lifted off in preparation for the day ahead. Eventually, Matthew climbed onto his bicycle, beginning to pedal, and when he had picked up enough speed, she hopped lightly onto the back carrier. She crossed her ankles, and placed one hand on Matthew's hip to steady herself. As they rose higher, the trees parted, and Ani could see the calmness of the bay, a silver mirror on which the clouds rested. Above them, the low moon was still visible, though pale as smoke.

Ani described the night fishing to him, and the baskets of fish and prawns that Lohkman would take to market this morning. He laughed at her description of the envious gazes that had followed them as they unloaded their catch. How the other fishermen had hurried to decorate their boats with garlands of flowers, knowing that a well-kept vessel would appease the spirits. "And it encourages the fish, too," she said, "because if they must be caught, they'd prefer to be caught by something beautiful."

As he pedalled, Matthew told her he had been awake for hours, had accompanied the rubber tappers through the plantation, helping to collect tins of syrup. In a few hours, when the syrup had thickened, he would return to help wash the latex and roll it into sheets, which they would hang to dry, smoking the rubber over a wood fire.

When they reached Halim's house, he coasted towards the front door, and she slid off the back of the bicycle. It was a weekday morning, and the house was quiet, everyone had left to begin their day. Inside, Ani lit the charcoal brazier and set a pot of water to boil. Matthew had brought her a paper bag full of warm bread and pastries from the market, and he took one out, placing it in her hand. "Eat a little something first," he said.

He took over the coffee-making, and after she had eaten, she carried the rest of the boiling water into the *mandi*. She filled the basin, adding a little hot water, and began by washing the saltwater from her hair. She could hear Matthew in the kitchen, taking the bundle of fish and prawns from her basket and setting them in the cool box. When her hair was clean, she twisted the length of it, then coiled it over her shoulder. She found a square of soap and began to wash herself.

He stood on the other side of the door, talking about acquaintances he had met, about his stepfather's sons, who might come up to visit from Tawau. They were interested in helping out on the rubber plantation. "Barely ten, and they want to be landowners already."

She tied a clean sarong around her waist and pulled on a cotton shirt. When she came out, he smiled to see her, and she went to him immediately.

"Ani," he said. "You look happier than I've ever seen you."

They came together, as they had often during the last month, their hands moving over each other's body. She unbuttoned his shirt, and he slipped his hand beneath the edge of her sarong, moving it across her stomach, cradling her hips. She felt her body relaxing, warmth spilling through her limbs. They did not rush as they had the first time, returning again to the plantation, barely concealed by the trees. There was no hurry now, no fear that the other might vanish. In her bedroom at the back of the house, she helped him undress, then she undid her own sarong. They lay in bed together, their movements slowing, kissing, then holding back.

Outside, they could hear people walking on the gravel road, trucks passing, a bicycle bell. Nothing had prepared her for love, the physical ache that overwhelmed her body, that diminished the world around her to sense, to touch. He was so close, moving on top of her, she had to fight to hold the sound in. She trapped her breath against his skin.

For a long time, he rested his head in the curve of her neck. Their breathing ran together, the slow, even comfort of it. Last night, he said, he couldn't sleep, thinking of all that he still wanted to tell her, about Tawau and of the terrible days after his father was killed, how he and his mother seemed invisible to all who knew them. Yet now that it was daylight, he found that words were useless to describe what had happened. She was already half dreaming by then, and the sound of his voice travelled in her thoughts, as if they were her own. He said that sometimes when he walked on Leila Road, he became confused, and he did not know where he was in time. "The houses, the buildings, everything is different," he said, "but the way the sun sets over the hill, the way it reflects off the sea, reminds me of being a child again. It reminds me of things I thought I had put away long ago."

She slept the rest of the morning, opening her eyes briefly when Matthew rose to return to the plantation. "Don't wake up," he whispered. When she dreamed, there were no faces, no people. Just lightness flooding her, lifting her away from the earth. She felt her mother's arms, felt the blanket of her mother's hair around her.

Around noon, she woke to the sound of voices. Someone had wheeled the neighbourhood radio out. She could hear the footsteps of children running towards the sound.

When she stood up and looked through the curtains, she saw them standing pressed together, transfixed by the voice, their mouths open as if to taste the words. The dial was fixed to Radio Sabah in Jesselton. When the announcer introduced a song, "Goodnight Irene," the children scuffed their bare feet in the dust, bringing up small clouds, the particles expanding as the first chords began. The hottest part of the day was just beginning. Someone brought out an umbrella, and the children gathered together under it, grateful for the shade.

Late in the afternoon, the rains came, and thunder broke in the sky. The two boys ran inside, soaking wet. Then, when they saw their father in his study, they hurriedly opened their schoolbooks. Ani and Mas sat together at the kitchen table, listening to the wind rattling the roof and the doors. Trees swooped and whistled, setting loose a downpouring of leaves.

"Wonderful," Mas said, smiling. "We haven't had a storm like this in months."

They unrolled several yards of fabric and laid the cloth across the kitchen table. Mas had an old shirt of Halim's, and she undid the seams, laying the pieces one on top of the other as she pulled them loose. Ani heated the iron. They worked slowly, Mas, seated at the treadle machine, keeping up a low, running monologue as she pulled threads. Ani smiled at Mas's laughing indignation at the latest teaching methods of the new Form One teacher: "All those children do," she said, "is sit in the grass and sing songs." She spat a piece of thread emphatically into her hand. "As if singing nursery rhymes will turn them magically into doctors."

When all the pieces lay neatly before her, Mas stood up to stretch her legs. The storm had begun to ease off, and she wandered into the sitting room and began to turn the dial of the radio. After a moment, music came through, the reception occasionally disturbed by faint crackling. "There's something I've been meaning to tell you," she said, when she returned to the kitchen. She spoke in English, wanting to keep the conversation private from the two boys. "We received a letter from my cousin Bashir. He is the eldest in your mother's family, and he lives in Tarakan."

Ani set the iron aside, listening.

"He says that if you can make the journey to Tarakan, he would like to see you. In two months, he is going into the hospital for treatment, and he thinks you should come before then." She sat down at the machine. "Will you go to see him?"

"I will."

"And then, afterwards? Will you stay in Tarakan, or will you come back here?"

Ani hesitated, unsure how to read Mas's question. "I'll come back."

Mas nodded. She nudged the hand crank and fixed the needle into place. But after laying down a few threads, she stopped again. "When I finished teaching my lessons this morning, Matthew Lim's uncle came to see me. He said that his nephew was accepted at the University of Melbourne." Mas paused, as if still in wonder at what came next. "It seems that Matthew is thinking about turning this opportunity down."

"Yes," Ani said. She felt a warmth in her cheeks as she went to sit at the low stool by Mas's knee. "He told me."

Mas reached out, smoothing Ani's hair. "I couldn't help but remember you, after the war. Thin as a sheet of paper, and so still, so quiet. I think of you as my own sister, my own child."

"I've never felt so at peace here, Mas."

"So it is you, as well, who wants to remain."

Mas looked at the two boys in the sitting room, holding their pencils, beginning to write. She said that, during the war, Halim had been forced into a work camp, and she had been left alone with the children. It was the jungle that had kept them safe. Nothing was what it appeared to be in the light, or in the darkness. There was even food to be found, if you knew where to look. So many people disappeared. A life had been worth no more than a bird feather, that's what she told herself, when first her eldest child, and then her youngest, died. When the war ended, she felt as if she had awoken from a deep sleep to find herself one of the lucky ones. She had survived, but at what cost? One part of her would always be buried with her children, no matter how many days accumulated, no matter how much distance she put between them. "Your life is changing, Ani," she said. "There is only one thing that I learned from that time. Try to decide what you want, now, before you are forced to choose."

Ani thought of her parents, her father walking each day to the airfield. "And if there is no right choice?"

But Mas went on as if she had not heard. "Before choice is taken from your hands," she said, turning away. "By then, it will always be too late."

When evening came, Ani walked down to the harbour. She was early, and she watched the last of the lift-net boats coming in. Twenty to thirty feet out, they let their sails fall slack, and their momentum carried them to shore.

It was busy tonight, the dealers and fishermen still bargaining over the last of the day's catch. Women sat with their children, mending nets, or packing up what had not been sold. On the beach, a group of fishermen lay one beside the other, their feet resting against their boat. They used sand and water and the rough, callused soles of their feet to scrub the hull. Every now and then, a burst of laughter would erupt, and the sand would go flying.

Tajuddin came and sat beside her. He was chewing betel nut and repairing one of a half-dozen metal rings he had set in his lap. "*Selamat petang*, Ani," he said, and she returned the greeting. He told her that he had caught four handsome *dorab* that afternoon, and he believed that the seas would be bountiful tonight.

After a pause, he said, "Are you well, Ani?"

"Yes, *datuk*."

He nodded, unconvinced, then returned his focus to the metal rings.

On the shore, Ani could see the high pyramid of fish, glistening with a sheen of water. Women and children gathered around, and the fishermen talked excitedly, gesturing as they spoke.

When Lohkman arrived, the two men went to see the catch. Ani watched their progress along the sand. They stopped every few steps to be greeted by other fishermen, to examine a newly mended net, or admire a neighbour's boat. With the wind moving against her face, she did not think about Matthew, or Tarakan, she let all feelings subside. She saw their boat waiting on the beach, the glow of the bird on the prow and the warmth of the orange hull. People gathered to carry a lift-net to its storage quarters. They came in a long line, spaced ten to fifteen feet apart, moving along the water's edge like a ribbon, each carrying a part of the rolled-up net. Children ducked between them, calling to each other as the men passed. The line moved past her, a slow and joyous procession, beads of water on the lines shimmering in the light.

The child that she remembered, the child walking along the ghost road, no longer hid from her. She could reach her hand across the barrier of time and grab hold. She could save her, finally. Don't be afraid, she thought. We are here, we have made it to the other side.

She saw the shoreline crowded with people, the bright colours of their sarongs, and then the sea, which she imagined hung like a curtain at the edge of the world.

In the days that followed, Matthew told her that he had made his decision. He did not want to leave Sandakan. "And

Australia?" she asked him. He said there was enough work on the plantation, and perhaps, later on, he could take a teaching position at the mission school. What he desired most of all was a life with her, a life free from uncertainty.

She pictured their lives unfolding like the casting of a net, when the lines left your hands, you knew where the entirety would fall.

Then one evening, walking in town together, they were approached by a young man she recognized from her years at the mission school. He wore a white shirt and slacks and carried a satchel over his shoulder. After he had confirmed Matthew's name, he said, "I remember your father." At first, the young man's voice was measured and calm. He told them that he still had the papers, signed by Matthew's father, that had been issued when his family's crops were confiscated during the war. Then his voice began to rise, and people passing by on the street stopped, curious, looking from one to the other. The young man took another step forward. "My mother and sisters died of starvation," he said, his voice shaking. "My father died a broken man." He gazed into Matthew's face, as if he could see through to the centre of him, to the man he would inevitably become. "You have no right to live amongst us." The young man leaned forward, his body tensed, rigid. Then he turned abruptly and walked away.

Matthew remained where he was, his arms loose at his sides. When the shock on his face faded, it was replaced by something else, grief, anger, hardening his expression. Eventually, the crowd retreated. The street flowed around them once more. Ani took his hand, cold to her touch, and pulled him along with her, away from Jalan Satu, towards the harbour. The heat bore down on them. Frogs chorused in the grass, a singing that filled her ears. She slipped her sandals off and walked into the water, Matthew following behind, and the tide slipped past them. She saw the boy that she remembered, a boy who loved his father. She recognized the heaviness of this devotion.

After the war, she told him, there had been trials. But Mas and Halim both said that these had brought no relief. A handful of Japanese soldiers had been sentenced, but the ones who had given the orders were never tried, and they received no punishment. "There was no one to hold responsible," she said. "No one to go to for justice. He carries those papers with your father's name because it is all he has, it is the only answer given to him."

"My father lived here from the time he was ten years old, but when he died, no one came to see us. No one grieved him. They looked away when they saw my mother. We were nothing to them."

He said that in Tawau, those memories had begun to fade. He did not know how such a thing was possible, but the past had become like a book submerged in the water, the ink running across the lines, all the detail lost.

She looked at him, bewildered. "You must have known that forgetting could not last. Not in this place."

Matthew continued as if he had not heard her. "I can't help but think about him. I wish to go back and save him somehow. He was an educated man, a good man. In the end, his desires were so ordinary, to protect us, to keep us safe, but he paid for this desire with his life. If I had to face what he did, would I not do the same? If it were you and I, Ani, if it were our children, there would be no choice."

The next day, Matthew did not come to meet her at the shore. She walked up the hill, searching for him, at each bend of the road hoping he would appear. When she came in sight of Halim's house, Matthew was there, sitting on the front step, but he did not turn as she approached. She sat down beside him. On the road, a line of schoolchildren walked side by side; a truck came behind them, and the children scattered like a flock of birds taking flight, jubilant and laughing.

He told her that he had woken suddenly in the night, had put on his clothes and let himself out of his uncle's house on the hillside. The humid air had enclosed him in warmth. He remembered looking up at the sky and thinking how beautiful the moon was, simple and round, as it sank towards the horizon. He had followed it, walking towards his father's former plantation. Once there, he saw that the kerosene lamps were lit, the flames floating in the dark. As he walked, he counted the trees aloud, turning at the thirtieth row, coming to a standstill at the thirtieth tree.

He knelt down, listening to the sound of night insects, of birds that he couldn't identify. Owls, babblers, even in his childhood he had not been able to distinguish them. He began to push the dirt away, seeing the child that he was kneeling there, scrabbling at the ground. "I thought he must have known everything. He sent me on this errand because he knew his fate and he wanted to keep me away. I did what he had asked, only by then it no longer mattered. But still I went into the plantation."

He dug at the ground for a long time, at first calm, but then, finding nothing, panic overwhelmed him. The lights blurred, he was sweating and could not see, but still he continued, with no idea of time or reason. Eventually, exhausted, he dropped into sleep. Some time later, one of the tappers must have found him and sent for his uncle. They were all gathered there at the thirtieth three, labourers, family, and the boy that only Matthew could see, standing in the shadows. When his uncle asked what had happened, Matthew could only point at the boy. He wanted to go to him, pick him up, but he could not move. His uncle tried to put a coat around his shoulders, but Matthew pushed him away. When his uncle approached him again, Matthew lashed out. Then a terrible numbness took hold of his body and his legs gave out from under him, and the men carried him back to the house.

"They tried to keep me from leaving," he said, looking at Ani now, "but I told them that I needed to sort out my thoughts, I needed to see you." He paused for a moment. "Sometimes, in my dreams, I am almost able to reach him. I am telling him how to escape, how to leave Sandakan, I am almost holding him, but then he turns away."

Later, lying together, his skin was damp and feverish, and he put his arms around himself as if he were cold. He said there was a story she told him once, long ago, about a man who harvested gold from the fields. All these years he had tried to recall it, but somehow it had become confused in his mind. Did she still remember? he asked.

She said yes, and as she told him, his breathing grew steady, lengthening out. In her story, the man walks towards the house standing alone in the middle of the field. The woman, old and stooped, promises him a gift more valuable than money. He will no longer be without land. For all eternity, he will not be at the mercy of the world.

That afternoon, while Matthew slept, his uncle came to the house. He was a tall, imposing man dressed in a jacket and tie. Ani had spoken to him before only in passing, but when Mas opened the door, it did not surprise her to see him, awkward and dignified on the front steps. Mas invited him in. They went together to the sitting room.

"Matthew is resting, I hope."

"Yes, *datuk*," Ani said.

His uncle nodded. He and Mas talked of other things, of the primary school and the construction of a new gymnasium on the grounds.

Ani's attention was distracted by the sounds drifting in from outside, the children running between the houses, their voices rising and falling with the momentum of their game.

At last, he turned to Ani, and what he had come to say was finally in the open. "Matthew should go to Tawau as soon as he is able. He does not belong in Sandakan." He paused, looking at her. She thought she saw pity in his eyes, a feeling of compassion. "I have said all this to him already. I suspect he knows it is true."

Her body tensed, and she kept her hands clasped in her lap.

Mas said softly but firmly, "They are adults now. We cannot make their choices for them."

"They are acting like children," he said. "And they must let go of it."

In her confusion, his words seemed to lose their meaning. She reached for an answer that would not come. "He has only just returned here."

"He is ill," his uncle said. "And he need not be." He began to describe Sydney and Melbourne, where young people from across Southeast Asia were being trained as doctors and engineers. When they returned home to their countries, they would bring with them a sea change.

She did not know how to respond to him, how to explain what he was asking of her. She said perhaps she could go with Matthew, they could travel to Australia together.

"No, Ani," Mas said. "Immigration is strict. That is not possible."

The silence seemed to stretch on for minutes until, finally, Matthew's uncle stood, preparing to go.

"In the end, the decision belongs to you both," he said. "But I am only thinking of Matthew's future. All I ask is that you do the same."

The next day, Ani went alone to the hospital clinic. An hour passed, and then another, as she sat in the waiting room. Beside her, a young woman drowsed, her baby sheltered in a sling tight against her chest, fast asleep. The doctor who eventually examined Ani, an elderly Chinese man, was hurried, preoccupied. He gave her the results of her test, saying that her baby was due in seven months. Then he smiled, congratulated her, and left the room to see his next patient. Ani sat in the room, unable, for a time, to stand and walk into the afternoon heat.

She remembered being underwater with Lohkman. How the glare of the world had disappeared, softened by the water. She had taken a breath, then dived straight down, exhaling, air escaping from her lips. Her body had sunk towards the sea floor, moving among the crevices of rock and the waving vegetation. There was a puffer fish that Lohkman had captured in his hands, rolling it through the water like a child's toy. He wanted her to listen for the shoals of fish, to learn this talent that he himself had acquired. But all she heard was a dull roar, every sound blurred and inseparable. She wondered if her child would soon be able to hear her voice through the echo chamber of her body, if it would be able to distinguish it from all the others – just as in dreams she heard her own mother, one voice rising from the din, calling to her across the divide, telling her to let go, to stop searching backwards. You cannot save us, she said. You cannot change our fate. The past is done.

Outside, the light, the brightness of the sky, caused her to stumble, and she grabbed hold of a railing for support.

An elderly man, standing on the steps, offered his umbrella to shade her from the sun, but she shook her head, recovering. She went slowly out into the road and turned in the direction of home.

So she was the one who began it, who turned their conversation in another direction. On a beach west of town, they walked together along the empty sand. In the distance, she could see the red hills of Berhala Island, the currents sweeping past, the tide curling against the shore. She said that now, after all these years, she was finally ready to leave Sandakan, to go to her mother's family.

His face, when he looked at her, shook her resolve. She saw his confusion giving way to fear. "When did you decide? Why have you decided this now?"

The words caught in her throat, but she forced herself to speak them aloud. "If things were different, if there was nothing to hold you here in Sandakan, what would you do?"

He refused to answer, but she would not relent. He shook his head. "Nothing has changed for me."

"But Australia."

"It doesn't matter."

The tide was going out, and it left a smooth plain of sand at their feet. This was the future, she said. He would stay in Sandakan, on the plantation, and they would never be free. Perhaps they could go to Australia together, find the way to begin a different life. But the love that she felt for him could not be separated from the childhood they shared; it could not admit forgetting. The words seemed to come from far away. "I won't let this happen to us," she said.

He took her hand, trying to draw her towards him, but she pulled back. "What is happening, Ani?" He asked if she truly meant to leave, to not return.

She felt cold, a chill radiating through her limbs. "I didn't realize it for so long. I thought as you did. But what we wanted is not possible." She struggled to keep her voice steady, but tears stung her eyes. "Our parents would not wish us to be bound by the past."

"I know you, Ani. Something has changed you."

She shut her ears to the disbelief in his voice, to her own grief. She told him that they were alike, two pieces of the same puzzle, but in the end, if you laid them down beside each other, you'd see an empty space, the jagged edges. And in this space, she knew there was no oxygen, no relief. It was a place they had made together when they were children. They had filled it with all the things they wanted to forget, a landscape of craters and bodies. She said that their feelings for one another had blinded them to the truth, what lay between them was too far-reaching, too vast. They could not hold it or push it down.

Some part of her was spinning loose, split open. She got to her feet and began to walk away from him.

He followed her, calling her name, and finally she turned and shouted at him to leave her, to let her alone. At the sudden noise, birds lifted up around them, fluttering up into the trees. He stared after her, shocked. But she continued along the beach to the harbour, where the last of the night boats were heading away from the shore.

As she walked, the water ran across her feet, and she imagined the tide sliding under her, pulling her away from Sandakan, this life and the pain that she kept adding to, as if she could bear any sacrifice, any tragedy, as if the war had made her strong enough to survive all that the future necessitated. She listened for Matthew's footsteps coming across the wet sand, coming to join her, but all she heard was the tide and the trees, the nightjars and insects.

These years in Jakarta have not changed the longing she feels. Sometimes, now, falling asleep, she imagines a different ending. One in which she stands up from the sand and she tells him the truth. Everything that she set in motion that night, the words that can never be taken back, comes to rest. Life moves in reverse. She tells him that she will go to Tarakan, she will wait for him to return from Australia. When we find one another again, we will know how to continue.

Tonight, after a light supper of rice and vegetables, Ani changes her son into his pyjamas, and they go downstairs to begin her shift in the photo studio.

Across the street, the Pondok Restaurant is overflowing, and the reflections of the neon signs flash slowly against the walls of the studio. Holding Wideh's hand, Ani unlocks the door, and they make their way through the foyer. The office is quiet. There are plastic covers on the telephone and type-writer to protect them from dust, and the curtains are tightly drawn. In the developing room, the day's prints are hanging neatly along several lines, and a dozen film canisters sit waiting on the counter.

Ani makes a place for Wideh on the tiled floor, opening blankets and fluffing cushions, then she lays him down. He is three years old already, and he smiles up at her, repeating the word *Ibu*, "Mother," playing with the sound until the word is lost amidst a jumble of different noises.

Each evening, she works here, in the darkroom, devel-oping rolls of negatives. In the day, someone else will come and use the enlarger to transform these negatives into prints, but this first step is hers. In the dark, Ani takes the lid off the first canister, removes the film spool and cuts it free. Feeling for the guides, she loads the film onto the tank reel. Only when this is secure, and the lid is firmly in place, does she reach her hand out and switch on the developing lamp.

Ani has never taken a photograph. All she knows of the process is this one part, but she knows it well. When, at Saskia's recommendation and with no experience, she had come to Frank Postma looking for work in the studio he owned, she had come halfheartedly, expecting little. Perhaps some evening shifts cleaning and tidying the office, she had suggested. But that was not what he wanted, he told her, first in fluent Malay, then switching to English, sometimes for-getting himself and lapsing into Dutch. "I need help," he had said, waving his arms at the stacks of film. "And Saskia spoke so highly of you."

He had served coffee, and, sitting in the studio, Ani told him that she had met Saskia and Siem Dertik in 1953, on the outer decks of the boat that had carried them to Jakarta. Ani had been on her way from Tarakan, where the last of her mother's family remained. From there, she had felt the wish to be a part of something greater, to lose herself in the city, and so she had continued to Jakarta.

"People come here from all over the world," he had said. "It's a good place to begin again." He set down his coffee and opened box after box of photographs. Pictures of Dutch families released from internment camps, Balinese dancers, canals shining like ribbons in the field. "Light on surface," he had said. "Most of the time, to each other, all we are is light on surface."

Then he had taken her into the developing room and shown her, as if it were no more difficult than preparing a meal, how to measure the chemicals, remove the film, soak and rinse it, then hang the finished negatives to dry.

In the corner of the studio now, Wideh raises his arms above him, turning his hands from side to side, delighting in the movement. While she works, Ani talks to herself and to him, walking herself through the steps. Start the timer, pour the developer, tap the container lightly on the counter. Agitate the contents and never lose track of the time.

She is at home in this studio, protected for a brief while from her memories, from the chaos and uncertainty of Jakarta. Studying the row of negatives, she follows the trajectory of the photographer's gaze. She travels beside him as he feels his way through the scene like a child in a darkened room.

At midnight, long after Wideh has fallen asleep, she is finally finished. The negatives are pinned on a line, and she dries each carefully with a small sponge. Picking up a magnifying glass, Ani examines the work. There are pictures of Indies families posed in front of their former plantations, the men dressed in Western slacks and shirts, the women in *kain* and *kebaya*. She cannot read their faces, they have taken care to cloak their emotions. But in one, there is a boy caught unaware. He stands at a gate that is closed to him, his entire body yearning towards the house.

She knows that these photographs, once printed, will be carefully wrapped, then tucked within soft materials and laid inside a piece of luggage. She has been doing the very same for Saskia. In some distant country, taken out and looked at again, these photographs will become the shadow that follows them, the past that never changes, that never disappears. When all other memories fade, these, at least, will not be lost.

When she left Sandakan, she brought almost nothing. Arriving in Tarakan, Ani had been two months pregnant. Bashir, her mother's oldest brother, was dying, and all the other family had scattered during the war years. If that is what you want, he had told her, go to Jakarta. He gave her the money and family keepsakes that remained. All our young people now, he said, are taking their dreams to the city. He brought her to the local magistrate, signing a declaration that her parents had been born here, in the former Dutch East Indies. When she left Tarakan, she had in her possession documents attesting to her Indonesian citizenship. She had, in some way, come home at last.

Ani lifts her son from the cushions and he wakes up, momentarily, reaching out to touch her face with one small hand. Then, sighing, his eyelids flutter, blink, and slowly close again.

With his body warm against hers, she leaves the studio, locking the door behind her. She climbs up the stairs to the apartment where they live. Inside, by the light of the street lamps, she lays him down and tucks the mosquito net around the edges of his cot.

Ani stretches out on the divan in the corner of the room, and eventually, as her mind lets go of the day, the street outside grows quiet, the traffic begins to lessen, and the neon lights of the Pondok Restaurant flicker and turn out. Surrounded by darkness, she sees him standing at the harbour, coming to meet her finally. In the face that she remembers so well, the glimmer of recognition, of understanding.

The next night, over dinner, Siem says that he has bought tickets for everyone to see the Shanghai Acrobats that evening. This is his family's last night in Jakarta, and though the tickets cost six hundred rupiahs apiece, a week's salary, Siem waves it off, grinning like a small boy. He says that they should not spend their last night morose, washing dishes, cleaning the house. It has become evident, he says, with a flourish of his hands, that there is too little magic in the world.

The night air is still warm when they near the theatre. Cars and scooters blur past them, and the blinking colours leave an image in Ani's eyes even after she looks away. At an intersection, the traffic lights are not working, and a large crowd gathers around them on the curb. When an opening comes, they move in unison, flooding into the street, bringing the vehicles to a standstill.

Ani and Saskia are walking arm in arm, and the children are clutching Siem's hands. On the front of a boarded-up building, someone has painted, *Dutch Get Out, Indos Go Home.* They both see it at the same time, and Saskia says, "We're going, we're going," so quietly that Ani just catches the words.

Up ahead, she can make out the form of a young girl who appears to hover above the crowd. She is sitting on the handlebars of a bicycle. The girl floats towards them, one hand on the crossbar to hold herself steady. Behind her, a young man pedals the bicycle at a leisurely speed, and they move across the pavement in perfect balance. Watching them, Ani's own body seems to lift. She sees Leila Road in the early morning, her bicycle slipping downhill, the sea opening before her.

Inside the performance hall, they are swept along by the rush of people, and the theatre is a commotion of voices. In her seat, Saskia frowns, worrying aloud over the last bits of packing still to be done. Siem puts his hand on her knee and says, "Forget tomorrow."

When the lights go down, Wideh leans forward on Ani's lap, gripping her hand in his. He points towards the stage.

The spotlight opens on a young man standing alone on a high platform. There is no music or sound of any sort. He has his eyes closed, as if deep in concentration, and while he stands there, alone and waiting, a hush falls over the theatre. His chest rises and falls, the seconds pass by. To Ani, it feels as if the audience waits in anticipation of the moment when he will open his eyes, step forward, and fall, which he does, as if releasing his spirit. He arches his back and dives into the empty space below. He is rushing towards the earth, but he doesn't flinch. A few people in the auditorium gasp, and the sound travels up along Ani's spine. At the last moment, an invisible wire catches him and he collapses his body into a ball and tumbles up again through the air.

In front of Ani's eyes, the lights seem to wane and blur. The boy's body, slender, he is only a child, passes across the stage.

When the war was finished, she and Matthew had gone down to the harbour, standing together on the docks. They were nine and ten years old. Still wearing their clothes, they swam out, leaving the few lights of Sandakan behind them. In the water, invisible to the eye, were shipwrecks and unexploded bombs; there were Japanese and American planes lying on the ocean floor. For a long time, she and Matthew floated on their backs staring up into the dark. Were the stars travelling away from them, Ani had wanted to know, or were they coming steadily nearer? He said that the stars were leaving; they were ships carrying people who had left the Earth a long time ago, not knowing that the heavens themselves were a vast desert. Now, it was only the ships that flew on, after the people had grown too old. She remembered Matthew saying that his father, too, had gone away, that he had been killed even though the war was over. The soldiers had lifted his father up and thrown him into the bed of a truck. If you had seen them from a distance, he said, from their movements, so casual, so indifferent, you would not have guessed that they were carrying a body.

Offstage, musicians begin to play, and three slender girls emerge into the lights. Their dance is slow and meticulous, a hand gesturing, wrists turning in delicate circles. Their bodies twist and open, legs extended in arabesques.

One steps up onto a platform, and then without hesitation the second climbs onto her shoulders. Finally, the last girl begins her ascent. At the summit, she sets her hand, palm to palm, on the hand of the girl below. Slowly, she lifts her legs up, balanced by the strength of one arm. She unfolds her body as if her limbs are as weightless as the flame of a candle.

Beside her, Wideh sighs deeply, clasps his hands together, looks out at the stage as if caught in his own dream. One day, she will find the words to explain her life to him. How, in the dark, in Sandakan, planes lifted off from the aerodrome, sending back a murmuring of lights. She had said goodbye to Mas and Halim, to Lohkman, then she had boarded the steamer and travelled across the sea. The note she had written to Matthew was safely in Mas's hands. Her love for him had not changed, she had written; for both of them, another kind of future must be made to exist. Could she explain it to Wideh like this, make him understand why she had made this choice, why she has kept the secret from his father all these years. When the time comes, she will find a way to tell him the truth.

In her mind, she sees the kerosene lamps, the still plantation. The air is filled with the sound of nocturnal birds and cicadas, the sound of a small boy counting aloud, the thirtieth row, the thirtieth tree. When he finds the place that he is looking for, he begins to remove the earth. He works desperately, steadily, and the shadows of the trees fall around him like the lines of an imaginary house. How far must he travel? At what point will the treasure that he carries be safe?

Onstage, the first two girls hold their position while the third arches her back and swings her legs until she is upside down. She tilts her face up and gazes calmly at the audience. For several seconds they remain motionless, and then the girl at the very bottom begins to walk from one side of the stage to the other. Their bodies tremble with exertion, and the girls sway back and forth.

On her lap, Wideh strains forward towards the stage. He is under the spell of the acrobats, the man who dove through the air, unafraid; and now this small girl who blooms like a flower atop the human ladder.

Beside her, Saskia takes Ani's hand, holding on as if she, too, can anchor her own body there, in the theatre.

The next morning, at the harbour, everything happens quickly. Siem and Saskia carry the luggage, while Ani gathers the children to her. Together, they make their way towards the registration desks.

The sun is starting to rise now, colouring the edges of the horizon. Ani kneels on the ground beside Wideh and

Tash, and the crowd passes around them. Dutch soldiers are trying to organize the emigrants. They hurry people towards the gangway, and the crying and laughing rises in pitch and volume. She does not want to say goodbye, but Saskia whispers in her ear the old saying: "All things change and we change with them." For a long time they stand holding one another.

By dawn, the great ship in the Jakarta harbour is boarded and sunrise floods over the sea, the water a deep and brilliant orange. The crowd on the dock has thinned now. As the horn sounds, some wave handkerchiefs, others lift both arms in the air, as if they, too, are floating on the water. Among the hundreds of people leaning over the ship's rail, Ani cannot find the Dertiks. It is Wideh who sees them first: Tash, perched on Siem's shoulders, and Saskia pressed close to them. They have almost disappeared into the multitude. The ship begins to move away from the harbour. She holds Wideh close to her as she watches the disappearing form.

6

The Garden of Numbers

VANCOUVER, CANADA

On the morning of her thirty-ninth birthday, Gail wakes up to the warmth of the light through the attic windows. Ansel is lying on his side, one hand on the curve of her waist. In Gail's vision, without her glasses or contact lenses, he is blurred and indistinct, like someone in the farthest reaches of a swimming pool. From their bed under the steep roof, she can see the change from night to day, evening stars, rainfall tapping insistently on the glass. Some mornings, Gail wakes up to the sound of their elderly neighbour across the street, Mrs. Cho, who trims her yard with a pair of children's scissors.

When Ansel wakes, they climb out from under the covers and dress in comfortable clothes. She takes a comb and does her best to calm Ansel's hair, which is tossed like grass on a wind farm. He makes the bed and picks her pyjamas off the floor. By the time they have stepped outside, they have spoken only a few sentences, yet she feels a tentative peace. They move as if in memory of a different day, of countless similar mornings.

They used to have a running joke, she and Ansel. When people asked how long they had been together, they'd say the first number that came into their heads. "Twenty-five years?" Ansel would respond, turning to Gail, eyebrows raised. "Or is it more?" Forty years, perhaps. What, in their minds, seems a lifetime, a history together. She remembers this joke with pleasure, because it returns her to a time when their relationship was carefree, when it harboured neither suspicion nor fear. For almost a month now, she has known about Ansel's affair with a woman named Mariana. It remains as a space between them, around which they carefully move.

They walk to the New Town Bakery, where they choose their breakfast from the display case and the high stacks of bamboo steamers. Then they continue, under the Georgia Viaduct, towards False Creek. It is early Sunday morning, and the city still drowses. Ansel counts two or three sails unfurled on the windless bay.

Tonight, her parents and a few close friends will come over for dinner. Her parents had wanted to host the party, but she had put them off. Knowing them, such a party would involve a ten-course dinner, towering cake and enough sparklers to light the neighbourhood. Even at the best of times, she has never felt comfortable as the centre of atten-tion. Perhaps, she had thought, handling it herself would keep things low-key, and take the pressure off the occasion.

They are sitting on a wooden bench, facing the creek. Ansel tells her to be alert for seagulls. Just the other day, he says, he saw one swoop towards the bus shelter and seize a sandwich straight from the hand of a young woman. A freak occurrence, Gail says, but she clutches her breakfast tighter and scans the skies warily for belligerent birds.

In the last few weeks, he has been solicitous, grieving; he watches Gail as if she might disappear. At first, she had imagined packing a suitcase, walking away. A thought that, for just an instant, sent a rush of weightlessness through her heart. She has never been one for dramatic entries or exits. People fall in and out of love, relationships change, she accepts this fact as truth. But the intensity, the depth of her feelings for Ansel has always frightened her. Once, long ago, he asked her to marry him, but she had pushed them both away from that possibility. She did not want to get married, she wanted a different kind of relationship. Each day choosing to be with one another. Each day deciding.

She remembers the first time she met Ansel. His white coat was too big for him, it drooped over his shoulders. She had been working for CBC-Radio, covering the crash of a six-seater Cessna, the pilot killed instantly, his son in critical condition. They had sat on the bench outside the hospital, looking up at the night sky, the hint of starlight. For a long time, they talked about nothing in particular, and then, finally, about the pilot who had been killed and his son who was slowly, but certainly, dying. "Hour by hour," Ansel had said. "And all we can do is try to make sure that he feels no pain." They had both been drawn out of their own private thoughts, out of their loneliness. This is what love was to Gail then, a line, a thread that she could follow, eyes closed, leading her out from the solitude of her mind. No secrets or revelation, just one person on Earth who could anchor her.

"Are you happy, Ans?" she asks him now, surprising even herself by the fearlessness of her question.

He looks at her searchingly.

"I just wonder if we ended up where we thought we'd be. I'm almost forty, and I don't know where the time went."

"Yes," he says, without hesitation. "I'm happy." He looks as if he wants to say something more. Then, stopping himself, he asks, "Are you?"

Gail nods, but it takes her aback that it is she who cannot give a straightforward answer. She closes her eyes, feels an ache in her chest, a physical pain that pulses slowly. Day by day, she thinks, the distance between them is growing, carrying them out of reach of each other.

Instead of speaking, she takes his hand, holding it carefully between her own.

That night, while she is setting the table for dinner, the phone rings, and a moment later Ansel appears beside her holding the cordless. "For you," he says. "Harry Jaarsma, calling from Amsterdam."

She glances at the clock. It is four in the morning in the Netherlands. She can see him in his apartment, the heavy brocade curtains, high stacks of paper obscuring the carpet.

"Jaarsma," she says, taking the phone from Ansel, watching his back as he disappears from the room. "How *are* you?"

He says, without greeting or introduction, "I have good news."

"Don't tell me –"

"It's true," Jaarsma says, unable to contain his joy. "Never underestimate the power of patience."

She says the only words that come to her mind. "You broke it."

"Indeed."

Gail sits down. Behind her, there is a low hum in the living room, the sound of the party, Ansel laughing with her mother, Ed Carney and Glyn playing a duet on the piano. Gail's father is standing by the window, looking into the room as if he is outside it. She puts a hand against her eyes, trying to concentrate on Jaarsma's voice as he tells her how he had woken in the night and an idea had come to him. He had leapt out of bed, turned on his computer and typed what he guessed to be the key phrase. "I sat back and waited. Then, right in front of my eyes, the numbers began to fade away. Letters, words, entire sentences. I felt as if William Sullivan's ghost had arrived in my office and was rudely typing upon my keyboard." He laughs. "I must enter the remaining the numbers, but I wanted to share the good news."

In her mind, Gail can see the first line of the diary: *5 9 24 8 26 9*. Numbers fill thirty single-spaced pages, without any visible order or pattern. She has repeated the line to herself for months, *5 9 24 8 26 9*, as she falls to sleep at night. She has awoken with it on the tip of her tongue.

She remembers how Jaarsma had been as excited as she was at the prospect of unlocking the secrets of Sullivan's journal. They had met in the Netherlands some fifteen years ago, through mutual friends now only vaguely remembered. Gail had been studying in Leiden, and during their first meeting they had found themselves arguing on the same side in a heated discussion about Robert Oppenheimer and the Manhattan Project, about science, ethics and history. Part way through the night, he had turned to her, eyes glassy from the beer, and said, "We think so much alike. Let's not ruin it by falling in love." They had raised their glasses to a long and enduring friendship.

Almost immediately, Jaarsma, whose specialty was chaos theory, had worked out the structure of the code, a version of the Vigenère Square. But rather than using the letters of the alphabet, Sullivan had used the numbers 1 through 26. The Vigenère Square, Jaarsma had explained to her, combines twenty-six different cipher, or code, alphabets. So far, so good: since the mid-nineteenth century, a means had existed to unlock it. But the final level of encryption, the key word that would allow the codebreaker to determine which of the twenty-six cipher alphabets was in use at any given time, had so far eluded him. A key word of *blue*, for instance, would alert the codebreaker to use the cipher alphabets *b*, *l*, *u* and *e*. The key used by Sullivan was not a simple word, and the longer the key, the more difficult it was to break the code. Perhaps the key was a list, a song, an entire book. It could be virtually anything.

Two months ago, Jaarsma had called her, exhausted,

saying that the effort was futile. "My computer runs for hours at a time," he had said, "but it is lacking in that most human of traits: intuition." He told her that he had ceased to function properly, was unable to eat or sleep. He carried the diary everywhere, studying it on the train, in his laboratory, at the dinner table. His colleagues were unforgiving. The journal was occupying him to distraction. Jaarsma and Gail had mutually decided to put the project on hold. The phone call this evening is the first time Gail has heard from him since then.

"What *was* the key phrase?" she asks him now, straining to hear through the noise of the room.

"It was their names. His son, his wife and himself. Just their full names spelled out. Nothing more." After a pause, he says, "I haven't read all the way through to the end, but I think the contents will surprise you. Her father was not the man I expected to find." He adds, "Is that enough to persuade you to visit me in Amsterdam?"

"I hardly need to be persuaded."

He laughs. "I'll have the champagne ready. Congratulations on your birthday, by the way."

The dinner progresses around her, laughter and conversation, and much clinking of glasses. Her thoughts drift in and out of the present. Over dessert, Ansel looks across the table at her, as if to say, *What is it? What's wrong?* She feels, for a brief moment, a wave of claustrophobia, and she stands up and begins clearing away the dishes.

Glyn rises to help her, and the two go into the kitchen, plates and coffee cups balanced precariously. When the dishes are safely stowed in the sink, Glyn leans against the counter, her expression concerned. "Thinking about work?" she asks.

Gail does not answer right away. She reaches up to the cupboard, brings down the bottle of port, and then enough glasses for everyone. As she opens the bottle and begins pouring, she tells Glyn about Jaarsma's phone call. Glyn is editing the documentary, a co-production for CBC-Radio and Radio Netherlands, but so far she has stayed in the background, allowing Gail time to research and gather tape. "When this project is finished," Gail says, "I think I'll take some time off. Sit back for a while. I'm a bit run down, is all."

They touch glasses, Glyn's infectious smile warming the room. "For years we've been planning to celebrate New Year's on the Gulf Islands," she says. "Why not this year? Rent a little house on the Pacific, do the Polar Bear Swim. Ansel must have vacation time coming up?"

"Yes," Gail says, sipping her port. "I think he does."

"You're exhausted. The curse of the freelancer." She reaches her fingers out, brushes a strand of hair from Gail's forehead. "Remember Prague? We sat under the stars together, knowing we were at the start of something, some grand adventure. Were we right or wrong, back then? You and I, what a pair of romantics."

That night, after everyone has gone, Gail leaves Ansel in the living room and goes into her office, shutting the door behind her. The curtains are open, and outside the street lamps glow, laying circles of light on the empty road.

She is surrounded by equipment worthy of a museum. Reel-to-reels, cassette recorders, record players. Lately, she has been working with Mini Discs and digital editing programs, but she cannot bring herself to dispose of the old tape, the old equipment. "They still work," she says to amused colleagues. "They still do what we asked of them."

She collects tape the way others collect records or rare books, safeguarding them with a feeling of reverence. She has fragments spliced together, dozens of conversations gathered on a single reel. Soundscapes, features, interviews. On days when her mind wanders, she randomly loads a reel onto the player, puts the earphones on, listens. For Gail, the devotion lies in more than the words spoken. It is the words spoken at a specific moment in time, in a particular place. A child singing in the background, a pause in the telling, an old woman wetting her lips, smoothing her dress. A man who forgets the presence of the microphone, who begins a conversation with himself. "And after that, nothing was ever the same. I wanted to go back, I needed to see him, but I couldn't."

Before going to bed, Ansel knocks on the door of her office, pushes it open. "It's your birthday," he says, casually. "Surely you can take the night off."

She saves the document she is working on, then turns to face him. "Jaarsma broke the code," she says. "That's what he called to say."

His eyes light up, happy for her.

"I've decided to go to Amsterdam. I set aside part of the funding for this, the plane ticket and travel, hoping everything would turn out."

She can see him wanting to say something, to argue against her going. Her response begins to take shape in her mind, *I have to do this. I need to be away.* But he does not fight her. Instead, from where he stands, he wishes her good night, then closes the door softly behind him.

Alone again, she opens files, then closes them once more. She thinks of another love affair two decades before, the feel of another man's hands on her body, the pull of desire. All this, a lifetime ago. At twenty-one, Gail had begun graduate work in the Netherlands. There, not even halfway through her M.A. in history, she took a leave from the University of Leiden, gave up her apartment, and travelled east. She was restless, tired of reading about *realpolitik*, about her thesis topic, Japanese militarism in the 1930s, anxious to make something concrete of her life. And she was in love. A floundering, impossible affair. The man, a professor of languages, was handsome, brilliant and married. So she cut her ties and applied for a visa to the Eastern Bloc.

By spring, she was living in Prague, in a tiny two-room flat, working afternoons in a haberdashery. Her roommate, Glyn Madden, was a radio producer. At thirty-six, divorced and at loose ends, Glyn had sold her house in Wales and gone off in search of adventure, which, they both agreed, had proven to be more elusive than it first seemed. They traded books between them, drove across the border to Germany in search of English-language novels, came home with strange, tattered copies of Karl May westerns. They walked at dusk, joyous, alive, up to the Prague Castle. The apartment they shared was in Na Kampa, and at night they sat at the window, staring down at the miniature heads gathered around the café tables. They took turns changing the records on Glyn's turntable: *Abbey Road*, Joni Mitchell, REM.

Each month, her mother sent her a small package of famous B.C. smoked salmon and a long, descriptive letter, filled with stories. Gail's father, she wrote at one point, had started a community garden in Strathcona. Every Sunday, children clustered around him, each one wearing tiny rubber boots, holding tight to a miniature spade. Business in the restaurant was steady, she said, and her father had decided to come on as a part owner. *He is well, though he misses you. We both do.* Gail went home only once each year, at Christmas time. It was the most she could afford, and she did not want to rely on her parents for money. "Too stubborn," her mother would say, holding her at the airport when she left. "Too independent." But the words, Gail thought, were filled with pride, too, that they had raised her to be so free, so fearless in the world.

In Prague one morning, Glyn had woken her at 4:00 a.m., holding a cassette recorder and a microphone. "Join me," she had said, her voice low and robotic, leaning over Gail's bed, eyes shining in the darkness.

"What is this? *Star Wars*? *Spaceballs*?"

"Let's go. We're late."

They loaded their bicycles into Glyn's van, then drove two hours east. Through the countryside, a Thermos of coffee between them, they watched the sun rise over the fading hills. In Brno, thousands of runners were gathered for a marathon. Glyn wired her to a cassette recorder, placed a microphone in her hand and headphones over her ears. The starting gun went off, and Gail, flustered, immediately dropped the recorder on the ground. On the tape, afterwards, she could hear Glyn laughing. But when she replaced the headphones, Gail heard details that she had never heard in life. Whispered conversations, the rhythm of hundreds of shoes striking cobblestone.

She hurriedly unlocked her bicycle and began pedalling after the runners. On the tape, later on, she heard the bicycle bell ringing ever so slightly as the wheels rattled over the stones. She heard runners drinking as they went, dropping the plastic cups on the road, and the light jaggedness, like cut glass, of their breathing.

That was the moment of revelation. Her degree fell by the wayside, and Glyn found her a job at Radio Netherlands, which had a small outpost there in Prague. They worked side by side each afternoon, pulling tape. Switching from grease pencil to razor blade, the reel of tape sliding back and forth, her right foot maneuvering the pedals. A swift diagonal cut, then a thumbprint of splicing tape to bind the pieces together. She laid the outtakes over her right shoulder, and then her left, in a carefully ordered fringe. Afterwards, they would eat dinner in the studio, potato dumplings soaked in gravy, washed down by bitter black coffee. Among her reels of tape, she has a recording Glyn made in 1989, in Wenceslas Square, when hundreds of thousands of people, laughing and crying, jingled their keys in unison to symbolize the fall of the Soviet regime and the opening of the door to democracy.

Somewhere in that decade, she had fallen in love with a print journalist, a goat herder and an art collector. The print journalist had been the last, while Gail was in the Arctic. That was much later, after Glyn had moved to London and Gail was on assignment for Deutsche Welle's English radio service, recording a feature about the beluga whales trapped in the ice-jammed waters of the Chukchi Peninsula, near the Bering Strait. The three thousand whales were slowly suffocating. Chukchi fishermen set out each morning, axes on their backs, attempting to open patches of ice. Up above, Russian helicopters circled like clumsy birds. They poured fish down from the sky.

For three weeks, Gail did not see her own body naked in its entirety; she was a walking bundle of fur and fleece. Swaddled, she carried her portable DAT recorder in an insulated bag. When she held her microphone out over the water, she could hear the whales themselves; they formed an endless line as they took turns breathing, one by one, at the air holes. A whistle of sound, a breath like water being swallowed. Sometimes, the whales allowed a seal to push into line, rising up, finding oxygen. She could not distinguish the sky from the ice, the snow from horizon.

The Chukchi gathered at her microphone to tell their stories. Before the waters were divided up, they said, before lines were drawn in the sea by Washington and Moscow, they used to cross the Bering Strait in skin boats. Once upon a time, their people lived nomadic lives; back then, the herds of reindeer had been thirty thousand strong. When she looked up from her recorder, Gail saw a group of young boys pirouetting their bicycles on the snow, their shadows, thin and graceful, reaching into the distance.

Eventually, a Soviet icebreaker arrived to clear a path for the whales. The icebreaker played Beethoven, and it thundered from the speakers. The whales, entranced, followed the Ninth Symphony back to open water.

Afterwards, Gail caught a flight to Fairbanks, and then on to Vancouver. Home to the house on Keefer Street, the wild, luxuriant garden that her father kept, the trellises bursting with roses, perfuming the air. She had been living in Europe for almost a decade. When they sat down to dinner, she felt as if she and her parents were travelling across a vast field, coming to meet one another. Her father, who had worked all his life in a restaurant, set down dish after dish, and each one was her favourite. They were so tentative with one another, as if circling in a room where the lights have gone out, trying to find their way by intuition, by memory alone.

After dinner, washing up in the kitchen, she had seen a letter lying on the countertop. The envelope was addressed to her father, and the stamps, she was surprised to see, were from the Netherlands. "What's this?" she had asked, picking the letter up.

He had taken the envelope from her, turning towards her mother. His expression is vivid in her mind, even now, and the way her mother had looked at him, the lightest touch against his arm. "Someone I knew once, in Sandakan," her father had said, seeming to search for the words. "She died recently. Her husband wrote to tell us."

"During the war," her mother said, "they were children together." Her father clutched the envelope in his hand, lost, unsure where to set it down.

Gail had busied herself with the dishes. When she turned back, the envelope had disappeared, and her father was hanging the dish cloth to dry, smoothing the creases away with his hands.

Standing up from her desk, she turns the lights off and climbs the stairs to their bedroom. Ansel has left the reading light on for her, and he is fast asleep. She slips into bed beside him. For a long time, she gazes up through the skylight at the stars. She connects the invisible lines between them, Lyra, Cassiopeia, Perseus, as she used to do when she was a child.

Beside her, Ansel sighs in his sleep, he rests his body against hers. Her feelings have not changed, though she no longer knows how to make them palpable, certain. Gail thinks of something he told her long ago, how the pattern of the wave is one of the most common in nature. Sound, light, X-rays. The revelatory pictures of an MRI scan, a machine that throws light on the shadows of the mind. And what does it see? The work of thousands of synapses. The chemical traces of memory and love. If it could peer into Gail's mind in a moment when she thinks of Ansel, how many patterns would it see awakened? The incoming tide, wave after wave of memory. The accelerated heartbeat, the charge Gail feels in his presence, none of this has changed. But for him? If she could see into the darkness, would she find in him what she hopes for? An echo of her own desire, as strong and sure as it was in the beginning, before something between them faltered and lost hope.

The next morning, after Ansel has left for the clinic, Gail finds the Bering Strait recording on a reel labelled *Whales, Ode to Joy, 1990*. She unwinds a foot of tape, blows the dust off, and has a memory of walking out across the shelves of ice. She remembers being taken, by snowmobile, to the Strait, seeing open water, still and crystalline, a mirror at the edge of the frozen tundra.

Two years ago, she had given up the security of her job as a producer. After another round of funding cuts at the CBC, she had been anxious. She wanted to make radio herself, to create features and documentaries on subjects that aroused her curiosity, that moved her. To make ends meet as a freelancer, she pitched her ideas to public radio stations around the world, calling up old contacts at Deutsche Welle or the Australian Broadcasting Corporation. She had a way of making every vacation into a work project. While other people carried cameras or mobile phones, she was never without a microphone and recorder.

As she sits down to work, a group of school children come laughing down the sidewalk, two by two, holding hands. Their teacher points out a blue jay, and the children erupt in yelling and finger pointing: "I see! I see!" or, heartache in their voices, "I *don't* see! I *don't* see!" An older woman shuffles past, pushing her groceries in a supermarket shopping cart. Viewed from her desk, her fingers poised over the keyboard, the scene seems to hang, suspended, before Gail's eyes.

5 9 24 8 26 9. She clicks an icon and an audio file flickers open across the screen. The interview that she plays was recorded in Prince George several months ago, on the verandah of Kathleen Sullivan's home. They had driven from the airport, through a landscape of open fields, along a single highway unrolling like a river. Kathleen had leaned forward as she spoke, strands of auburn hair slipping loose from a low ponytail, each sentence clear and insistent.

"Even now," she says, her voice coming through the speakers in Gail's office, "I remember the way the diary smelled and the sound it made when my father opened it. The book literally creaked. He had found it laid away in a drawer, and he wanted to decode it for us. He set a notepad on the table in front of him, then he picked up a pencil and started to copy down the numbers." Kathleen tells how, when she had first become fascinated by the diary, she had been ten years old. She had believed in the possibility of a perfect answer to the mystery of her father. Rain was the result of condensation in the atmosphere; the sun was an exploding star. There was a solution to her father, too, a cause and an effect.

She describes watching her father write out a row of numbers. Underneath this row, he wrote a line of letters. More letters, chaotic on the surface. It went on this way for some time while the television murmured in the living room, where her older brother was watching a soccer game.

Kathleen had turned to watch it, the Vancouver Whitecaps, the rain of white jerseys, a soccer ball drummed across the pitch. Her father put his pencil down, stared at the numbers as if willing them to form a meaning. He erased what he had written and began again. He ran his hand across his face, shook his head. Kathleen remembered looking at his terribly scarred hand, a strange hollow in the index finger where he told her a bullet had passed too close. Her father became confused as he worked backwards through the code. Still, he went on staring at the numbers as if, given enough time, the method of decryption would magically present itself.

Kathleen sat at his feet. Eventually, she felt them shift, opened her eyes to see them walking away, the diary abandoned on the table.

On the tape, Gail's voice: "And if the code is broken. Can you put into words the thing that you hope to find?"

There is a long pause, the muted sound of a truck passing on the back roads. Then, silence. "He drank," she says finally. "He drank himself into oblivion. In his worst moments, he couldn't even recognize us. There was so much violence in our lives. In the end, it was his drinking that drove my brother away, that broke my family apart. I need to know what happened to my father in those camps, what he lived through. And if it isn't in the diary, then where did he keep those thoughts? What did he do with all those memories?"

The sound waves roll across her computer screen. Gail edits in a fragment of Jaarsma's interview.

"Cryptography," he says, "holds a particular danger of its own. People expect to find patterns. You are handed a code, someone says, 'Break this,' and then it becomes like a game, a chase. It can drive you mad. Once you begin to doubt your skill, once you begin to lose faith, to wonder if the code is indeed a code, if it contains any meaning at all, it throws your life into disorder. What if, in the end, this book is no more and no less than a book of numbers? What if the surface is all there is?" He pauses and then says, "I think codebreaking is part of a very human desire, the desire for revelation, for meaning. To have every secret, every private thought, laid bare, regardless of what that might cost us."

In front of her, the recording has come to an end, and the soundwaves disappear from the screen.

The phone rings, and Gail blinks, coming back to her surroundings. When she picks up, she hears her father's voice, already speaking, halfway through a sentence.

She takes the phone and walks out of her office, into the living room, where the windows are open. A sudden breeze shivers the newspapers across the coffee table. Her father is talking about arranging a vacation, two weeks along the coast of British Columbia, north to Haida Gwaii, the Queen Charlotte Islands. "And with our anniversary coming up," he is saying, "it could be a nice present. But will she like it? Perhaps it's too extravagant?"

Gail smiles, leaning out the window now, and she pictures her parents walking hand-in-hand in the hush of the rainforest. Outside, fall leaves scatter on the wind. "I think it's a lovely idea."

"It's our fortieth wedding anniversary," he says, in wonder at the thought.

His voice sounds grainy, worn at the edges, and she asks him if he slept well last night. Her father makes a noise that means, Not to worry. But when she presses him, he says that he slept for an hour or two, then watched *The King and I* on television.

Night after night during her childhood, her father, the insomniac, would pace the house, haunting it like a restless spirit. Before leaving for school each morning, Gail would see the remnants of his night. An empty teapot on the counter, the sleeve of a record on the floor. In university, her father had studied history. Occasionally, a book, Gibbon or Toynbee, the pages dog-eared, would lie open on his chest.

Sometimes, the insomnia slid into depression. Then, for a week, he would not step out of his room. She remembers her mother standing at the doorway, leaning her ear against the door, as if listening for the sound of his breathing.

What do you dream about? Gail had asked him once. My childhood, he said, after a pause. What was your childhood like? Her father had smiled fondly at her before turning away. "Like every childhood. Mine was no different." Ever the curious daughter, she would take his hand. "Tell me one thing about it. Anything."

He told her how to tap a rubber tree, how to hold a cigarette tin against the trunk and catch the precious liquid. How to carve an orange into a lantern, or a radish into the petals of a rose.

She once kept a list of his eccentricities. Her father was afraid of the dark. He could not eat certain foods: sweet potato, cassava and tapioca, which he called *ubi kayu*. Every weekday morning, before leaving for his job at the restaurant, he would stretch his arms and back, a kind of calisthenics that he said they had learned in school, when he was a boy. He had a fascination with Japan, a quick temper, and a disconcerting knowledge of British Columbian history. The First Nations, he once told her, have an archaeological history here that can be traced back ten thousand years. "Imagine that," he would say, shaking his head, peering down at Gail as if he could read the span of years in his daughter's face. He said that he tried to picture what first contact was like, when the Haida stumbled across the ship of Juan Perez, when they saw the white sails open and fluttering in the wind.

On the phone now, he is still talking about *The King and I*, describing how he first saw the film in Melbourne, in 1958. "All the boys I knew, they wanted to grow up to be Yul Brynner," he says, laughing. Once, he had woken to the sight of his roommate practising his ballroom dancing, twirling an imaginary partner.

"And who did you imagine *you* might dance with?" Gail asks teasingly.

"I always danced with same person. In Sandakan, when I was young. But she died a long time ago. I thought I might see her again, but it was impossible." She hears him shifting the phone to his other ear. "Don't forget," he says. "I want to surprise your mother. It's been so long since we took a trip together." When she puts down the phone, something in her mind seems to stop and catch, a word, a name, hovers on the edge of her memory.

The phone rings again, but she doesn't pick it up. On the answering machine, Ansel's voice. "It's me." A pause, and then he says, "Are you there? I didn't want to wake you this morning before I left. Are you there, Gail? Anyway, that's all right. It was nothing important. You looked so peaceful this morning. That's all." Something in his voice causes her to sit down, exhausted, unsure. "I love you."

The message light on the machine begins to glow. She thinks of her mother, sitting at the kitchen table, polishing the glass beads of the chandelier, a task she did when Gail's father was ill, when he slipped into a depression and she could not pull him back. Long ago, when she was a child, Gail would fall asleep in her mother's lap, face pressed against the fabric of her dress. The familiar smell of soap and sweetness. Across the room, her father sat for hours in his armchair, his cup of tea gone cold, and it seemed to Gail that he had disappeared, cut himself loose from his body. Her mother would lift Gail from her lap, rise from her chair. She would place her hands on his shoulders, rubbing his neck and back. Touch calling another person back to this world, warmth flowing from one body into another.

A few months ago, she had helped her mother clean and organize her workroom. While her mother went to the kitchen to prepare lunch, Gail had got started, wiping the bookshelf. It was crammed with sewing manuals, but there were also cookbooks, magazines and novels: Balzac, Dickens, Thackeray, coated in a thin layer of dust. Gail had sat cross-legged on the floor, turning the worn pages. She was replacing the books on the shelf when she saw a handful of envelopes that must have fallen on the carpet. She recognized one of them immediately. It was addressed to her father, and the Dutch stamps, now yellowed and dry, curled up at the edges. She had slid the letter out, a single page, fragile and creased.

I am heartbroken to write that Ani passed away on November 29, 1992, at home, of cancer. Wideh has returned from Jakarta, and he is here now. He was with his mother at the end.

Before her death, Ani requested that I write to you, and she provided me with your last known address. I hope that this letter reaches you.

I am very sorry to have to write to you with this news.

The name at the bottom of the page was Sipke Vermeulen.

She goes back to her office. At her desk, she scans the list of sound files, trying to focus on her work. She chooses one and hits Play. The recording that emerges from the computer is her own voice, the interview with Jaarsma about cryptography and the Vigenère Square. "The ciphers leave a shadow," Jaarsma says, in response to her question. "However faint, you cannot erase that. This is the narrow, almost invisible opening for the codebreaker. At Bletchley Park, during the Second World War, cryptographers often recognized a pattern they had seen weeks, even months ago. They would walk across the room, fish out the correct fragment from a stack of paper. As if it were all a dream. It was the subconscious memory of a pattern."

In radio, in the countless scripts that she has written, Gail works with the belief that histories touch. Follow the undercurrent and you will arrive at the meeting place. So she weaves together interviews, narration, music and sound in the hope that stories will not be lost in the chaos of never touching one another, never overlapping in any true way. Each element a strand, and the story itself a work of design. Out of the disparate pieces, let something pure, something true, emerge. Let it remain there, visible.

And in this documentary, where is the truth in the story of William Sullivan?

Gail runs her pen along the script, making notes in the margin.

Years ago, in Prague, she had interviewed a woman whose teenaged son had drowned in the Vltava River, a tragic accident. In the midst of recalling that day, the woman had looked up at Gail, suddenly angry, asking why she dared to ask these questions, what right she had. Gail had opened the recorder, removed the cassette tape. She had placed it carefully in the older woman's hand. "If only you could understand," the woman had said, clutching the tape. "The words that I put in the world can never be taken back."

She remembered the woman's frantic gestures, the ribbon pulled out of the cassette, spooling onto the ground.

She opens a browser on her computer and begins to book her flight to Amsterdam. Dates, flights, times: the numbers swim before her eyes. When she has an itinerary ready, she prints it up, and emails a copy to Jaarsma.

Outside, a woman calls out, then a screen door opens and slowly closes, the hinges creaking. She types Sipke Vermeulen's name into the computer and watches the results scroll down the screen. The Nederlands Fotomuseum in Rotterdam. World Press Photo. She follows a link, and a series of black-and-white photographs open up before her. The caption underneath reads, *Algiers, 1959. The Algerian War.*

For a long time she studies the photos. In one, a child plays on an abandoned tank, he hangs upside down, suspended from the barrel of the gun.

She opens one image after another, seeing images from the Netherlands, Germany, Indonesia, and it becomes clear that Sipke Vermeulen is a Dutch photojournalist, a war photographer.

Gail closes the browser, picks up the printed itinerary from her desk, and walks out of her office. She climbs the stairs to their attic bedroom. Standing at the window, she can see a dozen tai chi practitioners gathered in the nearby schoolyard, moving, out-of-phase, in a lengthening ballet. Elderly men and women flick their heels, stretch their arms away from their bodies, turn with a strange and gorgeous precision. Movement after movement unfolding, an outgoing tide, spreading towards the edges.

Many times in her childhood, she had woken to the sound of her father's nightmares. A screaming in the dark, lights coming on in the house. She would creep to their bedroom door, holding on to the sound of her mother's voice comforting him. Once, unable to go back to sleep, she had found her way, in the dark, to the living room. There, she lay on the carpet, her arms open, as if to gather up the air, to hold the weight of the room. From where she lay, she reached out and turned on the antique radio. The panel glowed and, after a few seconds, music, something jazzy, began to drift through the speakers. Eyes closed, she pressed her hand to the wooden cabinet, drew the vibrations through her fingertips, all the way to her heart.

When dawn came, she went to her parents' bedroom, inched the door open, stood at the border of their room as they slept. She gazed at them with a boldness that she would not otherwise dare. Asleep, it was as if they had gone away together, leaving the worries of their life behind. She imagined casting a spell over them. When they woke, they would find themselves in a place where no secrets existed, where all the sorrows of the past had been laid to rest. What sorrows? She did not know. She knew so little about their lives. Privacy, her parents believed, was sacred.

For as long as she can remember, she had wanted to save them. She imagined her parents turning to her, seeing her finally, and the past would fall away. That is what she had hoped for when she was a child. To say the right thing, to pull off a feat of such perfection, they could be distracted, if only for a time.

From the window, she can see the myriad cracks in the sidewalk, the antique waste bins. A few blocks over, the sound of Chinatown like a swirling body of water. Here, in the oldest neighbourhood in the city, the trees are surprisingly young. They are planted each in a square of soil, a gesture towards the future. In the playground at Strathcona Elementary, children run in looping paths. They dribble balls on the basketball court, run three steps for a lay-up. For a

fleeting moment, as she watches, their bodies hover motionless in the air.

The clouds open in a rainstorm, a kind of sheeting monsoon
that rarely appears in Vancouver. In the bedroom, Gail listens
to it clattering on the house, onto the glass skylight. Downstairs, Ansel is making dinner, a casserole of leeks, tofu and
potatoes, spiced with curry. She gets up and goes downstairs,
where she uncorks a bottle of red wine, drinks one glass and
then another too quickly. The alcohol warms her, and she
remains by Ansel as he assembles dinner, leaning her head
into the hollow between his shoulder blades. A familiar
gesture. He slides the casserole in the oven, and together they
go into the living room. It is dimly lit, and on the couch he
gathers Gail into his arms.

There is a recklessness to the way they undress one
another. Perhaps such release is a gift; perhaps it is only the
wine passing through her bloodstream. He kisses her mouth,
along her neck, and it is a kind of betrayal, the way her
body responds to him. But she does not want to stop it, stop
the momentum that accumulates between them, she cannot
imagine how such a thing, something so treasured, could
come to an end.

Later, when they are lying together on the couch, she
tells him that she has booked her flight to Amsterdam, and
that she will remain there for six days. She will finally be able
to move ahead on this project.

The silence lingers between them.

"I need this time away," she says.

"From us."

Long ago, any sign of pain in him would cause her deep anxiety, because it hinted of a future of possible loss, more loss than she could imagine. But now, seeing his expression, she feels confused.

"Gail?" he says, her name a question. "Just come home."

My love, she thinks, and the words are true.

He kisses her, and she knows, somehow, that he is asking for help, for an end to the sadness they are causing one another. Asking because, after all these years together, it is the only thing that might save them. Together they stand up, they find their clothes and pull them on. Then they go into the kitchen, leaning on one another.

Harry Jaarsma's home in Amsterdam is a three-storey brick rowhouse, tall and narrow. Inside, the staircase to his office is so steep that, climbing up, Gail feels a sensation of vertigo, the walls pitching towards her. She grips the bannister, takes a deep breath, and climbs the last few steps. She and Jaarsma emerge into an open space, glass walled and high-ceilinged. The room is a container of light.

"My thinking space," Jaarsma says. He is a few feet ahead of her, dressed in jeans and a T-shirt bearing a diagram of a caffeine molecule.

She had arrived last night. "Lovely," he had said, on seeing her at the airport. "But careworn." They had taken the train from the airport into central Amsterdam, then walked through the cold, winding streets to Jaarsma's home. Past the train station, where thousands of bicycles leaned together in the night, continuing across the canals that ring the city, rippling away from the centre. Her breath trailed behind her, a white fog in the darkness. They passed brick facades, topped with delicate gables. Almost twenty years have passed since she studied in the Netherlands, but the sound of the Dutch language now fell reassuringly on her ears. He set her luggage in the spare room, and, over the course of a few hours, they had moved from coffee to beer to Beerenburg, a sweet liquor distilled from juniper berries, which had dulled her senses and caused her to fall asleep on the couch, but not before she and Jaarsma had managed to talk enough politics, art and science to make up for years apart. "Having children," he had proclaimed, at the end of the night, before nodding off on the carpet, "is an essentially hopeful act. But I, Harry Jaarsma, have always been an essentially hopeless man. And I will never, never, be persuaded otherwise. Bring on the worst. I am ready."

Now, standing in the sunlit office, they are both fatigued and pale, nursing cups of steaming black coffee.

He goes to his desk, lifts up a stack of pages, and brings them to her. She recognizes the photocopied pages of the diary at once, and her heart begins to thrill in her chest. She sets her coffee down and starts to turn the pages, finding where the numbers end and the text begins: *20 December*

1941. *Hong Kong.* "You said that he surprised you," she says.

He smiles, an expression both gentle and melancholy. "Read it and discover for yourself."

She had wanted to believe that once the code was broken so much in William Sullivan's life, in his children's lives, would come clear, that a line could be drawn from beginning to end and a true narrative emerge. She sets the pages down, unable to begin, not wanting to finish. It isn't disappointment she fears, but trespass. To awaken a memory that has no consolation. She remembers a conversation with her mother, from years ago. Gail had asked her mother to tell her about her first love, and her mother had smiled at the question. Your father, she had answered. Your father was my first love, and my first heartbreak.

When they have finished drinking their coffee, she opens her equipment bag and removes the Mini Disc recorder, microphone and cords. They set up a space by the windows, William Sullivan's diary laid on a table between them. She tells him that she will read the pages this afternoon. Perhaps, for now, they can fill in a few missing pieces about code-breaking, and tomorrow they will talk specifically about the diary.

He nods, one hand brushing the tip of the microphone that she has affixed to him with her usual trick, the bent coat hanger around the neck. "How do I look?" he asks, smiling.

"Sharp. Very sharp."

They settle into place and Gail listens, assessing the sound of the room. There are no refrigerators, no computer fans whirring. She readies her equipment, then does a sound check, adjusting the needle as Jaarsma rambles on about his hangover. In her earphones, his voice has a low, rich timbre, a melodious accent.

Guided by her questions, he begins to talk about the Vigenère Square, and then cryptography in general. She asks him to assess the personality of someone suited to the work of codebreaking.

He begins to describe the repetitive nature of the work, how codebreakers were recruited from mathematics departments, orchestral groups and crossword puzzle competitions. He beams. "Do you know football?"

Gail shakes her head.

"I'm reminded of a famous quote by Johann Cruyff. He said, 'If I wanted you to understand, I would have explained it better.' He was talking about football, but I think what he meant is to trust pure intuition. Follow something less explicit. It is perhaps very unscientific to say, but I think that to break a code you must inhabit the mind of the code-maker. To unravel the clues, you must, to some extent, place yourself within his consciousness."

Outside, she can hear the whistle of a train passing, and they wait a few moments for the noise to subside. On the far side of the room, a blur of colour catches her attention.

"The print on your wall, Jaarsma. I feel like I should recognize it."

He smiles, pushing his chair back, stands and walks to the other side of the room. Gail follows closely behind him, wondering whether to pause the tape. She lets the recording continue, taking care to ensure that the wires of the microphone stay clear. Framed beneath the glass, the pictures, six in total, are strange and wild. They hint of seahorse tails, the spiral of a winding nautilus, electric sparks.

"The Mandelbrot Set," Jaarsma says, running his fingertips over one of the prints. "A collection of points derived from the quadratic equation $z = z^2 + c$. The equation itself is very simple, but the Mandelbrot Set is one of the most complex objects in mathematics. See this boundary here," he says, indicating a shape enclosed by a band of colour. "Any part of this edge, this cartoid, no matter where, no matter how small, will, if magnified, reveal new points. And these, if further magnified, will also reveal new points, *ad infinitum*."

Gail moves closer to the wall, gazing at the pictures. Each successive print is a magnification of a detail of the last. The last frame is labelled as being a ratio of 1:1 million.

"The boundary encloses a finite area, but the boundary itself is infinite. No matter how much we increase the magnification, the same shapes appear and reappear in the border, though never quite the same. The image reveals a kind of symmetry, not of left and right, but of large scales and small ones.

"Imagine that we are standing here," he says. Unexpectedly, he takes her hand, ever so gently, and places it on a corner of the print. "I can imagine what the rest of the picture is like because this is a fractal image, and it is self-similar. It repeats. But to imagine the entire picture is akin to standing on a street corner and trying to imagine what

England looks like from an airplane, or from Mars. I can extrapolate, but what I see at this level may not conform to my expectations of what it will look like as we move in space and time.

"Do you know how birds fly in formation? As far as we know, they hold no picture in their minds of the V formation, let alone the vast pattern of migration. They are aware only of the other birds in their immediate proximity. And the same is true for me; I respond to what is immediately around me. But the pattern that I cannot see, that I have no knowledge of, exists. My mind, my brain, is not made to imagine distances of great magnitude. Or infinite time, eternity. We glimpse a part of the puzzle and intimate, however vaguely, an answer. But if I read a book about geography, or the history of the Earth, or the universe, for that matter, how does that change the way I place myself within this formation?"

She gazes at the boundary, the intricate details. "It changes nothing and everything."

Jaarsma smiles, delighted. "Precisely."

She turns off the recorder and removes her headphones. "If I wanted to find someone in the Netherlands," she says, "how would I go about it?"

He is taken aback by the question. "The telephone book?" he says, finally, not sure if she is serious.

"There is someone I want to find."

Jaarsma walks across the room to his computer. He opens a browser and enters a Dutch Internet address. When the page has opened, he looks up at her, fingers resting on the keyboard.

Gail retrieves her notebook from her bag and opens it to the last page, where she had written, this morning, the name that she cannot shake loose: *Sipke Vermeulen*. Jaarsma studies the page, then types in the words. Almost instantaneously, an address and phone number appear on the screen.

That night, Gail stays awake. Her suitcase is open, the contents still neatly packed. Jaarsma's translation of the diary is open before her, twelve pages of single-spaced type. William Sullivan, she thinks, all his thoughts transcribed into numbers, multiplied and added to themselves, a testament to what a person might do to make all their words disappear.

She imagines him working with pencil in hand, copying the numbers onto a sheet of looseleaf. Over and over, he erases his numbers and begins again. How is it possible to forget pain, to be unable to recall something that was once so inescapable?

In the diary, there is no detailing of violence witnessed and endured, of friends executed, of resistance. That, in the end, is what Gail finds so startling. She knows, through her research, that in the Hong Kong camp, a third of the men died before the war ended. In the prisoner-of-war camp in Sandakan, only six of three thousand men lived to see liberation. William Sullivan kept the diary as proof of a different kind of existence, where part of him still saw the world as if he were free. He wrote about their rituals, what time they got up in the morning, the kind of trees that grew outside the camp, the food they ate, the girl smugglers who passed by outside. "Some are as young as ten years old. Their clothes hang together with invisible thread." And another entry: "My most prized possession is a set of three tin dishes. They came to me through various hands, and they are useful for all sorts of things. Food, chiefly. But also to gather leaves for tea, to hold on to a bit of water. They are valuable also because, in a time of necessity, they can be traded for pills or medicine." Through these sentences, these pages, he would make the world cohere.

For three years, the men in the camp were starved and brutalized, treated as less than animals, but he had continued the journal, as if through it he could maintain some part of his dignity. In entry after entry, he imagines the days to come. "When I see you next," he writes, addressing Kathleen's mother. "After the war is finished."

When the camp was liberated in August 1945, he had been twenty-five years old. Gail had learned that the physicians and psychologists of the time had all agreed: the war was finished, these men who had survived should go on with their lives in the best way possible. They should not burden their families with the misery of what they had endured. So he had gone on, honourably discharged from the army, and he had kept his silence.

Earlier, she had telephoned the number for Sipke Vermeulen. The voice of an elderly man had answered, his words clear and lightly accented. When she said her name, a silence followed, and she feared the conversation had come to an end, that Sipke Vermeulen would put down the phone, without her understanding the reason why. But then time had begun again. He had repeated her name, in surprise, in recognition.

Arrangements were made. Sipke Vermeulen had told her he would come down to Amsterdam in two days' time, and then they would travel up north together to his home in rural Friesland.

Jaarsma had been standing in the window, watching the moonrise, the gleam of light clouding the city. He had poured two glasses of wine and ordered dinner from the neighbourhood Indonesian restaurant, sticks of satay, *babi pangang*, a container of rice. When he looked at her, his face held a question. She told him about the letter that she had found years ago. She wondered if it was possible to know a person truly. And if we did, would we know what we had, would we recognize it?

At one point in the evening, Jaarsma had put his fingers to the window, indicating the light. He told her that people believe that the moon changes in size as it moves across the sky, becoming larger and fuller as it nears the horizon. But the size of the moon, he said, remains constant no matter where it is, and the idea of a larger moon is an optical illusion. We could measure it, he said, with a paper clip, shaped into a caliper. He still remembered the day his father, an astronomer, told him this fact.

"And what did you feel," Gail had asked him, "when you learned it was only an illusion?"

At first, disbelief. He had been standing beside his father, the moon, low and immense, before them. "It was so large," he said, "I felt we could get in the car, drive across the city, reach out and hold it in our hands. Every night after that, I twisted a paperclip just as my father had taught me, proving over and over again that even the largest moon is no different in size from all the rest." Was it our perception of the sky that was in error, he had wondered, or our perception of the moon relative to the buildings on the horizon? Did we compare the current moon to an inaccurate memory of a previous one? What was it, within our own minds, within the wires and creases of our visual cortex, our internal map of the world, that allowed this distortion to happen?

She had sat in silence, the wineglass in her hands, waiting for Jaarsma to continue.

"There is no definitive theory," he said at last. "The question itself is thousands of years old, spanning from the time of the ancient Greeks. Maybe if we are lucky, within our own lifetime, we will find not only the right answer, but also the one that satisfies us."

That night, she falls asleep, the lamp still burning, the transcribed pages of the diary laid out beside her.

7

The Island

YSBRECHTUM, THE NETHERLANDS

*W*hen Gail Lim arrived in the Netherlands, Sipke Vermeulen was seventy-four years old, and Canada was the country of the pilot who fell from the sky over Ysbrechtum in 1940. That night, almost sixty years ago, the parachute had come down like a balloon returning from the heavens. Sipke had heard the explosion, turned his face towards the glint of fire, and run out into the grass with his three brothers. They were older, and they ran ahead of him, their eyes focused on the sky. Above the farmhouse, the parachute floated out from beneath the clouds, it looked like a part of the moon torn away. He watched the figure cradled in the harness, the slender lines of the body growing ever clearer. When the parachute collapsed into the ground, the folds fluttered in the breeze. Sipke's brothers pushed their way through the buttresses of silk.

They hid the Canadian pilot in their barn. When the Germans came, his father described the explosion and the ball of light, and then the parachute that had appeared in the flames. The Germans asked where the parachute had landed, and his father made a drawing. He told them that the remains had been carried off by the wind, west towards the sea.

Sipke was twelve years old. Three times each day, he brought food and drink to the injured pilot, and then sat with him. The pilot taught him his first English word, which was *thirsty*. Sipke's mother took the parachute, cut it into pieces, and made new dresses for each of his sisters. In time, with the covert assistance of the village doctor, the pilot's broken bones mended. One day, the pilot disappeared, having been taken in the night by Resistance workers who had come up from the south.

When the war ended, Sipke was seventeen years old. Each of his three brothers had married, moving out of his parents' farmhouse and into homes of their own, but Sipke had a longing to see the world. He studied languages, English, French and German at the university in Groningen, and after he had finished his schooling, he went to London. There, in the evenings, he wandered the museums, which were free and warm. In one, there was an exhibition of Robert Capa's photographs. He saw the famous Spanish Civil War soldier, arms flung out in the moment of death; across the room, in the grainy photos of the D-Day landing at Normandy, Allied soldiers, munitions on their backs, laboured through the water. Night after night, he returned to this gallery, he sat on a bench and stared at the images for hours at a time. Walking home under the street lamps, through the crowds of people, he came to believe that only in stillness, only if he were able to step outside of time, could he begin to make sense of the world.

For half a year, he worked as a window washer, saving enough money to buy a Leica. He travelled across England, then Europe, honing his skills, improving his English. In Berlin, he photographed gaunt, skeletal men, German POWs, walking home to their villages from labour camps in the Soviet Union. The pictures sold to a Dutch magazine, and he told the photo editor that he was willing to travel, ready to go anywhere. Shortly after, he was offered a job as a war photographer. A split-second decision, one that he did not hesitate over, and his life changed. Sipke sent a letter home, telling his mother that he was leaving for Indochina. She called the boarding house where he was staying, and tried, across the crackling lines, to persuade him to come home. How could he explain it? He needed to see things for himself, to know what he was capable of.

Later on, others told him that he had a gift; he was able to catch and distinguish the defining moment. When he was working, he had the sensation of walking into a deep tunnel, the edges of his body dissolving into the scene around him. Yet he was capable – he does not know how or why – of pulling something tangible from the deep. His photographs were picked up by *Elsevier*, *Life* and *Réalités*. He tried to follow Robert Capa's famous dictum: "If your pictures aren't good enough, you aren't close enough." It was the golden age of photojournalism, and the magazines and newspapers were hungry for images. In Indochina and afterwards, in Algeria, South Africa and Indonesia, he ceased to feel hunger or fear. He felt that his life was precariously balanced, and all he did to prevent his fall was click the shutter, this sound more real to him than his own heartbeat. For twelve years, he travelled from assignment to assignment, living without a fixed address. In Algeria, he photographed the mutilated bodies of men and women who had been tortured and killed, by guerillas, by the FLN or *colon vigilante* units. He photographed two small children, crawling through the bombed wreckage of their home; and then, that same day, in a neighbouring village, an entire family who had been murdered, in retaliation, by a mob. He felt as if a part of his mind was decaying, he was ashamed of the pictures that he took, and he was confused by their beauty. A dead child abandoned in a field, his face unmarked, the light on his skin. Tiny flowers rising between his fingers.

Nothing made sense, and he tried to separate himself from his emotions, focusing on the sights of his camera to dull the turmoil, the sickness. *The only possible negotiation is war*, François Mitterrand's famous line, rang in his ears, and he knew he was witnessing the destruction of the middle ground. By the time he left Algeria, the estimated casualties stood between three hundred thousand and a million. Everywhere he went, he held his camera to his eyes and saw only the dead.

His first memory of beauty was when the Canadian pilot had fallen into the fields, wrapped in his silk parachute, and since that day, he had tried to recapture what he felt, staring up at the sky. *I am watching you*, he had thought, running across the grass. *You must be alive, because I am watching you*.

Exhausted, he accepted an assignment from *Elsevier* to travel to Indonesia and shoot a photo essay: Borobudur, dancers in Bali, Khrushchev's visit to the capital. It was 1963. One morning, walking through a slum in Jakarta, he gave a few cents to a fortune teller who offered to read his future. She warned him that his gift would disappear. "Not this year or the next," she said. "But somehow you will lose your talents. You will receive something of great value in return."

Sipke tells all this to Gail as he drives her from Amsterdam towards the north, to his home in Ysbrechtum, in Friesland. Gail Lim is a young woman, perhaps in her late thirties. The first thing he noticed about her, at her friend Harry Jaarsma's apartment, was her smile, which seemed to travel across the room and push him lightly in the chest. She had opened the door, her eyes brightening immediately. They went out to his car, and she carried only a small, old-fashioned suitcase and a canvas bag over her shoulder.

Driving, now, he talks about the three thousand kilometres of fortifications that surround the country, protecting it from the sea. They pass the gleaming propellers of the new windmills, the neat rows of poplars lined up like sentries to buffer the wind. When they cross the Afsluitdijk, and the North Sea opens to the west, she says that the landscape is hypnotic. Their car runs down the highway as if they are moving across the beautiful flatness of the ocean itself. "This is a country so small," he tells her, "that on a map it must write its name upon the sea." She is a good listener, she allows him to talk, to ramble, until he runs out of words. An hour and a half, and the highway has already carried them far north, to fields and shining canals. "When I was a boy," Sipke says, "I would ride my bicycle on the farm roads. I would open my arms and use my coat as a sail to catch the wind."

He asks about her schedule, and Gail tells him that she is not due to fly home to Vancouver until Thursday. She has arranged for a rental car and will drive herself back to Amsterdam. He counts the days in his head. "Three days to see this part of the country," he says.

He reaches into his shirt pocket and takes out a small black-and-white photograph showing Ani and Wideh, standing at the train station in Heerenveen, on the day that Wideh left home to begin university.

"My wife and son," Sipke says. For the last thirty years he has thought of Wideh as his own child, and the word comes out before he realizes his mistake.

Gail does not seem to notice. She takes the photo from him, and her expression as she studies it is intent.

She is waiting for him to continue, Sipke knows, but he keeps driving, unable to speak. The realization takes root in his mind: she has not come because of Wideh. It was Ani she asked about over the phone, Ani whose story she wishes to hear. The photograph remains in her hands.

On the side of the highway, they pass an abandoned

farmhouse with the words, painted in blue across the wooden slats, "Too much ocean."

His wife was fifty-seven years old when she died of ovarian cancer. At first, the disease had seemed under control, and then, when illness came, it was so sudden. She had told him that she wished to be buried under a tree, and so he scattered her ashes around the willow in their backyard. Wideh had come home and stayed for half a year. Then the boy, now a man, had left again. He had Sipke's restlessness in him, and the world was calling.

Before she died, the radiation had weakened Ani, causing her hands to tremble; she could not hold a pen or write a sentence. In her patched white housecoat, she would sit beside him at the kitchen table. She dictated her letters to him, and Sipke wrote them out in his own neat script. He and Ani had moved easily between Dutch, English and Indonesian; they had many languages within their reach. When they were younger, the exchange of words, of ideas, was important. But later, less so. He believes that the human body has some other means of communicating, some way that is yet to be categorized by science, or by language itself. Two people can swim in the same memories, the same dreams; that is how it had become for him and Ani.

He had written down her words on paper: letters to Wideh, to the Dertiks and Frank Postma, to friends in Sandakan and Jakarta.

When Ani died, his world had come to an end. In the days that followed, he sat in his living room, staring out at the canal, the great willows, and felt as if he, too, were passing into a kind of darkness. Outside, the days and nights went on, school children went by on their bicycles, but he chose to stand still. He did not want time to pull him away from the centre of his life. Wideh called every night, and sometimes, across the long-distance lines, they simply sat together, without needing to speak. He was comforted by his son's presence. He would fall asleep with the phone cupped to his ear.

One day, he took up Ani's correspondence again. It was like reaching for air. There were one or two people who did not know, would have no way of knowing, that she had died. From Sandakan, her friends Mas and Halim still sent the occasional letter. In his grief, he had not written them. She was not dead to him. He could not live with such a reality. Instead of writing of Ani's illness, he had simply continued Ani's letters as if she were still pacing behind him, dictating the words. To Sipke, the letters, her continued existence, seemed one of the few things in his life that was right.

Two nights ago, when the telephone rang and the young woman, Gail Lim, had said her name, he had felt as if decades of his life had collapsed, returned him to that time long ago in Jakarta. Now that Matthew's daughter is here, he has made a promise to himself, he will try to tell her all that he knows is true.

Standing in Jaarsma's apartment, her luggage beside her, Gail experiences an unexpected wave of feeling when Sipke Vermeulen takes her hand and says his name. She senses that she is not a stranger to him, but someone known.

Now, in the car, she glances at Sipke, who talks continuously, filling the air with a stream of words. His hair is almost completely white, grand and windswept, and he keeps his scarf on against the chill. The expression on his face is open and kind. He tells her that, next year, he will celebrate his seventy-fifth birthday.

An hour and a half later, Sipke turns down a country road and they pull alongside a house with a high, red roof, surrounded by farmland. To their right, a tidy lawn opens onto a garden. In the cold, the branches of the trees appear crystallized.

"This is our house," Sipke says.

He looks as if he wants to say something more, but then he takes her suitcase from the car and together they go up the front walk, where he stands briefly, searching for his keys. When he finds them, he unlocks the door, pushing it open.

They pass through a foyer and then into a sitting room where the walls are covered with photographs. This house does not feel like a place of absence, as Gail realizes she had come to expect. There are pictures of canals, a field of devastatingly green maize, a windmill that appears to be floating on the water. Among the landscapes are pictures of a woman and a child. Ani Vermeulen, she knows, and their son, Wideh. "These are *your* photographs," Gail says quietly, more to herself than to Sipke.

"Yes. They go back many years."

She returns to the front door, slips her shoes off, and re-enters. Slowly, she walks along the wall. For a long time, her gaze lingers on the boy, Wideh, captured from childhood to adulthood. She is absorbed by his face, the serious eyes. In one photo, he gazes at a heron facing him, the two standing opposite one another in the grass. Her eyes fall on a portrait of Ani Vermeulen; she is in a café somewhere, not in Holland, perhaps in Asia, light filtering in through horizontal blinds. She appears to be in her twenties, and she is turning her face away as she laughs. Light and shadow play across the picture, across her face, and the portrait is so tender that Gail feels as if she is trespassing into a territory that is both private and revered.

Sipke comes to stand beside her. He indicates a photo, and Gail recognizes a much older Ani, sitting on the grass with her son. "Before, when Ani was here, we kept the walls bare, because she always liked to have a sense of openness, of space. But afterwards, after she died," he stops, his hands clasped together. "I wanted the house to mirror what was in my thoughts." He looks past her, towards the photos, then meets her gaze again. "It was seven years ago that she passed away. In 1992."

When Gail looks into his eyes, she feels as if no time has passed for him. A breath of grief moves through her.

Sipke picks up her suitcase, and she follows him into a

bedroom at the back of the house with a view of the farmland. They admire the landscape together. The sun, bright
and full, is just beginning to slip below the horizon. "I will
leave you to rest," he says. "We will have dinner at seven?"

She nods, takes his hand, and thanks him.

On the bookshelf in her room is a clear jar, filled with
shining marbles. There are kites suspended from the ceiling,
and as she walks they brush delicately against the top of her
head. The hideaway of a young boy. Wideh's room.

She lies down on the bed, on top of the covers, fatigued
by the long drive north. From her bag, she removes the copy
of Sullivan's diary, stares at the lines for a time. Somewhere
in the house, a television or radio comes on, and she can hear
the smooth tones of a woman's voice. Gail closes her eyes,
and in her memory the light of a television screen flickers in
a dark room. Her father sleeps in an armchair, she has found
him there, and the room is quiet but for the sound of his
breathing. Outside the window, the branches of the tall trees
are outlined in morning light. She can see the clouds moving
steadily across the sky, and she cannot shake the sensation
that they are adrift on a boat at sea.

She turns onto her back, rests the pages against her chest.

When she opens her eyes, she sees a photograph on the
bedside table. In it, Ani Vermeulen is much older, and her
hair is tinged with grey. Her eyes, dark and shimmering, are
focused on something, someone, that Gail cannot see. Her

expression is that of a person catching sight of herself in a mirror, half surprised, half relieved to see the face in front of her.

~

Over a dinner of potatoes and kale, Sipke watches her eyes as they move from photograph to photograph. He tells her that he had arrived in Jakarta in 1963, on assignment for a Dutch magazine.

Gail is sitting across the table from him. Her dark hair is pulled back, gathered at the nape of her neck, and her face, trusting, is pale in the candlelight. She asks, "Why photography?"

He sets down his fork and takes a sip of wine, thinking. "I started taking pictures when I was very young. I felt, then, that a photograph could change the way events transpired. The photograph is revealing, it triggers something that you know, a truth that you haven't yet found a way to express. I saw what was happening around me, and I wanted to change it." He stops and says, only now remembering, "That was a question that Ani asked me, too. You see, after I arrived in Jakarta, I gave up war photography. I went into portraiture, for a time. That's how I first met her."

"Was Ani a photographer, too, then?"

He shakes his head. "She worked in the studio because it was a living."

Outside, the wind picks up, and a sound, like low whistling, moves between the trees. Gail looks towards the window, as if to catch the movement with her eyes before it disappears. "My father knew her once. I think it was when they were children, during the war."

For a moment, he remains silent, unsure how to answer. "Perhaps I should start at the beginning of what I know," he says. "I should start with Ani's life in Jakarta."

She nods, gratefully. "Have you ever met my parents, Sipke?"

"No, I have not." He looks up at the wall, at a photo of Wideh taken when he was just eleven years old. He is sitting at a table, oblivious to the camera, moving his hands across the map laid open before him, one elbow leaning on North America, one hand curved around the islands of Indonesia. "But you are right. Ani knew your father. She knew of you, too, once, a long time ago."

As twilight fades behind them, Sipke tells Gail that he has not been back in Jakarta for almost forty years. In the letters from Wideh, from Ani's friends Saskia and Siem Dertik, he hears of a place that is at once foreign and familiar. Street names, coffee shops, places he thought were lodged forever in his memory, the sharpness of his recollection has been ground down by the passing of time. But the important places, Jalan Kamboja, the photography studio and Ani's apartment above, all of these remain distinct, as if he could turn a corner and find himself there again.

When he arrived in Jakarta, he was thirty-five years old. The war of independence between Indonesia and the

Netherlands had ended more than ten years before, but the hostilities had not ceased. Still the paint could be seen on the occasional bank or business, *Dutch Get Out, Indos Go Home.*

One day, while photographing along one of the main canals, he happened by a photography studio on a busy street. There was a sign in the window, *Te koop*, and without thinking, he pushed open the door and walked inside. The owner, Frank Postma, was Dutch, and the language fell reassuringly on Sipke's ears. He told Sipke the asking price, barely six hundred Dutch guilders, for the studio and the small apartment beside it. It wasn't the money, Postma had said, showing him the well-kept studio, and then the darkroom. He wanted to return to Amsterdam, to live once more in the city of his birth. The living space, though small, looked comfortable. Gesturing towards the ceiling, Postma said that a young woman and her son lived in the apartment upstairs. For the last six years, she had worked for him, developing negatives, and she was helpful and skilled. Sipke had left, walking for hours along the canals. He stayed awake most of the night, and in the morning he returned and told Frank Postma that he would buy the studio.

He went into portraiture, keeping Ani on as his assistant. In the darkroom, working with his back to her, he was so absorbed in his own thoughts that he sometimes forgot she was there. He thought that the sound of running tap water, of the pouring of chemicals, came from his own hand. She was a young mother, with beautiful, curious eyes and a gift for languages. Malay was her mother tongue, and she had learned English in school. The scattering of Dutch spoken in the portrait studio, and on the street, had proved no obstacle to her. Ani was reserved and thoughtful, but sometimes, in the evenings, he heard the sound of her laughter drifting through the ceiling. Her son, Wideh, was nine years old, polite, fiercely protective of his mother.

On the other side of the world, it was winter in the Netherlands. His mother wrote long, poetic letters describing their lives, and the lives of his brothers' families. The canals had frozen, she said, and the Elfstedentocht, a skating race on the canals of Friesland, was taking place for the first time since 1956. Outside, the children tied their skates, their *houtjes*, to the soles of their shoes, just as Sipke himself had done when he was young. If he closed his eyes, did he still see the wide sky, the tumult of clouds? He reread the letter again and again, as if through it he could enter the life he had once known.

He had moved into the ground-floor apartment, and each night, beneath the mosquito net, Sipke fell asleep to the whirr of the fan, his sleep heavy and dreamless. *Elsevier* offered him an assignment that would bring him back to Europe, to photograph life alongside the newly constructed Berlin Wall, but he felt indecisive, as if he were in some kind of stupor. He could not bring himself to venture out of Jakarta. He applied for a residence permit and was granted a one-year stay.

In Freedom Square, electricity was skimmed away from the houses and shops and directed to Sukarno's monument. As electricity faltered across the rest of Jakarta, the monument shone in the night, luminous. At the very top of the column was an effigy of the president. According to rumours, Sukarno's fortune teller had told him that he would die when his statue was set on top of the column, and so he had decreed it would not be finished until his death.

During the day, while Wideh was at school, Ani took care of appointments and bookkeeping. Each morning, the boy kissed his mother goodbye and fell in line behind the other children, with their satchels and neatly combed hair, walking to the nearby primary school. When school let out, he sat with Ani at a desk in the studio, the radio a whisper behind them. Wideh explained to her very seriously whatever he had learned that day, the nature of clouds or the cycle of rainfall. When Sipke addressed him, the boy said, in Dutch, "*Praat u tegen mij?*" Are you talking to me?

In the darkroom, she was always an arm's length away. Under the pale glow of the lamps, occupied by work, they found it easy to speak about personal things. Early on, he asked her what kind of man Wideh's father had been.

"A good man," she had said. "We were both young, and we had known each other since we were children. It was natural to fall in love."

"Does he live in Indonesia now?"

She said that she did not know where he was. "I left before Wideh was born and came here on my own. He never knew the real reason why I had left Sandakan. Afterwards, I no longer knew how to change what had happened. It is better this way."

"A mistake?" he asked gently.

She shook her head. After a moment, she said, "I think, in some ways, we will always be attached."

A year passed, and Sipke renewed his residence permit. They began to take their meals together. At night, while Wideh worked through his multiplication tables, they sat in Ani's apartment. There, on the second floor, they seemed to step away from the city below. She told him that both her parents had died during the war and that a part of herself still lived and breathed in Sandakan. "It must be difficult for you," she said, "living in Jakarta. Being so far away from your family."

He nodded. "My brothers still live in the village where I grew up. I suppose I've always been the restless one, the person who longs to go away, to see the world."

"Yet you stay here, in Jakarta."

"How can I explain it? Sometimes I feel as if time has stopped. As if I've stepped back from my life, because I don't know where I'm going."

"There's danger in thinking like that."

"What kind of danger?"

"Because time continues," she said. "Because this moment, this place, is real."

When the studio was busy, they would work into the evenings, after Wideh had gone to sleep. They unwound the film in the dark, the can opener, reel and tank laid in a tidy row between them. Once, she told him about a journey she had made when she was a child, from Kalimantan to British North Borneo. How her father traded with different peoples along the way, providing rattan and jungle produce, bird's nests, and so on. He knew the names of different trees and flowers, of birds and insects. "He was a merchant, just as his father was. My grandfather used to sell skins to the British and Dutch who came to Borneo. They wanted everything. Beetles. Many kinds of butterflies. Frogs, civets, birds of paradise. He had this great store of knowledge. When he died, I was only ten years old, and he had taught me only a small part of what he knew." She held the reel in her hands, turning it thoughtfully. "I told Wideh about his own father not long ago. It's a difficult thing for a child to understand, and yet he seems to accept it. He has not asked about it since."

"I was in Jesselton once," Sipke said. "In North Borneo. I was waiting for a boat that would take me to Phnom Penh."

"Yes, Jesselton is the capital now."

He turned and brought the developing lights up.

"What is it that drew you to it?" she asked. "Going to distant places. Photographing wars. I suppose many people find it exciting."

"Some people, yes. Excitement, adrenaline. Maybe, once, I felt the same."

He poured the developer into the tank and covered it. They did not speak for several minutes, and then he said, "There is a very famous picture of a man walking towards a house with kerosene and a torch. The house is barred, and there's a family inside. You can't see them in the photograph. It's a dirt road, and there is a mob behind him."

"The man has a cut above his eye."

He nodded, surprised. "Where did you see it?"

"It was in the newspapers. I still remember the expression on the man's face."

"The mob thought the father was a collaborator, so they set fire to the house and waited for the family to come out."

Ani had been removing a roll of film, and now her hands stilled over the canister, her body tensing. For a moment, he did not want to continue, felt that he would hurt her somehow. He said, "It was in Algiers. There were other photographs. Of the man who tried to escape from the house, and of his family."

She said nothing.

Sipke continued, trying to explain himself to her. "The mob surrounded them. I was down on the ground and I begged, in French, in English, for the men to back off, not to go further. And then when it became clear that this family would be killed and nothing I said could stop it, I picked up my camera and I photographed it. I thought, I can't look away now. I don't have the right to turn away.

"Afterwards, no one wanted to publish what I had seen. I had failed to compose a picture, something whole that could make sense of the pieces. The pictures were senseless, gruesome. A bloodstained hand, a face. But the man with the kerosene and torch became famous. That photograph is different, it's alive. It's the last good photograph I have taken, but I can't bear to look at it. I keep asking myself, what happens when the context is lost and only the image remains? People look at that picture now, in magazines and books, and they speculate about it. They don't know what happened before or after. All they see is this one moment, disconnected from the past or the future. It feeds their imagination, but it doesn't give them knowledge."

Ani looked at him, and he felt that she could see into the core of his memories, to the emotions that overwhelmed him, even now.

"Perhaps you are asking too much of a picture."

He shook his head. "The picture shows us that this suffering is made by people, and because it is made by us, it is not inevitable. That was the reason I wanted to be a photographer." Carefully, he mixed a stop bath and poured it into the spout. His hands trembled and the liquid spilled. "There is something that I've always remembered. The war photographer George Rodger's response to Bergen-Belsen. He was one of the first to enter the camp after Liberation. He said that he walked through the camp, saw thousands of bodies and was horrified. He wanted people to confront what had happened, he wanted to compose photographs that could never be forgotten, and so he arranged the bodies, moved arms and legs. Afterwards, he swore he would never take another war picture as long as he lived."

"And then, what happens when people know?"

He met her gaze, unable to answer.

She told him, then, that she had found her father's body on the airfield in Sandakan, and she had been unable to carry him home, to bury him. She remembered that when the Allies finally arrived in Sandakan, in September 1945, they found people whose homes were gone, whose crops had failed, and who, even though the war was over, would still die of starvation and disease. What good did it do, after all, to remember, she said, to hold on to the past, if the most crucial events in life could not be changed? What good did memory do if one could never make amends?

She turned away from him, towards the sink, taking the chemicals she had mixed and adding them to the tank. "There was a time when I tried to imagine that things could arrange themselves in a different order," she said, "because I couldn't bear the thought that the past was irrevocable." She paused, looking down at the liquid. "Are there days you wish you could erase from your life?"

It took him only a moment to answer. "I would forget that day in Algeria, if I could."

She nodded. "If it were possible, perhaps I would do it, too. Not only my memories of the war, but the things that I regret. But how much would be enough?" she said. "Would I recognize the point at which I had gone too far, when I was changing so much that I was losing more than I imagined possible?"

They went to the Pondok Restaurant, the *kedai kopi* across the street. The road was crowded with people, motorbikes weaving between cars. The *betjak* drivers gathered at the far end of Jalan Kamboja. They lined up behind one another, carrying their own tin plates and bowls, wiping their faces clean with handkerchiefs as they waited their turn at the food stalls. Ani told him about the forests outside of Sandakan, how some of the trees were as high as 150 feet. When you looked up at the canopy, the outstretched branches did not overlap, they formed an intricate pattern of dark and light, of leaves and air. Those trees, she told him, were the height of an eighteen-storey building. Wideh had calculated it for her one evening, an exercise in mathematics.

She smiled. "I must have been seven years old. My father took me to the forest, because the largest trees were flowering and this happened only once every ten years. I had never seen it before. When the flowers fall, they fall in such great quantity that they cover everything on the ground. They pile up in the same way that snow piles up in cold places." Ani had walked through the petals. She remembered the feel of them covering her feet, shifting smoothly around her legs. "My father told me that there were insects who laid their eggs in the buds. After the flowers had fallen to the ground, the newborns emerged, covered with pollen, and then they flew away to other flowers in other trees. He said that the insects are so tiny that for them the air feels very thick. Flying for them is like swimming in water for us."

Sipke told her about his father's farm. At dawn each morning, he had walked across the open pastures where no trees grew that tall, the way Ani described them. He remembered the horizon, trees and barns miniature against the sky. The heavens were a dome. He described the heat of a cow's nose against his skin. They were curious animals; they would walk across the field to greet a visitor. He showed her photographs, glimmering canals, the geometric lines of a football game, the coastline of the North Sea. There was a game he had played with his brothers, *polsstok-springen*, in which they used a pole to leap across the canals.

He remembered running across the grass, planting the pole in the water and using it to propel his body through the air. At the height of the arc, he would press his body forward, urging the pole to begin its descent, and then at the perfect moment, leap off to the other side. She laughed when he told her about the wooden shoes he'd had as a boy, made of willow, how he had worn a hole in them from all his days walking in the fields.

Ani asked him, "What kind of future do you see, Sipke?"

Perhaps, somewhere in his body, he knew the direction of his life had changed. There was only one answer he could give her. "Your son growing up. You and I in the world beside one another."

"Yes," she said, and her voice was just a whisper to him. "I imagine that, too."

Outside of Sipke's house, the lines of the canal have blurred into the night. His words are suddenly gone, and some feeling, distant and almost forgotten, is hovering on the edges of his consciousness. The room seems very dim, and his knees ache more than usual. He gets up to turn on the lamp and the room immediately brightens. "Do you mind if I stop and make a pot of coffee?"

"No," Gail says. "Let me help."

She fills the percolator, and Sipke rummages in the fridge for some bread and cheese. He can hear frogs croaking in the canal, the faraway *hush* of cars. For a moment, he cannot remember how they arrived here, from which direction they came. He feels as if they are adrift in another time, another country.

"If it's difficult to talk about . . . ," she says.

Sipke looks at her standing at the counter, and her expression, so patient and watchful, reminds him of Wideh, the way he sat with his mother in the garden near the end of her life. Wideh would beguile with her stories. He would remain beside her, counting the birds at the feeder, the boaters drifting by along the canals, watching his mother's face as she slept, as day by day the world grew quiet.

"I love to say her name," he tells Gail. "After she died, our friends told me that I had to go on, that I couldn't remain in the past. But when I think of Ani, so much of myself, my own life, comes back to me."

They stand together, sipping their coffee, and he remembers how Ani would come home from the market, her bicycle laden with groceries. Her skin smelled both sweet and cold. He used to wake in the night, open his eyes to find how she had wrapped herself around his body, as if to follow him into the world of his dreaming.

People hold other lives inside them, this is what Sipke believes. When Ani died, her friends and loved ones had gathered together, and in the stories they told, he had felt her presence again, more palpably than in his own familiar memories.

The three years in Jakarta will always remain another life inside him, untouched by future events. In the streets of the city, he had felt himself to be a foreigner, a stranger, but with

Ani, in her apartment, they had created a kind of sanctuary for themselves. One part of his life had come to an end, and another, richer, more surprising, opened before him. "Are you married?" he says, meeting Gail's eyes.

She says no, but she tells him she has been with Ansel for almost a decade.

"In Jakarta, everything in my life changed. There was something about the way we were together that was, that felt, essential." He stops, searching for the words.

"Necessary," she says. Her face is turned away from him, and he cannot see her expression.

"Yes," he says, nodding. He follows her gaze towards the darkened fields. "Yes, like that."

He had been in Jakarta for over two years, he tells Gail, and Ani and Wideh had become the centrepoint of his life. He would make dinner each night while Ani helped her son with his studies. In the evenings they walked to Freedom Square, or to the nearby park to watch the kite flyers, to be a part of the crowd. Business in the portrait studio was steady, and for a while he had felt as if he could stay there forever, that the peace in his life and in this country would hold. But by 1965 the political and economic situation in Indonesia had grown precarious. A quarter of the population in Jakarta were squatters, more coming in each day from the surrounding countryside. There were guerillas in the villages and a rising dissatisfaction. The papers hinted that President

Sukarno was terminally ill. In private conversations, people wondered how much longer before the government splintered. How strong was the army. To Sipke, it seemed that only Wideh remained untouched by the turmoil. The boy spent hours gazing at maps, leafing through the heavy atlas that Ani had given him for his birthday. At night, lit by the glow of a kerosene lamp, he played marbles by himself, rolling them across the tiled floor.

He remembers the three of them sitting in the upstairs apartment, all the lights off, windows flung wide to let in the breeze. Ani's apartment was only one room, divided by curtains into a sleeping area and a kitchen. Her bed was a thin mattress that during the day she kept behind the divan. Outside, pedicabs jostled in the road.

One night, as he stood gazing out at the traffic, Sipke listened to the sound of Wideh whispering a story in Indonesian, a traditional folk tale, to his mother. "In the beginning of the world," he said, "there was the sea and the sky, and a single bird who had nowhere to rest. He flew from east to west, searching for a breeze to hold him aloft. One night, exhausted, falling through the clouds, he came up with a plan. And when morning came, he provoked a terrible quarrel between the sea and the sky."

Wideh was lying on his side as he spoke, on his cot in the far side of the room. Ani sat next him, the mosquito net sheltering them both. The child seemed utterly contented. Sipke was reminded of something Ani had told him once, about the crater in Sandakan where she would go. How, when she was a child, this scar in the earth had been a place of safety.

"I don't know what the quarrel was, but the sea was very angry. She raged and paced and shouted curses at the sky. Waves touched the clouds, and when they fell, they crashed into the sea like drums.

"The sky, too, raged and wept. Night after night, he threw boulders down upon the sea. For months on end, the sea and the sky stormed, and at the end of it all, when the quiet came, many islands were standing on the water. The bird flew from one to the next, very satisfied with his cleverness."

When Wideh fell asleep, Ani got up carefully. She lit a kerosene lamp and they sat beside one another at the window, whispering so as not to disturb the child. She asked him, "What stories do you remember, Sipke?"

"Stories," he said, almost as a question.

"When your mother sat at your bedside, and you could hear the wind on the farmhouse windows . . ."

He smiled. "There is something that I remember. *Nooit vergeet je de taal waarin je moeder van je hield.* Translated it means, Never do you forget the language in which your mother loved you."

As he spoke, Sipke felt he could see her thoughts lifting away from them, trace their trajectory across the night sky. To where? he wondered. To North Borneo, to Sandakan. "Frisian words, Frisian phrases," he said, continuing. "I remember waking up each morning, opening the curtains, and seeing my father in the fields. My mother going out to meet him. It isn't the country that I miss, but the person I was then. I used to be afraid to go home and find that everything had changed, that I no longer belonged there."

She nodded. "Every year that goes by makes it more difficult to return."

Outside, vendors called their wares, pushing carts and trolleys around the potholes, through the crowds of people idling on the sidewalk.

They sat in silence for a few moments, and then he said, "If things keep going as they are, I may be forced to leave Indonesia. My papers may be revoked. I haven't made any plans, but I've been thinking —"

"Do you really believe it will come to that?"

"Those are the rumours."

"But only rumours."

"Ani," he said, "would you consider leaving Jakarta?"

She lifted her eyes, and he could sense her surprise, her confusion.

"Come with me," he said. "I'll arrange everything."

"It's the other side of the world, Sipke."

"Come with me."

He had the sense she could see something that he did not. "We could," she said, finally. "Perhaps it could be possible."

That night, they fell asleep together, Ani gathered in his arms.

In the morning, they woke to the sound of rifles. People fighting or celebrating, it was hard to tell which. They did not go downstairs or open the studio. On the radio, a commentator described how, here in Jakarta, rioters had set fire to the British embassy in protest over the proclamation of the new Malaysia. This was *konfrontasi*, the commentator said, and Indonesia must stand firm against the threat of British imperialism.

Outside, demonstrators gathered, a sea of black caps, of *pitjis*, growing in number as the morning wore on. Banners printed with slogans, *In the name of Allah Ever Onward No Retreat*. Wideh, a sarong tied around his waist, gazed down at the crowds, his bare shoulders, slender and fragile, leaning dangerously out the window. He had been examining one of Sipke's cameras and now he held it to his eye. He moved slowly, framing shot after shot, practising without ever touching the shutter release.

On the radio, one official after another denounced the presence of British and Australian troops in North Borneo. Malaysia, they said, was a threat to Indonesian independence, an incitement to war. Sipke switched off the set. The floor seemed to tremble as the angry crowd marched, chanting. An effigy of the prime minister of Malaysia was set alight, and the smell of burning cut through the air. He and Ani moved as if in a dream, washing the dishes, cleaning the floors. Outside, they heard what sounded like firecrackers or gunshots.

At noon, when they sat down to a meal of rice and curry, Wideh still wore the camera around his neck. While they ate, Sipke began to talk about setting the light metre, adjusting the depth of field, the basics of composition. "The first pictures I took," he told Wideh, in broken Indonesian, "were landscapes, because I was too shy to speak to anyone. Later on, an older photographer gave me advice. He said that if I was patient, if I waited, then people would forget the camera. Another part of them would drift up into view."

Wideh surprised him by saying that he had been studying Sipke's contact sheets. "What I wish for," he said, politely, in English, "is to have a roll of film of my own."

Sipke reached into his pocket, and placed a small plastic canister on the table between them. Wideh was ten years old. Below, the noise of the protests grew in volume, waves of sound cascading along the narrow streets. Wideh took the canister in his hand, the way Sipke and his brothers used to hold precious stones, newborn birds, or treasures unearthed from the depths of the canals.

That night, Sipke sat up with Ani beside the radio. The light from the street lamps wavered, occasionally cutting out. "The West can help us," a speaker said. He sounded like an older man, perhaps one who had fought in the wars of the last two decades. "But they must let us find our own way; and the best it can do is to set examples and help us to reach up to them. It should not be concerned whether our director of agriculture or education or health is a Communist or a Nationalist: that is our affair. If you honestly want to help us, you must not ask questions. You must not demand that we love you. You must earn our respect and then learn to return it."

Sipke watched her eyes. To him, they were full of anxiety, her fingers adjusting the dial as she listened to the voice distorted by static. The curtain had not been closed, and on the other side of the room, Wideh was still visible, asleep behind the mosquito net.

Together they lifted her mattress out from behind the divan and set it on the floor, then she lay down, leaving a space beside her.

Soon, she said, she would celebrate her thirtieth birthday, she would be older than her parents had been when they died. She spoke openly, her thoughts spilling free in a way he had not heard before. She told him that, often, her thoughts returned to Sandakan, that the pull of home had not diminished. She still imagined going back there some day. It was the place where her parents were buried. In the war, so many lives had been destroyed, others forever altered. Even if she tried, she could not measure what she had lost, or know what she had never attempted. In 1953, when she left Sandakan, she had carried a single hope, that Wideh would be one of this new, modern generation. That he would make his way in the world, unhindered, free to make his own destiny.

Afterwards, he remained by the window while she drifted to sleep. So many voices rose up, carried by the heat and air, a ghostly sound, moving against the walls.

In the house, the phone rings. Gail does not start, but Sipke's hands jump out in front of him, instinctually, towards the sound. He takes the receiver, turns his face to the darkened window. "Sipke Vermeulen."

It is Joos, from the farmhouse down the road.

Gail stands up, puts her hands on her hips and tilts her upper body to one side and then the other. She walks into the kitchen. Sipke can hear the refrigerator door opening and swishing shut. Two glasses filling with water.

He finds himself in a rambling conversation with Joos about a kind of bird that seems to have disappeared from the Netherlands. "We saw them when we were boys, didn't we?" Joos says, in his usual mournful voice. "*Ooievaars*, swooping across the fields. And now they've disappeared to some other country. Probably Norway or Canada, like everyone else. Even so, this country is so crowded, Sipke. When we die they will have to bury us standing upright."

After he finally manages to comfort Joos, Sipke asks Gail if she would like to go for a walk. Smiling, she agrees, and they bundle themselves in big coats and pull on woollen toques. Outside, there's the sound of wind moving through the banks of reeds and the swaying alders. As they walk, he tells her that Wideh lives in Jakarta now. "He is a photojournalist. Perhaps, later on, you would like to see some of his work."

"Yes, I would love that."

A light snow begins to fall. Gradually, she tells him about her documentaries, about Ansel and the life that they share in Vancouver.

"And your Ansel," Sipke says. "He also works in radio?"

"He's a doctor, a pulmonary specialist."

"Ah, wonderful. And you have children."

They curve along the water's edge. "No, not yet."

"One day?"

"Maybe one day." His questions seem to relax a reserve in her and she begins to talk. She tells him that she had seen his letter one day at her parents' house, the letter telling her father of Ani's death. "Hers was a name my parents both knew," Gail says, "and between them, it seemed to have a meaning, a weight."

She says that she held on to the memory as if it were a touchstone, something that could anchor her. She knows, has always believed, that there is a secret that has coloured her life, her childhood. In the last few months, she has felt as if, day by day, she is losing her footing. There are fissures, openings, that she no longer knows how to cover over.

They are surrounded by darkness, lights from the distant farmhouses just visible. Her face, so reminiscent of Wideh, is filled with yearning.

"And so you came here," he says, "looking for an answer to your questions."

For a long time, she looks at the ice that is beginning to form in the canal, the silvery sheen of the surface. "I don't know," she says, finally. "Perhaps I'm looking for an answer that isn't real. That doesn't exist."

He closes his eyes, opens them again, sees the snow disappearing in her hair.

They continue walking, and their path takes them back along the road, past the sweep of farmland that divides each property here. They come in sight of Sipke's house, where he has left a single light burning.

Inside, after they have shed their layers of coats and scarves, Gail tends to the fire. Then, he and Gail sit down once more, across from each other at the kitchen table.

Between them, Sipke has laid out a handful of black-and-white photos: the studio, Ani and Wideh at the harbour in Sunda Kelapa, the canal that runs along Jalan Kamboja. He tells her that, by mid-1965, Indonesia was on the brink of collapse. Sukarno was ill, it seemed. Possibly dying. Already the speculation was rife as to which faction – the army, the Communists, or Darul Islam – would set the inevitable coup in motion. Sipke's request to extend his residence permit had been denied, and he had been given three months to leave the country.

"It was in June of that year," he says, "when Ani received a letter from Canada, from your father, saying that he wished to see her."

Sipke watches Gail as he speaks, more than anything not wanting to injure her. All her movements are stilled, but she does not look away.

"Some time later, Ani told me something that I've always remembered. She said that it was your mother who had encouraged your father to travel to Jakarta. She asked him to go, to find what he needed to know, believing that the truth was capable of bringing about a change in all their lives."

Gail picks up a photograph from the table, and in her hands it appears fragile, aged, the edges curving up.

The photo catches the light, and Sipke sees Wideh, just a child, kneeling on the ground in Ani's apartment in Jakarta, carefully setting up a game of marbles. His hands reach out towards the small glass spheres, but the aperture is narrow, and only his face is clear and in focus. In the foreground, the marbles blur like stars. Gail lifts her face, meeting his eyes, and she holds his gaze silently. What he sees in her face is not hurt, not anger. Her expression reminds him of Wideh's face on the day Sipke taught him to develop his own negatives, how the boy had clutched the film in his hands, watching the lines come clear, grow together. As if a shadow, a darkness, was becoming more than its form, as if something barely glimpsed had now been breathed into life.

After a moment, she says, "How old is Wideh now?"

"Next month he will turn forty-five."

At first, because she does not respond, he thinks she has not heard him. But then she sets the photo down. Outside, the snow has painted the darkness white. He can hear the low whistling of the wind.

"When I was a child," she says, "my father had just one ritual. He would gather us into the car each Sunday, my mother in the passenger seat and me in the back, and we would drive away from our house, towards downtown, the ocean. He loved the city at night. When he was a student at university, my father studied history. He thought he would teach one day, but that never came to pass. The books are still there on the shelves, remnants of a different life. As we drove, he would keep up a running commentary, proudly pointing things out to me, to my mother. Naming the landmarks, wanting us to see the things he saw."

He reaches out his hand, and rests it on hers.

She says, "You said you would show me Wideh's photographs."

He gets up and leaves her for a moment. When he returns, he has an archival box containing tear sheets and prints, and he sets it on the table.

She rests her hands on the lid, but she does not open it. Exhaustion seems to shape the air around her.

"It's late," he says. "Perhaps we should rest."

"Yes." She is lost in her own thoughts. He can see her as a child, the car that winds back through the city, the same roads traced and retraced.

"Tomorrow, there is a place I would like to show you. I used to go there often with Ani and Wideh, a long time ago. It is called Schokland, and in the past it was an island, surrounded by the sea."

Slowly they gather the cups and dishes and set them in the sink. She smoothes the cloth on the table, then, leaning forward, her face young in the candlelight, she blows out the flames.

Sipke finds a place by the windows. When he closes his eyes, the morning humidity of Jakarta sits heavily, once more, on his skin. Outside, the first calls of the vendors are audible, the ringing of bells, makeshift carts clattering over the sidewalk.

That day when the letter from Matthew Lim arrived, Sipke had asked her what it was that she wished to do. "I don't know," she had said, over and over. But, along with the surprise that he saw, there was a thread of hope running through her, so fine as to be almost invisible. He could not help but see it.

Over the next month, he busied himself with things that needed to be done. He prepared to close the studio down and put the space up for sale. He sat for hours in the Dutch embassy, beside Indonesian mothers and grandmothers, flanked by the children they brought with them. Sipke took forms to one building to get stamped, another to get signed. To obtain departure permits for both Wideh and Ani, he visited as many as a dozen offices, continuously taking out his wallet and laying bills on the table. He returned to the Dutch embassy, took a number, and fell asleep under the tall windows.

He did not know if Ani had written to Wideh's father. He could not bring himself to ask the question, he tried to go on as if nothing had changed. He closed his eyes against her pain, because to acknowledge it would mean admitting the possibility that she would remain here, that she would allow him to leave and not follow.

One night, a few weeks after the letter had arrived, he and Ani stood at the window of their upstairs flat, looking down at the street. The power had been cut again and the kitchen taps were running only a muddy froth. The night was humid, and the air thin. He told her that their visas had been approved, that they could leave before the end of the dry season. "When we arrive in Amsterdam," he said, "I'll apply for citizenship for you and Wideh."

"I don't know if I can do this, Sipke."

A strange panic, one he had never known before, seized his chest. What was decided now would be unalterable. He bowed his head against hers. "The decision belongs to you," he said. "You do not need to be afraid."

In the days that followed, Sipke found ways to distract himself, to avoid Ani. He walked through the crowded market, along the canals, taking photographs of faces, of children laughing as they splashed in the water. Military exercises were taking place every hour, growing in intensity, blocking the roads. He had no ideas, no plans, only a feeling of deep foreboding. He papered up the windows of the studio, and taped a sign to the door. *Tutup.* Closed. *Gesloten.*

Each day, he left the apartment early and walked along Jalan Kamboja. Those who slept on the street were just beginning to wake. One morning, Sipke watched a woman and her two children, a boy and a girl, barefoot, in faded sarongs, washing themselves with the water that trickled from a pipe alongside a house. He had his camera with him. He held it to his eyes, framing the children in the view-finder, releasing the shutter a half-dozen times. The children cupped their hands together, catching the water patiently. Behind them, the paint was stained and peeling. The little girl watched him for a moment, then she stood up and ran towards him, followed by her brother. He was overwhelmed. Without thinking, he slipped a few rupiahs, all the money he carried, into their open hands.

That week, the paperwork for Ani's visa was concluded,

and he brought the documents home and showed them to her.

She said the words that he dreaded hearing. "Sipke, we are not coming with you."

For several seconds, he did not answer. "I'll stay, then," he said. "There must be some way."

She said that she had written to Wideh's father, and that she had decided to remain in Jakarta until his arrival. That much she must do for him. For herself. They both had to have the truth between them, to understand what had been lost, to know how to go forward. For the rest, she could only wait and see.

Fear rose up inside him, but most alarming to him, a feeling of acceptance that it could be no other way. *Sipke*, she said, but he left the apartment and went downstairs to the studio. The front windows were covered, but all the equipment remained in place. A line of negatives rested on the light box, waiting for him. There, in the half-light, he carried on working, trying to lose himself in the stillness of the room.

Ani let herself in. He was mixing chemicals in the bath, and he concentrated on the movements of his hands. They stood side by side, watching as he poured a measure of liquid into the tank.

There were photos scattered on the table. Sunset on the harbour at Sunda Kelapa, the tall masts of painted boats glowing, luminous. In the foreground, Wideh and Ani stood in the water, laughing as they looked up to see him.

She put her hand on his shoulder, the faintest touch, as if afraid he would turn away. She said that no choice existed for her.

That night, lying alone in his own apartment, unable to sleep, he got up and dressed quietly in the dark. Outside, he crossed the street and sat at a table in the *kedai kopi*. A man was coming along the road now, drunk and staggering. He was reciting poetry or singing a song. "Turn your heads as you pass," he said. "We shall die soon enough from a surfeit of words. We do not need the slow poison of your pity."

In the empty restaurant, Sipke closed his eyes and was back in Algiers, crawling on his hands and knees towards the man, the stranger. He had wanted the camera to speak for him, to make something out of this suffering that, in the end, could never be forgotten. But the photograph was only a shadow, a question waiting for a response, for someone else to take it in his hands and recognize all that it wished to say, all that it had failed to express. He wanted to call her down, to throw stones at the window, break the glass and tell her that for the rest of his life he would love her. He said her name over and over, but only the noise of the city answered.

He asked Ani if he could take a portrait of her, and she agreed. They went into the studio, which was almost empty now, ready for the new proprietor. Rain cascaded against the exterior walls. Ani wore a blue batik *kain* and *kebaya*, and the silk of the material was flecked with gold. Her hair was tied back, swept cleanly off her face so that it was her eyes that arrested you. He set his camera on the tripod, and framed her face in his view. They did not say anything to each other, and it came to him that their affair, what they had been to one another, had been redefined, had become another relationship entirely. A photographer and his subject, separate people in parallel worlds, and at the end of it all, no way that he knew to bring them together.

He laid all their papers on a table in the studio: visa documents, departure permits, plane tickets. "I would find some way to stay if you asked me to."

She took his hand, looking into his face, her body still. "I can't," she said. "That is the one thing I could never do." The space between them grew, expanding out, until she seemed as insubstantial, as ghostly as the dust in the light. She stepped away, releasing his hand so gently that he almost missed the moment when it slipped from his.

At the airport, the departure lounge was chaotic. Thousands of Indonesians, of expatriates, eager to leave the country. He was moved forward by the crowd, through the terminal, onto the tarmac, which blurred in the heat. He boarded the plane, carrying almost nothing, no extra clothes, no keepsakes. Only his cameras.

The airplane gathered speed on the runway. Alongside it, a hundred yards back, ran a dirt road lined by small huts. People were visible, crouched on the ground at makeshift kitchens, outdoor fires, their laundry drying under the hot sun, chickens scrabbling beneath papaya trees. The plane lifted into the air, and the thatched roofs gave way to the harbour, to the city and red-tiled houses, and then the swirling patterns of rice fields. "Peace go with you, Sipke," she had said when he left her, the traditional Indonesian words of parting. Peace remain. Below, he saw the tiny shadow of the plane growing smaller, until at the coastline it disappeared and all he could see was the reflection of the sun on the ocean. He closed his eyes. When he opened them again, a surface of clouds was all that remained, what was below had disappeared.

Early the next morning, Sipke and Gail drive south, out of the province of Friesland. The snow has stopped falling, but the ground is covered, a field of white. Through the mist, a pale, diffuse light falls to the ground, reminding her of a Rembrandt landscape. She looks for the horizon, trying to make out the dividing line between land and air, but one seems to run into the other, the snow having erased all distinction. Far away, on a lake that is not visible to her, there is a single boat sailing.

"This province we are entering, Flevoland," Sipke tells her, "was created in the 1930s, when a dike was built connecting North Holland to the province of Friesland, cutting the Southern Sea off from the North Sea, and thus from the Atlantic Ocean. When the water was pumped out, a new province was born.

"This road that we are driving on now," he says, one hand gesturing out the window, "was once the bottom of the sea floor. We have a famous saying here, God made the world, but the Dutch made Holland.

"The island of Schokland stayed where it was, but all around it, the water disappeared. One morning, it woke up to find itself a part of the continent again. An island sitting on a sea of land."

She peers out the window, and the flat fields rolling by are suddenly strange, miraculous.

Last night, she had remained awake, sifting through Wideh Vermeulen's photographs. One of the tear sheets was as recent as this year, a photo essay documenting the graves that had finally been opened in Jakarta and in villages across Indonesia. In the text that Wideh had written, accompanying the images, she read that even now, there is no agreement about what happened in 1965, who initiated the coup that took Sukarno from power, that placed Suharto in his stead. And there is no agreement over the number of people who died in the aftermath, a few hundred thousand, perhaps up to a million dead in the Communist purges. The facts of what happened have been covered in silence, lost in the passage of time.

The photographs are familiar to her somehow. Such images have become too common, the bones in sunlight, the people standing near. In one photo, a woman in her sixties kneels in the dirt before an open grave. In her hand, she holds a small square photo of a young man. The woman looks over the scene as if all the memories of her life are colliding in this moment, nightmare and hope and wish. In the caption at the bottom, her words are translated. For thirty-five years, she says, I did not know where he lay. Now I know, and all my hopes are here, they will not wake again.

Gail had fallen asleep with the box still open on the bed. In her mind, she had returned to Sipke's kitchen table, smoothed her hands across the photographs. In some ways, this story that he told her felt like one she had always known, as if it had been told to her while she slept, and on waking, she had confused it with her dreams.

They drive on in silence, turning up a country lane that begins to rise above the surrounding landscape. He tells her that they are now driving onto the island.

Remembering something that Ed Carney told her once, she says, "Did you know that the Dutch are statistically the tallest people on earth?"

Sipke laughs. "People say that we long for the vertical because our country is so flat. So we make narrow staircases and tall houses. Even our ambulances are too short for us now. People's feet protrude out the back doors. Really, though, our height has nothing to do with psychology and everything to do with dairy consumption. Milk, cheese and yogourt."

He guides the car into a parking lot, then they step out into the snowy landscape. Sipke opens the trunk and removes a small knapsack.

They walk together through a village of half a dozen houses surrounding a church. All the buildings had been abandoned, Sipke tells her, decades before, when the water level around the island had grown too high. Gail tightens her scarf around her neck. The sound of the wind rushing across the fields is high-pitched and ghostly.

"When the sea was pumped out, many objects came to the surface. Bones from the graveyards, centuries old, would rise up as the water receded and float past their wheelbarrows. They found shipwrecks from the middle ages, as old as the twelfth century. In the 1960s, they uncovered Allied planes shot down during the war. The remains inside were perfectly preserved, because of the peat." Sipke takes Gail's arm in his and guides her along a tree-lined walkway. "Even now," he says, smiling, "this is Wideh's favourite place."

In front of them, the island comes to an end. The edge is bordered by assorted wooden pilings, and a cliff falls in a sheer drop of ten metres.

"We are standing on what used to be the harbour of Schokland." Sipke taps his foot against the wood, which has now been supported by stones set in concrete. "This is the old pier."

He tells her that, since the time of Van Ruisdael and Vermeer, people have speculated about the nature of the light here, in the Netherlands. How it inspired the greatest painters of the age, and taught a new way of looking, of truly seeing, the land and sky. He says that when the dike was built and the sea pumped out, people wondered how the change in the landscape would affect the light. The sea, they said, had been a vast mirror, and perhaps, in draining the water, they had changed the sky irrevocably.

Sipke opens a blanket and they sit down together, dangling their legs off the pier. From his knapsack, he takes out a stainless steel Thermos and two cups and proceeds to serve the coffee. In the distance, below them, there are herds of sheep walking on the snow, gathering in groups. He says that there are plans to flood the land around Schokland, to keep the island visible above the surrounding fields, so that it does not subside, as time and nature would insist.

On the snow, a single heron has come to rest, its slender legs, poised and graceful, almost invisible to her. Far away, the land is divided into squares and rectangles, and steep roofs angle towards the sky. Here, amidst the dependable geometry of this northern landscape, she feels relief, a calmness taking root in her body. Gail wraps her hands around the cup, grateful for the warmth. She thinks of Wideh, somewhere in Jakarta now. About Ansel. She imagines him standing beside her.

Sipke gazes out at the horizon, his white hair beating in the wind. She tells him that she fell asleep last night remembering words from Bertrand Russell. Philosophy, Russell had said, was a means to teach one how to live without certainty, and yet without being paralyzed by hesitation.

"To live like this," Sipke says, "means we give up hope of an answer. We respect what is mysterious, while all the while we seek to unravel it."

She asks him the question that has followed her here, that remains with her still. "Do you think it's possible to know another person? In the end, when everything is put to rest, is it really possible?"

"By know, what do you mean?"

"To understand."

"Understand, yes. But to *know* another person." He pauses. "Think of knowing like beauty. The lines that we see are clear, we can trace them, study them in minute detail. But the depth that emerges is still mysterious. How to explain why it reverberates in our minds? When we know another person, I think it is just as mysterious. Knowing another is a kind of belief, an act of faith."

Later, she asks him what it was like to return to the Netherlands after so many years away. He tells her how he had gone back to the old farmhouse in Ysbrechtum where he grew up, the same one in which he is living now. He says that people recognized him in the street, they saw his father in his eyes, in the shape of his face. They stopped and shook his hand. "Aren't you the son of Willem Vermeulen?" "Aren't you Ankie's youngest?" "Come, my child," they said, even though Sipke was almost forty years old. "Let's have a drink together."

There had been an influx of Indonesians into the country. Even in Ysbrechtum, he said, a tiny village, he thought he saw Ani out of the corner of his eye, a young woman, wearing a sarong underneath a wool sweater, despite the wind and cold.

He says that he remembers waking at night, imagining the tickle of the mosquito net against his skin. The loss came to him again. This ache that people told him would subside. In the farmhouse, he set up a darkroom, and he developed the rolls of film he had brought back from Jakarta. Two children washing themselves at the water pipe, running towards him, their mother out of focus in the background. The young girl with the watchful eyes. A single portrait of Ani.

His older brother Wim had taken him to the bar, where they sat and drank glass after glass of Bols. Wim had told him, "Try to forget that place. This is where your life is now."

"Sipke," she says. "Tell me, did Wideh ever try to find my father?"

He turns, looking into her face, thinking back. At last, he says, "I thought, after Ani died, that he would. But I don't believe he ever did. He put all his energy into his work, into his photographs. His love for his mother was so great, you know, I think he wasn't ready to let anything interfere with the memories he had."

Around them, the snow begins to fall again. Sipke and Gail gather their cups, pick up the blanket, and walk back through the abandoned village. She stops and runs her hands over an anchor, rusted and heavy, that lies on the ground.

"Your father arrived in Jakarta in September," Sipke says. Beside him, Gail turns back to the edge of the island, to the boundaries that are now disappearing into the surrounding land.

8

Certainty

YSBRECHTUM

1992

She and Sipke walk arm in arm along a country road. The clouds above, stretched fine, gather the light and spill it down. They are alone but for the occasional bicycle trundling past, a car that speeds by, giving them a wide berth. The road becomes a gravel track, continuing through a farmer's field where, from time to time, a sleeping sheep lies across the path, and she and Sipke must detour around it.

When Ani grows tired, they stop and sit in the grass, eating the chocolate that Sipke now knows to carry with him. In the distance, she can see a wind turbine, sleek and white, propellers cutting through the air.

When she left Jakarta almost thirty years ago, this place had been mysterious to her. Standing in the open fields, the late autumn chill in the air, she could see in every direction, a storm or sunshine moving in, a distant wash of rain.

Sipke had continued to work as a photographer, and for a time they lived in the nearby city of Groningen, coming to Ysbrechtum only a decade ago. The community here, rural and tight-knit, had been welcoming, not unkind, but she has always felt an outsider. To ease her loneliness, they had travelled frequently, going often to The Hague, where Siem, Saskia, and Tash Dertik had made their home, to Maastricht, then across the border into France. Indonesia was a world away, an item on the newscast, a photograph. But in her mind, it joined all things, a background to all that she saw.

Sipke touches her cheek. "You were far away."

"I was thinking about this field, the first time we walked here together. About Jakarta."

A cool breeze skims across the grass and the sheep nearby turn their faces away, hunching their ruffled shoulders. Some of the sheep are marked by a cheerful red or blue circle, as if a child had come through this field with a paintbrush. Sipke moves so that he is sitting close beside her and she leans back, her head against his chest.

He says, "I always thought we would go back, eventually."

It was true. They had put it off time and again, saving the journey for a future date.

"It was me. I hesitated for too long."

He shakes his head, as if to say, *No, us.*

"I woke up one day," she says, "and realized the moment had passed, I no longer needed to return."

In the last month, Wideh has come home from his travels. He is Sipke of an earlier time, a restless spirit. For years he has lived from assignment to assignment, but here, in Ysbrechtum, he seems content to lay his camera aside. Dark haired, slim, and tall, he has a confidence that moves Ani, a face that is open to the world. Even as an adult, becoming set in his ways, he surprises her still.

This morning, after breakfast, he had laid out a dozen photographs on the kitchen table, a series on Borobudur in Indonesia. When Sipke had visited the temple in 1963, Borobudur, more than a thousand years old, had been in near ruins. Back then, people would bring small tools to the site, and when they left they carried the relics and carvings away in their arms. He told her that the monument, with its Hindu and Buddhist elements, is now fully restored, rising up, offering its peaks and domes to the sky. On the day he went, the grounds were almost deserted. He had followed the walkway that spiralled up through the terraces, the bas-relief sculptures decorating the walls illustrating a journey, an ascent, away from the world of suffering. She sifted through the photographs. I thought of you, he said, turning to Ani. His dark eyes imploring her, to get well again, not to leave him. He told her how the stupas, shaped like bells, surrounded him, each one containing a statue, a boddhisatva. He had watched the sunrise, not wanting to lift the camera, to place it between himself and what he saw. The valley around him was a startling colour, a golden inlay on the deep green fields. "How peaceful it was," he said. "The silence seemed to move like a being across the valley. I thought you would have felt at home there, just as I did."

"Yes," she had said, watching his face, so known to her, the grief concealed. "When I put your photos down, I can close my eyes and see the place, as if I were standing in Indonesia again."

The wind picks up, cutting a swath in the grass. Light edges the high, cumulus clouds, throwing them into relief. She thinks of a kite in the air, of a September day in Jakarta. When Matthew arrived, he had sent a note from the hotel where he was staying, and they arranged to meet in the park on Jalan Kamboja, alongside the canal.

The night before, she had lain awake. On the table were a half-dozen letters addressed to Sipke, begun but left unfinished. He had been gone for almost a month, and without him the days had an air of unreality. She wanted to write to him, to tell him something concrete, but she could not find a way to express the rush of feelings that she herself did not fully understand. Sipke had sent her a photograph, one of the last he had taken before he left for the Netherlands. In the picture, Wideh, lying on his stomach on the floor, was setting up a game of marbles. The glass beads shimmered, and her son's face was half in darkness. It was his father's face that she saw, clearer than any recollection.

In the park the next day, Matthew walked towards her. She saw the curve of his shoulders, the set of his mouth, all intimately known to her, as if she had conjured the young man she once knew. He wore glasses, wire-rimmed, silver. He took her hand, holding on to it for a moment. There were dark shadows below his eyes, a weariness.

They found shade on a bench beneath a cassia, with its thousands of shifting leaves. Kites of every shape and hue swam in the air above them.

At first, their conversation rambled, a skittish bird moving from branch to branch, unsure. He told her he had flown to Tawau, staying there for a few days with his mother and her family, then continuing to Sandakan where his uncle still lived. There had been a film crew in the town, making a movie. Within days, the prisoner-of-war camps had been reconstructed, in the same place where once they had stood before.

He spoke in Malay, the language of their childhood. "I had not seen the town in more than a decade. Since before I left for Australia.

"There," he said, after a moment, "even the trees were different. Every day, I went past a golf course. At twilight, hundreds of kangaroos would gather together. They sat like statues in the grass." He said that the realization of growing older had come upon him suddenly. The speed at which the years had gone by. He took a breath. "In Melbourne, I thought of you. I thought of you often."

To Ani, the girl that she had been, turning away from him, was both near and blurred. She wanted to find the words that would call her into being, some thread that would connect her back to that time. She began to speak about the day, twelve years before, when they had walked together on the beach, the tide washing out. He listened, his face open towards her, vulnerable. She told him that she had held the truth from him, that at the time she believed there had been no other choice to make. When she spoke Wideh's name, he looked down. There was exhaustion in his face, but not surprise.

"And so you left Sandakan," he said. "All these years, that was the reason."

She nodded, remembering how she had stood on the steamboat, watching as the harbour she had known all her life slid away from her. "When I went to my mother's family in Tarakan, my uncle helped me. Wideh was born here in Jakarta. Afterwards, I wanted to write to you. I wanted to make it right. This dishonesty. But I was not brave enough. I feared what the words might do. When Wideh asked about his father, I told him that I was the one who had left. That I had come to Jakarta on my own. I said that I believed you had remained in Australia."

From somewhere in the distance, she heard the din of Jalan Kamboja, a clattering of sound. She saw *betjak*s weaving between the trucks, crowds of people slipping through.

His voice, when he began to speak, was tentative. He told her that he could not pinpoint the moment when he had begun to understand. Information had reached him slowly. That she lived in Jakarta. That she had a child. Then, a year ago, when he learned that the child had been born in 1954, it was as if some part of him had come awake. He could not explain why he had not seen it before. Perhaps he had suspected all along, perhaps he had pushed the knowledge away, he no longer knew.

An older man carrying a birdcage passed them, the bamboo cage covered by a dark cloth. They could hear the bird, the claws against the fabric, the trilling of its voice.

He went on, telling her about Clara, the woman he had met while studying in Australia. "We married," he said, "two years ago. We have a child now, a daughter, Gail. It was Clara who said that I should come, travel to Jakarta, find what I had to know."

He said, "I would have given up Australia. I would not have abandoned you."

"Yes," she said. "And so I was the one to leave." Around her, the park seemed to fade out of focus, the shapes, indistinct, weaving together. "Last month, when your letter arrived . . ."

"I needed to make sure. I needed to know, once and for all."

For a time, they sat in silence, and she felt as if they were floating on the surface of the sea and the current alone pushed them on.

"Ani," he said. "Have you told him that I'm here?"

"No. I wanted to see you first. To know what you wished."

"I would like to see him."

"You'll be surprised by Wideh," she said. "How tall he is, how gentle. Even when he was a small child, he was older than his years, already curious about the world." She looked out across the grass, to where the park ended, giving way to a series of low buildings. "In another hour, he'll walk through this park on his way home from school."

"Wideh," he said. "I remember. Your father's name."

Waves of heat hovered above the ground. They crossed the grass, to where the canal shone, reflecting the afternoon light. He began to tell her of the last few days in Sandakan. The film crew had hauled in lumber from the mills north of the harbour, he said, and transported it up Leila Road. The prisoner-of-war camps had seemed to him more familiar than the town itself. On the film set, men, looking emaciated and haggard, had wandered through the barracks. Beside them, Japanese actors practised their lines, rifles set with bayonets dangling casually from their shoulders. Curiosity had brought people from as far away as Semporna and Tawau to watch; they sat on blankets around the periphery. When the cameras rolled, a hush fell over the clearing. Every gesture was mapped out beforehand, and each phrase laboured over. The actors' words, spoken so intently, fell like needles into the quiet.

In one scene, he told her, a prisoner was separated from the others. He was beaten, and then a soldier standing behind him placed his pistol against the man's head. The man struggled, but he was forced to his knees. The soldier fired, and the man's body jerked, then slumped into the dust. His head was twisted to the right, ear to the ground, eyes still open. When the filming stopped, he relaxed his body and turned over, staring for a moment up at the heavens above. Then he pushed himself to standing and wiped the dust from his clothes. Immediately, the blood in his hair and on the ground was cleaned away.

The scene was repeated many times, the cameras moving towards the man and then away. Sitting in the crowd, surrounded by people who dared not breathe, Matthew had closed his eyes against the scene. He felt as if a stone at the bottom of his life had rolled loose, as if the contents of his memory could no longer be contained. They spilled into the air around him, vivid and uncontrolled. Why was this happening, he had wondered, when he had tried so hard, given up so much, to leave it behind?

Ani could see the drift of smoke rising from the ruins of the camp. In a crater, two children sat back-to-back, the bowl of the sky above them. They had believed in a world reborn, that the life they remembered would come into existence again. It had not and yet the days had gone on for them both. Now, when she looked at him, she could imagine the way in which his face would age, filling out, the lines radiating from his eyes. Strands of white were already visible in his dark hair.

He said he had stood on the hillside, asking himself how it was possible to continue. At what point would he finally step forward, would he make, decisively, the shape of his life? When would the war be over for him? Sometimes, he said, one had to let go of the living just as surely as one grieved the dead. Some things, lost long ago, could not be returned.

Across the street from the park, children began to emerge from the school, their jubilant voices filling the air. They scattered in every direction. She could sense Matthew following her gaze.

Wideh walked into the park head down, absorbed in his own thoughts. He stopped at the canal, where a newspaper had been left on the steps leading down to the water. He was no more than a hundred yards away, but he did not notice them. Putting his satchel down, he opened the paper, then he removed a sheet and began to fold it, deftly constructing a paper boat. He made one after another, lining the finished pieces up on the steps, a fleet at rest.

Eventually, he looked up and saw them and he began to run towards the place where they were sitting. When he reached Ani and Matthew, he held back, suddenly shy. "Have you come to watch the kite-flying?"

She smiled, embracing him. "No, it was only a happy accident."

He leaned his forehead against hers.

"Wideh," she said. "There is someone here I would like you to meet."

She was about to say something more when Matthew reached out tentatively, placing one hand on Wideh's shoulder. When he spoke, his voice was casual, but she saw in his eyes what the effort cost him. He told Wideh that he had known Ani once, long ago, in the years before she had come to Jakarta.

Wideh turned to Matthew, looking curiously into his face. "In Sandakan?"

"Yes, but I no longer live there."

Wideh set his satchel on the embankment where Ani and Matthew were sitting. He fiddled with the buckle, all the while looking down at the grass.

"Do you fly kites, Wideh?"

He shook his head. "But I'm going to build one some time. A swallow. The pattern isn't complicated, not like some of the others." He motioned towards an older man in a quilted jacket standing nearby. His three kites, attached to one another in a triangle, were painted to resemble birds. They spun and fell sharply, their tails tracing patterns in the sky. The man stepped sideways and they plummeted to the ground, somersaulting over the grass before lifting up once more.

Wideh turned back to Matthew. "What is it like in Sandakan?"

"Nowadays, it's peaceful. Not as vibrant as Jakarta, but the harbour is very busy; ships come in from many places. When I was small, I used to imagine the town was a child, standing with his back to the jungle, and his face to the sea."

"As if to set foot in the water and sail away," said Wideh.

"A swimming city!"

Ani laughed. "You never told me."

"I still remember walking down to the harbour in the early morning," Matthew said. "Seeing you there on Tajuddin's boat."

"She hardly speaks about it," Wideh said, his voice filled with wonder.

"It was so long ago."

"Everyone knew her. In Sandakan, Tajuddin's boat was famous."

Matthew and Wideh continued to talk, about kite-flying, then distant cities, and Ani did not interrupt them. She listened to their voices, this knitting together, felt as if she were balanced within, a soul sheltered between the past and the present.

A civilian regiment, recognizable by their khaki shirts and trousers, swept onto the road, stopping traffic. They moved in unison, chanting slogans whose words she could not make out. Beside them, the canal was busy with people bathing and swimming, the womens' clothing blurring in kaleidoscopic patterns.

"One day, I'll go to Sandakan," Wideh said. "I'll put flowers on the graves of my grandparents. Ibu told me both my grandfathers died there, and also my grandmother."

"And if there are no graves?"

"Then the sea."

Matthew nodded. "I, too, was glad to go back. If only to say goodbye."

They sat together as the sun faded behind the trees, lowering through the branches. The kites drifted to the ground, a swirl of colour, and children ran to gather them up.

When they parted, he left as if he would be seeing them again, shaking Wideh's hand, then putting his lips to the boy's hair. She knew that what she and Matthew had shared in childhood had carried them safely through, a net where all other lines had been torn away. All these years, the net had held. His eyes rested on Ani's face. They said goodbye to one another, and then he stepped away from them. She saw what he had given her, the one thing her parents had been unable to do, prepare her for this parting, this letting go.

A *betjak* came along and he climbed in. She watched the vehicle pull out onto the busy street, watched for as long as she could, until it was one among so many others. Wideh took her arm and pulled her lightly, and together they walked along the crowded road, eventually crossing back into the park, towards Jalan Kamboja.

In the late afternoon, Wideh sleeps on a blanket in the grass, a magazine open on his chest. The fuchsia shrubs, planted in a border along the canal, reach out luxuriantly. Low against the sky, a flock of avocet, or *kluut*, veer and dip in unison. They are familiar to Ani now, these elegant northern birds, the *kluut* with their black-tipped wings; the heron that stand in the fields, watchful.

The birds tip towards the east, their movement coinciding with the appearance of Frank Postma, who steps with a flourish into the garden, his daughter, Ingrid, close behind him. Ani walks across the grass to meet them, and he puts his hands on her shoulders, kissing her on both cheeks. Ingrid presents the box of pastries that she says they bought in the Indonesian market in The Hague. *Spekkoek*, Frank announces, *klepon* and *ongol-ongol*. Only the best. Ingrid nods. "A veritable dessert buffet." At these words, Wideh gets to his feet.

Frank asks to see Wideh's photographs, and, after some prodding, Wideh brings out an envelope of prints taken during a recent trip to Southeast Asia. In one, the harbour at Sunda Kelapa, a study of the myriad lines of rigging that criss-cross the sky. In another, a stand of trees half concealed by fog, the trunks, otherworldly, crooked and gnarled. "Mount Kinabalu," he says. "A cloud forest in North Borneo. In the high altitude, the clouds deposit drops of water on the trees, and this provides what little moisture they need." He selects a print and shows it to Frank. "Here's a pitcher plant, one of the carnivorous plants of the region."

For a moment, Ani believes it is her father speaking. In her memory, they are walking single-file through the jungle,

Ani between her parents, their voices layering into the canopy above her.

Sipke appears, bringing beer and wine and a half-dozen glasses. In the last few months, his hair has begun to grey, a brush of white at the edges. Ani pours the drinks and Sipke stands with one hand on the small of her back, listening as Wideh describes Jakarta, the neighbourhoods bulldozed or rezoned, made over into something entirely different. Walking on Jalan Kamboja, he had searched among the remaining businesses, finding an elderly woman who remembered the street the way it was in the early 1960s, the Pondok Restaurant, the Dutch portrait studio. "They went away with their little boy," she had told him. "I'm not sure where they've gotten to now."

"Up to no good, of course," Frank says. He lifts his glass, takes a sip of beer. "I remember it all so clearly. Now, when I look at these young kids, going off with their cameras to Bosnia, to Croatia, I want to pack my bags and follow them. Being a photographer is what I've always done. I'm not equipped for any other life."

"That time is gone," Ingrid says, reaching out to touch her father's shoulder. "You'll have to content yourself with dusty old Holland. What was that line again?" She looks up at the cloudless sky, remembering. "'O starshine on the fields of long ago.'"

Sipke finishes the words. "'Bring me the darkness and the nightingale . . . and the faces of my friends.'"

Twilight comes, and the frogs are a chorus on the banks. Joos, their neighbour and Sipke's boyhood friend, shows up with box wine. Quantity, Joos says, is the order of the night. Beside him, Sipke frowns at the seal. While the glasses are being refilled, Ingrid stands up and finds Wideh's guitar leaning against the wall. She sets it on her lap, her fingers moving lightly over the strings, and the notes disperse, weaving together the space around them. Their voices rise, enclosing her, Frank's erudite and Joos's bombastic. Her heart eases to see Sipke and Wideh relaxed and laughing. It does not feel as if it is she who is leaving. Rather, the world is withdrawing from her, stepping back; it is taking its leave.

There is a child in the canal, barely visible. In the dim light, Ani can see her floating on her back, her hair in pig-tails, her arms flung wide. Around her, tall fronds reach above the water, interrupting the reflection of the evening sky. Slowly, the girl drifts past. Then, as if aware of someone watching, she turns onto her stomach, swimming, her shoulders appearing then submerging, her pale feet taking turns to break the surface.

When Ani looks up, she sees Sipke, and the tenderness in his expression returns her to a morning almost thirty years ago. She and Wideh are in the airport in Amsterdam, their one trunk on the ground. She sees the mass of people, the high wavering lights, and then Sipke coming towards them.

Together they leave the airport. Outside, they find that a light snow is falling. Sipke has borrowed his brother's car, and they drive under a series of concrete bridges, into the open. The colours transfix her, muted shades of green and brown, ice beneath a pearl-white sky. Everywhere, the land is unfamiliar, unimagined, canals slipping across the fields.

For a moment, the future comes to her, as vivid and clear as a memory unfolding. The highway rises onto a plateau, the land falls away. The North Sea opens before her, wind rippling the water.

9

The Glass Jar

January

*I*t had been one of those rare winter days, almost a year ago now, Ansel recalls, when the chill of the season seemed, for a few hours, a thing of the past. He had just arrived home from work, and Gail was sitting on the front porch. She had earphones on and she was listening to music. This is the way he remembers it. Gail in jeans and a cardigan, watching the life of the street go by.

What are you listening to? he asked. She told him to guess, and then, smiling, she took both of his hands, doing a jive. Somebody across the street whistled long and low. Car doors slammed, talk radio spilled out a nearby window. She was all energy, all heat. They were dancing on their hand-kerchief of lawn, and he felt as if something he had lost was, for a moment, within reach again. Later, her feet on his lap as she read the newspaper. This is good, she had said. Her voice was hopeful. This is right.

Overhead, the fluorescent lights in the hospital corridor waver. Ansel takes the stairs up, emerging on the fifth floor, into the quiet of the ICU. He stops at the nurses' station to take his bearings. The phone rings, the head nurse turns his face away, speaking in a low voice, and Ansel continues along the corridor.

At the far end of the ward, he can see Alistair in the last bed. A nurse is checking his IV lines. Alistair's eyes are closed, and he gives the impression not of sleeping but of being deeply absorbed, preoccupied by his own thoughts. Ansel scans the monitor, then picks up the chart from the foot of the bed. He runs a finger over the lines as he reads, and the movement reminds him of his own father, of how once, when he was a child, he had stood at his father's side in this same ICU. They had walked from bed to bed and his father had told him to be very still, that he should not be there, but he wanted Ansel to see how things were. The hush and gravity of the ward made Ansel want to run outside, swing a bat, stomp up and down on the pavement. His anxiety must have shown. His father bent down, hands on Ansel's shoulders, holding his gaze. "Sooner or later," he said, gently, "we all end up in the care of another."

Ansel hears the sound of a chair scraping. He had not seen her, a woman near his own age, so close to the curtains that her outline seems to disappear into the folds.

She nods slightly when he introduces himself. "I'm family," she says. "Al is my brother. I only arrived last night."

"There's a private room in this ward. A place to rest and be alone, if you need it. He's stable now."

"It's okay. I just want to be near."

He returns the chart to its holding place. Through the windows behind her, he can see down to the bay where the water gleams. The fierce light of the sun comes in, shining off the glass walls of the ward. They listen to the heart-rate monitor, the slow measured blips of electronic sound. Alistair, his face partly obscured by an oxygen mask, is still.

"Are you the doctor that got him into Kafka?"

"Pardon?"

"Kafka. Al phoned up one night and said, when I came, I should bring along some books. He says Kafka had tuber-culosis." She reaches towards the windowsill, holds up a tat-tered paperback. "So I went to the library and found this."

"Oh, yes," Ansel says, and then nods. "I think it was me."

"He was always a big reader, even when we were kids. I used to tease him about it. He was my older brother, and I thought he was showing off." Her voice sounds exhausted, but she continues speaking, filling the silence between them. "Always with his nose in a book and it didn't matter what, novels, comic books, even the magazines our mother kept around the apartment when she was still there. Al was full of surprises. Not everyone would want to be sent off with Kafka."

"I don't think that I would."

She smiles briefly before glancing away. "What would you have instead? A piece of music, maybe."

"No." He gathers his thoughts. "Someone beside me. No radio, no television. Just the sound of the world going by."

She puts the book down. Dr. Singh, the attending physician, appears in the doorway. His eyes skim the folder in his hand and then he steps into the room. Al's sister stands up. He can see the resemblance between siblings, the way Al might have looked before terminal illness set in. Her eyes are red from weeping.

Ansel listens while Singh speaks. He is kind when he details the prognosis, but he holds nothing back. When Singh leaves, Al's sister comes to stand beside Ansel. The light falls against her hair, casting her face in shadow. They watch Singh through the plate-glass walls, the multiple reflections of his white coat.

"If there's other family to contact, we should do it soon."

"No, I'm the last."

The room floats in silence, and then she says, "I'd been trying to get Al to come to Victoria, to stay with me and my kids. A few years ago, I almost had him convinced, but then he got the diagnosis, the HIV. He changed his mind." She pauses after each sentence, as if to gather strength for the next. "We've always been close. Things never came easy for him, he was sixteen when he left home. He was reckless with himself. I knew I couldn't save him if he didn't want to be saved. And even then," she crosses her arms in front of herself, "sometimes one thing doesn't go right, and then another, and then it all snowballs. But he put all the blame on his own shoulders, he tried to be the one to carry the weight, and it hurt him in the end.

"Some things I only realize in hindsight. How someone caught me at a time I didn't even realize I was slipping. And then, those times when I failed to reach out. Failed to see that someone I cared for was losing their footing."

"But you're here now," Ansel says. "When he wakes up, you'll be here."

Outside, in the hallway, time continues. They can hear the voices of nurses, of visitors in a nearby room. An elderly man is wheeled out on a gurney, his wife holding his hand as he glides past.

Ansel says, "Would you tell him I'll come back this evening?"

"I will."

"Do you need anything?"

He cannot read her expression. She seems lost in her own thoughts, trying to turn over a line, a word, that she cannot quite comprehend. What was it Alistair had said, so many months ago? No more questions, no more doubts.

"I'm fine," she says. "I am."

Behind the words, he sees loss as if it were a tremor of light around her. Ansel walks towards the doorway, is about to leave the room when she returns to the window. Her back is to him, dark hair against her shoulders, and she gazes out over the shining city.

At home, after nightfall, the house is unbearably quiet. In the kitchen, he switches the radio on, listens as a physicist describes the latest images transmitted back by the Hubble Telescope. Ansel has seen them on the Internet: a nebula six light-years wide, impossibly strange and glorious. The shape,

with its swirling tentacles of dust clouds, is somehow familiar. To him, it resembles a deep-sea creature let loose in
space. Or one could imagine it miniscule, a dot in a Petri
dish, now magnified large.

He tries to imagine Gail in the kitchen, preparing a meal
as the radio plays. She stands with one hand resting on the
counter, her eyes closed, listening intently.

On that night when she returned from Amsterdam, he
had been waiting for her at the airport, watching the unend-
ing line of travellers emerging through the double doors,
pushing their baggage ahead of them as they crushed into
the waiting crowd.

For a long time she did not see him. At last Ansel reached
her. "There you are," she said.

"Here I am."

The crowd parted around them as if they were an island
in a flowing river.

In the car on the way home, she had asked him to detour
towards the peninsula, to the cliffs on the west side where
the city ended and the ocean began. It was a clear night, and
sitting on the hood of the car she had pointed out the glow
of a lighthouse on the tip of the northern bank. The air
smelled of brine and the cold.

She seemed exhausted from the flight, distracted, and yet
she had not wanted to go home. They talked at first about
Harry Jaarsma, then she told him about travelling north to
the province of Friesland, about someone she had met there,
a man named Sipke Vermeulen. She said that he had known
her father. "There was a place we visited," she said. "To

arrive there, we drove across a piece of land that, fifty years ago, lay beneath the sea. Maybe one day, we can go back together and I'll be able to show you."

Neither of them had wanted to leave, and so they had remained there, despite the lateness of the hour, wrapped in their winter coats. She told him about William Sullivan's diary. Something about it had moved her, the numbers now transformed into sentences. She said that Kathleen had wanted to open a window from her father's life onto her own.

"Remember when we were kids," she said, "and the world consisted of the streets we knew, the streets we'd walked on. I always wanted to keep going, to roam as far as I could and make everything a part of me."

For a moment, he cannot move. His grief takes hold again, the pain worse than it has been in many months. He goes upstairs to their bedroom. Gail's clothes lie neatly folded on the bed, on the floor, and he gathers them into plastic bags. Each one is familiar, it has a scent and a memory. He lays her sweaters in a box, covers them with her winter coat. When the last piece of clothing is put away, he feels a spreading numbness, a distant calm. He sits down on the bed, then lies back.

The skylight above frames the evening sky. He remembers how, when he was a child, he and his sister would climb onto the roof of the garage. They would stretch out on the warm tiles, gazing up at the heavens. His sister told him to hold still. Could he see the clouds moving? He must have been only six or seven years old, and he remembers, even now, how the ground seemed to lose its substance. He felt the Earth making its rotation and he saw himself as a tiny thing, a breath, carried along with it. When he sat up, the sky retreated, giving way to the tips of the highest trees. Giving way to the house, the familiar details.

Now, he feels that same vertigo, a sense that he is falling. He gets to his feet, imagining her near. Love, this heaviness, this weight, holds him steady.

The rain begins, but Matthew remains outside for a little while longer. In the park, there are boys playing soccer, a blur of green and red jerseys looping across the grass. They clap their hands, calling to one another, put on a burst of speed to keep the ball in play. He sees a young man coming towards him. He wears a suit and an overcoat, as if he has just come from work, and he makes his way across the wet grass to a child who stands waiting, knapsack over one shoulder. Together they watch the game. The father stands awkwardly, trying to shield them both from the rain with a folded newspaper. The child looks straight ahead, but slowly, imperceptibly, he shifts his body sideways so that he is resting against his father's legs.

He tries to remember himself at that age, so small and serious. He sees the mission school as it was in the late 1930s, *atap* roofs in Sandakan town, the little boats anchored in the harbour. When he went back for the last time, people still could not talk about the war. If he mentioned it, they would shake their heads, their eyes would grow distant. "Terrible times," they said. Opening and closing the memory in the same breath. "But it was long ago, wasn't it? Those days are behind us."

"Yes," he had said, nodding, agreeing.

Days later, when the plane touched down in Jakarta, he'd felt as if he had awoken in a country that had no markers, no guides. There, with Ani, the past was no longer just a memory, a fog, it had the face and shape of a boy. Wideh had stood with his hand resting on his mother's knee, the gesture reminding Matthew of one he himself had made long ago. He saw in Wideh's face the resemblance to both Ani and himself, a gathering together of what had once been lost.

His son had been shy at first, gazing at the grass by Matthew's feet. But when Wideh lifted his face and pointed out the kites above them, some part of him seemed to unfold, delight emanating from him. Between mother and child, another language existed. He could not bring himself to disturb Wideh's happiness, he could not let the truth be spoken, tell him that his father had returned only to disappear and leave them again. He saw that this part of his life must always remain broken.

He went home to Canada. When he opened the door of the house, all the lights were off. Upstairs, in the doorway to her bedroom, he listened to the even sigh of his daughter's breath, and then he found Clara, already asleep, the lamp still on, a book open on the pillow beside her. When she woke, he would find the way to tell her. She would not look away, she would know what the future could be.

He had remembered this last night, when Ansel came to the house and they'd sat together on the front porch, in the unusually mild night. As Clara had requested, Ansel had brought with him a copy of Gail's documentary, which had just been finished. Clara set the CD into the player and then there was the sound of an airplane lifting off. Newsreels announced the start of the war. Harry Jaarsma, the cryptographer, was introduced, and then Sullivan's two children.

It was a little more than a year ago now, Matthew remembered, that he had walked with his daughter near this field. Gail had just returned from the Netherlands. He thought she looked well and told her so.

At first, she had seemed anxious, unable to settle. It reminded Matthew of when she was a child, the bursts of energy that left both him and Clara amazed. Gail would race around the house like a being possessed, then collapse on the living room floor, gazing up, dreaming. He asked about her work in Amsterdam, and as she spoke she seemed to calm, telling him about William Sullivan and the diary he had kept some fifty years ago during the war. How, when she read the pages, her own emotions had unsettled her, the intensity of them, the compassion she felt for all that he had set aside.

After so many years, Matthew thought, silence had become a habit for him, a way of being in the world. As his daughter spoke, fragments drifted through his mind. His mother's hand gripping his, as they ran into the jungle. The sound of a bicycle skimming along a dirt road. How he had loved his father all his life without ever truly knowing him.

He said to Gail that sometimes the past could not be made right, not every experience could be made to fit. "I left Sandakan believing that I had to push pieces of my life away. I thought the worst thing would be to lose a sense of balance, to fall. This is how it seemed to me. But I was wrong to hold back." He hesitated, but something in her expression pushed him to continue. "I never told you how your mother saved me."

"But I knew," she had said. In her bearing, in her words, there was an understanding, a recognition that shook him to the core, that now, sitting here, makes him weep. "All along, I knew."

Beside the soccer field, parents stand beneath coloured umbrellas, sipping their coffee, their chatter soothing to him. He could be in Tawau or Sandakan, a bystander on the *padang*, a child at the edge of the field.

The first maps, he knows, were drawn in the dirt, a picture of a place set tenuously down. He can close his eyes and see the road leading to Mile 8, curving down to the sea. A boy's hand tracing a circle on the ground, the soil warm against his fingers. He had once gone back to find it, the place between the rows of trees, but what he had tried to keep safe was lost. His childhood, a time before the war. A glass jar that moves from his father's hand to his, a continuous question that asks, how am I to live now, when all is said and done and grief must finally be set aside. Ani in a park on the other side

of the world, the words his father could not say, the remembered voice of his daughter. So many things, he thinks, that
we carry all our lives, in the hope that what we know will
finally redeem us, that we will find something that abides,
even now, in the indefinite, the uncertain, hereafter.

NOTES AND ACKNOWLEDGEMENTS

While many books were an immense help to me in the course of my research, I would like to acknowledge, in particular, Erna Paris's *Long Shadows: Truth, Lies and History* (Toronto: Knopf, 2000); Maslyn Williams's *Five Journeys from Jakarta: Inside Sukarno's Indonesia* (New York: William Morrow, 1965); Thomas Dormandy's *The White Death: A History of Tuberculosis* (New York: New York University Press, 1999); K.G. Tregonning's *North Borneo* (London: Her Majesty's Stationery Office, 1960); Stephen Budiansky's *Battle of Wits: The Complete Story of Codebreaking in World War II* (New York: Touchstone, 2002); Thomas Looker's *The Sound and the Story: NPR and the Art of Radio.* (New York: Houghton Mifflin, 1995); Russell Miller's *Magnum: Fifty Years at the Front Line of History* (New York: Grove Press, 1997); Raymond Firth's *Malay Fishermen: Their Peasant Economy* (New York: W.W. Norton, 1975); and Gavan Daws and Marty Fujita's *Archipelago: The Islands of Indonesia* (University of California Press, 1999). I would also like to acknowledge two documentaries, Karen Levine's "Hana's Suitcase" and Jane Lewis's "My Father's Story," both of which originally aired on CBC Radio and served as the inspiration for Gail's radio project. Karen Levine's book, *Hana's Suitcase*, based on her radio documentary, is published in Canada by Second Story Press.

I gratefully acknowledge the support of the Canada Council for the Arts and the BC Arts Council.

In Sandakan, Tawau, Singapore, and Melbourne, I was able to interview many people who shared their stories with me. I thank you, from the bottom of my heart, for your generosity and trust. To my parents, and to my extended family in Canada, Malaysia, Australia, China, the United States and the Netherlands, all my gratitude and love.

Although aspects of this novel – the Japanese Occupation of British North Borneo, the Sandakan Death Marches, and the events leading to the fall of Sukarno in Indonesia in 1965 – are based on the historical record, the characters in this novel are fictional creations. The geography of Sandakan town has been slightly altered for the sake of simplicity.

William Sullivan's diary is inspired by the story of Donald Hill, an RAF pilot stationed in Hong Kong who was taken prisoner by the Japanese Army in 1941. For those wishing to know more, the story is beautifully told by Andro Linklater in his book *The Code of Love* (London: Weidenfeld & Nicolson, 2000).

For their unwavering support, I am deeply grateful to Asya Muchnick at Little, Brown, and to Marilyn Biderman, Anita Chong, and all those at McClelland & Stewart with whom I have had the pleasure to work. My heartfelt thanks to Alex Schultz for his fine work copyediting this novel. To my editor, Ellen Seligman: I am fortunate indeed, and so grateful to her for sharing this journey with me. My thanks for her faith in this book, and for her wisdom and guidance in helping me to get the words right.

Jane Eaton Hamilton, Joy Masuhara, and Steven Dang generously shared their insights and answered my many and diffuse questions, as did Jeroen Kemperman at the Netherlands Institute for War Documentation. My thanks and great admiration to Don Mowatt, for opening my eyes to the world of radio. To Amanda Okopski and Dean Bakopoulos, my dear ones, unstinting in their love, generous in their joy, I am blessed by our friendship. And to Willem, my anchor and my love.

To Carol Hudgins, Cynthia Leung, and to my mother, Matilda Thien: no words can express how I miss you.

The epigraph from *The Needs of Strangers* by Michael Ignatieff, copyright © 1985 by Michael Ignatieff. Used by permission of Viking Penguin, a division of Penguin Group (USA) Inc.

The quotation about the origins of empathy on page 16 is from Richard Dawkins's *The Selfish Gene* (London: Oxford University Press, 1976).

The newspaper quotation on page 117 is from the article "Shortest time interval measured." BBC News, February 25, 2004. http://news.bbc.co.uk/2/hi/science/nature/3486160.stm.

The words heard on the radio on page 256 and spoken by the man on the street on page 266 are from Maslyn Williams's *Five Journeys from Jakarta: Inside Sukarno's Indonesia* (New York: William Morrow, 1965).

The quotation on page 290 is from Siegfried Sassoon's poem "Memory."